Don't Look Away

ALSO BY LINDA STREVER

Against My Dreams: An Immigrant's Story
poetry

Don't Look Away
A NOVEL

by Linda Strever

PAINTED SNAKE PRESS
Olympia, Washington

Don't Look Away
Copyright © 2015 by Linda Strever
All rights reserved

No part of this book may be used or reproduced in any form, except for the inclusion of brief quotations in review, without the written permission of the author.

www.LindaStrever.com

ISBN 978-0-9896228-1-3

Library of Congress Control Number: 2014958274

Cover and book design by Debi Bodett
www.DebiBodett.com

Printed in the United States of America

First Edition
Published by Painted Snake Press
Olympia, Washington

For Barry

Author's Note

The story of Vita Sackville-West and Violet Keppel Trefusis contained in this novel involves historical people and therefore includes some factual elements. I was intrigued by their relationship when I read Violet's letters collected in *Violet to Vita*, edited by Mitchell A. Leaska and John Phillips. Vita's letters to Violet did not survive. While Vita is perhaps best known as the lover of Virginia Woolf, she was a poet and novelist in her own right. Her affair with Violet Trefusis, lasting from 1918 to 1921, was radical and tempestuous, its painful ending orchestrated by their families. I wondered what might have happened if their relationship had been able to outlast the vulnerabilities of youth and the pressures of family and society. My story is a re-imagining of their time together, a long musing on the ways a different relationship with Violet might have altered Vita's life. It is fiction, as is Vita's voice.

Bill and Madeline's story grew out of family history. My mother once told me that when Bruno Hauptmann's arrest for the kidnapping and murder of the Lindbergh baby hit the newspapers in 1934, she was astonished to discover that she'd been walking past Hauptmann's house whenever she went to visit her cousins as a young teenager living in the Bronx. My father was a prisoner of war, captured in the Battle of the Bulge in December 1944 and held by the Germans for six months. He was one of many green troops newly arrived in the European theater, and his entire war experience consisted of imprisonment following just a few days of intense, overwhelming battle in severe winter conditions. Those two seeds sprouted into the fictional story of Bill and Madeline presented here.

The story of Anna and Thomas is also fictional, though it has an autobiographical element, in that I lost someone I loved to suicide and rebuilt my life in the aftermath.

The transatlantic flight of Charles Lindbergh in 1927 was, in his time, as monumental as the moon landing was in mine. And the kidnapping and murder of the Lindbergh baby in 1932, along with the subsequent arrest and trial of Bruno Hauptmann in 1934-35, riveted the nation's attention during the Great Depression. Controversy about Lindbergh's beliefs and actions leading up to World War II still lingers, as do theories about Hauptmann's possible innocence. These threads weave loosely into the three stories contained in *Don't Look Away.*

DON'T LOOK AWAY

Thomas

I have seen these things:

Wings made of starlight
Children made of rain
Men made of ocean
Women made of moon
Places made of nothing
Worlds beyond the sun

I will show you now
And then not again

When you meet me
I will be gone

Part 1

She followed slowly, taking a long time,
as though there were some obstacle in the way;
and yet: as though, once it was overcome,
she would be beyond all walking, and would fly.

Rainer Maria Rilke
translation by Stephen Mitchell

Vita & Violet

1918

"Do you remember the first time you kissed me?" Violet asked, her eyes closed, her head heavy against Vita's shoulder. The train's rhythm and the familiar scents of rain and pipe smoke on Vita's overcoat pulled Violet toward a restless sleep.

"Of course," Vita answered. For hours—on the first long train ride, the boat, and then on this train—she'd kept her back straight, her boots flat on the floor, her eyes watchful. Out the window the landscape dimmed, as dusk quieted colours into sameness, and Vita into a wary sense of peace. "Do you remember the first time we met? When you're sleepy, I almost hear your child voice—you were so smart in that little lavender dress, with its wide sash and scads of lace."

"You were so tall and stately. I scarcely believed such a one as you would pay me any attention." Fully awake now, Violet didn't open her eyes or lift her head, wanting to keep this moment and Vita's closeness. "And to think we ended up at school together. The Fates and the Muses, all the Greek and Roman and Norse gods, must have met in High Council to make it happen. And the gods of Hindustan and Africa and Stonehenge showered us with chanting and petals and fire. I was a willing sacrifice. Do you know when I first knew I loved you?"

"Of course. You were almost as lovely at fourteen as you are now, I must say. And always precocious." Vita smiled, remembering.

"No, I knew I loved you far ahead of giving you the ring."

"Did you? And when was that, my Violet, my beautiful Lushka?"

"The day I arrived at school, when I spied you kissing Rosamund in the garden. I wanted so badly to take her place, dearest Mitya."

"But what does a twelve-year-old know of love?"

"Everything, every day, ever since. I grew into it, and it grew into me, where it rests the way a mountain rests in the sky." Violet sat up as she spoke, studied Vita's reflection in the window, then Vita's face. "What if they find us and make us come back? I have tried to still my fear into the wool of your overcoat, but there really is no stillness, is there? How many times must we run away?"

"If only I could live in two worlds, Violet. I was so forsaken when your mother spirited you away to the Continent, convinced that you were really gone," Vita said, reaching for Violet's hand, offering the explanation she'd given herself dozens of times. "And Harold was a good match. I know it hurts you when I say it— but I love Harold and I love my boys. They are the ground that underlies everything. But my love for you is like the sky, overarching, making the rain and sun that create all life below. I have no idea how to live without you."

"But my mother was worried only about her own scandal, not anything to do with us. I thought you'd understood." Violet squeezed Vita's hand to underscore her statement. "She had to escape her notoriety after the king's death, let it diminish beyond a whisper. She no longer had his protection, so she had to forge her own—you cannot have forgotten, can you? Oh, if only you had waited." Her words had a pleading quality that Violet hated in herself, but it was too late to take them back. She squeezed Vita's hand again. "Please, Mitya, hear what I mean, not my words. I do not wish you to stop loving your family. I am just so frightened." A sudden knock at the compartment door made Violet jump.

"Yes." Vita kept her voice low and deep, a voice to match her trousers and boots. The single word came out with authority, a statement rather than a question. The porter opened the door, leaned in.

"Thirty kilometres to Paris, sir." He looked directly at Vita as he spoke, then bowed and closed the door softly.

"I must tell you now, I must." Violet delivered her words all in one breath. "I think my mother will force me to marry Denys. I hate her hypocrisy—all of a sudden she cannot abide a scandal. She thinks she can save me from you. I cannot marry him. I will not. I shall run away for as long as I can. But I fear I cannot run forever. Oh, what will become of us?" Violet slowed down, took control of her voice. "In thirty kilometres we must forget the other world, Vita. It is the only way."

Vita

1918

If only I had wings. I would arch my back
slightly, lift from the earth—when trapped
by dull actors at the theatre, perhaps, or I
could wait for a grand occasion, a state funeral,
and then rise slowly, a vision in black, veils
streaming behind, over the crowd of dignified
mourners. In stagnant settings I amuse myself
by fluttering the wings inside my head—
I have been in Istanbul under a starry sky
while the others in Lady Griswold's
drawing room think I smile at their wit.

When I was a girl, I dreamt of flying: if I
was good enough at my lessons or prayers,
perhaps I'd find the magic word or gesture
that would open my wings. Oh, Violet—
closest being to me in this life—our passion
is akin to flying. But flying must be done alone.
With you, I see all realms of possibility:
I could sing opera, write the epic to outlast
Beowulf, grow a penis and marry you.
But flying I must save for myself.

This is the kingdom of heaven. And I shall
find a way to live here. No, I will not fly
frivolously. Wings counter gravity, the force
that presses me to earth. What force must
I apply to give me lightness? After tonight,
I shall never be the same. Oh, my Violet—
I trust you will protect my private longing.
Burn my letters, burn the lock of my hair
you wear at your throat. Your keepsake
will be what I do when I am not with you,

how I return to life outside this villa,
yet keep my wings. When I think of you,
I will see far reaches of sky, upper sides
of clouds. You are my promise of flight.

I cannot sleep. The stars are too bright. My
eyes feel like prisms—too much light to hold.
I must refract it, break it into fragments, let it
vibrate all over the room. Except for the chime
of far-off bells, the air is quiet. In London,
Shanghai, New York, people are waking
or sleeping in rhythm with night. Morning
will not strike here for some time, and so
I am free to feel the cool air on my skin,
to muse on the stars. I do not need sleep.
I do not need to dream. I need only to stand
here at the open window, the night's door.

I hear your soft breath. Let your sleep
be sound. Let me stay awake to my heartbeat,
awake to what my eyes do with starlight.
I have ventured unaccompanied into the wood,
slept in the vault of my bedroom, no sound
of anyone near. I have been alone in a ballroom,
whirling among dancers, paced the gardens
waiting for childbirth. Yes, I have carried
another human being inside me, and still, I
was alone. When will I be alone enough to fly?

Questions have no answers. Why do I ask them,
what earthly good does it do? Why not accept
the life I have been dealt, the duties I am
destined to assume? The weight of the shadow
across my life is immense. If only I could lift it.

I have taken to dressing in trousers and boots—
to feel my muscled strength, to feel my steps
move me somewhere. In the mirror I have

the same bony face, pale skin, unruly hair.
But inside I am made new by each breath.

Can I know my mind, my heart? I look
at my diary from last year or last week,
and a stranger stares from the page. One day
I love my beautiful, living sons tenderly,
without limit, the next I could abandon them
without a thought. It is frightening to imagine
what I might do. I thought marriage would be
a way to slow myself. I thought facing the same
man over the same sugar bowl and pattern
of silver each morning would give me pause—
a past and future anchored in time. Now I am
a delighted wife and mother whose very joy
depends on comforting others. Now a cold,
fiery bard looking for virgins to seduce.

Yesterday a sugar cube in my tea was all I
desired. Today I could turn over the long
mahogany table, let generations of china
smash on the floor—all this while I am
seated, smiling, at breakfast. Love and hate
occupy the two sides of my face. I am like
Janus guarding my own door, two-faced,
jailer and liberator. Who am I now?

I have tried to burn desire away, clean it
from my fingernails like so much dirt.
I have tried wanting everything
with a desperate, inconsolable howl—
the very trees to bloom in January, the sun
to rise at midnight. I have tried something
between, a gray of hope and peace, a dull
ache, a small satisfaction. Just when I think
myself calm, I am startled by the force
of my denial or claim, by the sobbing
a blade of grass can inspire, the laughter

that comes from air, by the wanton
urge to flee from my family name.

Am I mad? Did I inherit the extremes
of my ancestors, passed to me like a hammer
on porcelain? I could raise a troupe of lords
and ladies from infancy to dutiful adulthood
or run off with a count or contessa
of dubious title, bask in the Mediterranean
without clothing or care. I am tired,
but I cannot sleep. Perhaps my wakeful
nights accumulate wisdom. If only
I could sleep forever, succumb to thick
darkness, where nothing matters:
not love or longing, duty or shame.

Icarus flew too near the sun and fell to the sea.
But I want to know if the height of his soaring
was worth the depth of his drowning. I shall fly.
To do otherwise would be a certain death. Perhaps
I will have better wings than poor Icarus. Perhaps
I shall reach the moon and bring back its light.
Let each of my flights teach me. Let my wings
beat their opposing rhythm and carry me higher.

Love and hate: let them beat together, take me
where they will. I will not think about landing.
will not expect it, nor long for it. I shall feel
my divided nature. Love and hate, pride
and shame, hope and fear—each a tendon
or muscle in my great wings. I will no longer
measure time, no longer be the slow tick.
The wider the pendulum's arcs, the higher
I will fly, the more unmeasured I'll become.
I will rise. I will fly. I will unmeasure myself.

Thomas

1981

I'll unmeasure myself. I'll unmeasure myself from this day forward. Forward into what? Life as I've known it has ended. I'm unmade in an instant, taken apart into molecules, into infinite particles of energy. I don't know how to reassemble myself. There's nothing here that I've known. The view out the back window down to the lake is altered, the grass bleached white. The trees shimmer in white light that rises from the ground and slides up their trunks. I can see it ooze, watch its slow spread as it takes over everything and the world remakes itself.

I'm inside this body. These are my hands and feet. I can make them move. I sit down, stand up, walk. I brew coffee. I chew toast. I swallow. I'm inside this body. That's all that seems to be the same. My hands feel cold. The skin of my arms feels warm against them. I'm still alive.

I'm still in the same body, and my body is alive. That's all I know right now. I look out the window. I have no idea what I'll do next. My bones are still inside my skin. My head is still attached to my neck. I'm breathing.

I'm in the same body, in the same house, and the back yard is out the window. But there's no way to imagine myself in a life, what will come next.

This is what it takes to start over. It's not that I want to be dead. That would be simple. What this morning is all about is simply not being dead. The white light flows up from the ground and soaks the trees. It's reaching the topmost branches. There's no wind.

Maybe if I start from the beginning, take a shower and wash off death. Maybe if I put on the new jogging suit I bought the other day. Yes, I'll take a shower and wash off death.

─────

My limbs move easily. My breath comes fast, steady. I could run a hundred miles at this pace. Mourning doves call their soft morning call. I imagine them, gray and sweet, in the branches overhead. I can't see them, but it doesn't matter. My heart is steady like my breath. Trees and houses move past, and the road glides under me. People drive by in cars, holding their commuter mugs to their lips. Dogs join me, then drift off.

That's the sun over the trees. That's the sky around the sun. I can feel the heat on the top of my head. The light is golden and warm. I don't know what I'll do next. I don't know how to remake myself or if I just want to stay unmade.

"Good morning," someone says, running the other way on the other side of the road. He looks me in the eye when he says it. I feel my breath swell my lungs, exhale. There's a rhythm to all this, breathing and moving my limbs.

I remember everything: how my face looks in the mirror, my mother's voice, my boss's nervous laugh. I remember driving my car and talking with my neighbor about politics. Last night I peeled potatoes over the sink. I ate a pork chop while I listened to the evening news, made a mental note to put the garbage out by the curb. I washed the dishes, dried them, put them away.

I remember all of it: reading the newspaper, reheating my old coffee, adding peanuts to the grocery list. What I can't remember is what I was thinking just before I decided to die. The decision wasn't a thought. It was more of an action that stirred through my body and came into my head. I wanted not to wake up this morning. I wanted just to die and stay dead. It was so simple: pills and water, and someone would find me, probably when I didn't show up for work for a few days or when the newspapers piled up on the stoop. I remember thinking that. There would be sad people, family, friends at work. But they'd go on and I'd eventually dim. All of this was clear to me when I took the pills.

I woke up this morning like it was an ordinary day. I opened my eyes, saw light coming under the drapes. The room was the same, but I was not. How could I ever be the same again when I wasn't dead? I held up my hand to the light. The palm was familiar. I spread my fingers wide, curled them into a fist, uncurled them. It was morning, and I was alive.

This is the day I'll find out what I do next. My heart is pumping blood. My breathing matches the rhythm of my legs. I could run forever.

It's strange not knowing my life anymore, strange and normal. I wanted to be dead, but this will do instead. Unearthing what I do next and after that, breathing, listening to mourning doves, moving my arms and legs. Yes, this will do. This will do just fine. There's nothing left. I have memories. They're intact. But really all that's left is what I'll do next.

This is morning. These are houses and trees and fences and my arms and legs. This is a road. That's sky. That's the sun.

∽⋱⋰∾

I want to look up. I want my eyes to carry me into the expanse of blue, the net of clouds. I've looked down long enough. I've studied my feet, dead leaves, pebbles and litter long enough.

Now let me have only sky. It seems too bright to stand at first, too big, too far away. How to take it all in, hold it? Yet I have to. Looking up changes the world. I wish I'd known this long ago. Regrets rise like the worms that inhabit my eyes when I focus on blank sky. I'll have to blink them away or learn to see past them.

I'm training myself to look up. How long I've spent with my head down, looking only from side to side, closed, trapped by my own fatal horizon. If only I'd known this before.

Come on, so much for *if only*. I didn't die. I'm not dead. With the finality of finding myself alive—how can I look down or back? It's not possible. I have to untrain myself. How many times have I had the idea that death is final? How absurd! It's not death that's final—it's life.

That's sky. It hurts my eyes, stabs my temples. I'll practice this looking until I don't feel it anymore. Every day I'll look into the sky's white light until it no longer hurts. I'll fight the impulse to look down, force my eyes up. It must be possible to take in more light. Surely, the more light I force in, the better.

I don't have a lot of time to waste on small matters. What my eyes do when faced with sky is important. This is what I do now, train my eyes to take in more light.

This is the seventh day. Each day I've lengthened the time before the pain becomes too intense. When I started, my eyes and my neck were overwhelmed within seconds, but now I can take in the sky for thirty minutes or more before I feel the stabbing and have to stop. It's my discipline to wake, to go outside, to lift my eyes until the pain forces me to look down. Then I rest, my eyes closed, my breathing deep. Then open and up, breathing deeper still, pushing longer. Today I made it to forty-five minutes up, then fifty. I've made fast progress. Good. I don't have time to waste. When I wanted to die, I could afford to throw my time away. But time is all I have now, and it's growing longer.

In the afternoons I train my body. I run until my breath hurts. Then I rest, rolled into a ball off the side of the road, breathe hard until it no longer pains me. Then I run again. Over and over until the hurting time lessens and the running time lengthens. This part of the training is about developing a body that can match my eyes. This is my afternoon discipline. This is what I have to do.

In the evening I prepare for the next day. I eat nourishing foods that please my eyes. It would not do to open my gaze and then pollute it with ugliness. Polluting my body would be just as absurd. I rest, study about light and eyes, about the lungs and the muscles of the leg and torso. Eventually I sleep, but only until first light. It's important that my eyes meet sunrise, just as it is that my body meets sunset. This is the measure of time.

It's also important to remember what I've seen in the sky, in my food, in my evening study, in my sleep. This is a part of the training of my eyes. It's important to feel my full body, the blood pumped by my heart, the exchange of oxygen and carbon dioxide in my lungs. Training my body supports the training of my eyes.

Everything else is replaced. I no longer need other memories, no longer do anything else with my body and eyes. Everything is erased but this.

Vita

1919

Everything had been erased. But suddenly
it was dawn. It was newness. It was the flood
of pink light all over the shadowed land.
Corners were revealed. Bushes took shape
out of darkened air. And I awoke.

I woke to your shadow, the shape of your face
cast over my face, the shape of your hand
over my hand. Then your shadow gave way
to you. You slept, your dark hair cast wide
over your pillow, your breath soft, barely
moving your breast. Your face was soft, too,
full, without any creases of joy or worry, perfect
beauty without thought. I lay looking at you
until the sun rose over your head and blinded me.

There was a moment before the blinding, when
your face eclipsed the sun's light, and a halo
surrounded your head, as if you were the real sun,
the dark sun. But nothing stays for long. The sun
rose higher and blinded me. You were nothing then,
taken, cast into darkness, and I could not see you—
the end of us. How I wish I could keep your aureoled
face, hold the sun still, and time. But the tide rises
and falls. The sun rises and sets. Life, with its utter
demands, comes spilling in, uncontrollable and bright.

And so I returned here, to a life crammed with duty
and prestige, where I cannot picture your face,
so blinded am I. I hold your letter in my hand, proof
that the gloried life existed. Here, amid stone walls
and groomed gardens, I struggle to remember.
Now, in the glaring light, your letter voice sounds

harsh, pleading. I cannot remember your true sound, teasing and musical, the sound of the haloed world.

Dear Violet,

You, too, have tried it, the expected life. You pleased your mother and married well, charming Denys with his sheathed sword, his war accomplishments. You have tried to love him and perhaps you do. Regardless, he is merely one more torture, unreal to me except as whip or rack, my body lashed and torn by the relentless fact that he exists. In spite of him, you call to me, but your voice is grating and rough. In spite of him, you wish to return to the forgotten life, the life that does not exist inside these walls, built so high and thick of ancient stone—

I shall plant a new garden. I shall plant a garden
without plan that can grow in riotous splendor.
I'll surround it with a rock wall to keep it safe,
protect myself from it. I will plant violets
everywhere inside and hope that some spill out
into the grassy lawn, just enough for me to know
that the eclipsed life always exists somewhere.
Then I will have the choice of cropping
their spread or letting them expand their unruly
invasion—lovely to have such a choice.

How does one choose between selves? How do I
weed one side of my nature and let the other grow?
Or shall I construct a tower of stone and mortar,
where I can live quietly, avoid the attack of petals
and leaves? What does it mean to choose? To hack
one self away and cement the other—that is what
I must do. Now you exist only on paper. Your
piercing voice bleeds its ink onto the page. A tower
and a garden wall—one to keep myself in and one
to keep you in. Perhaps I can live in weeded peace.

If another choice existed, what would be its name,
its place? Where could I go to live with you, without
my dear husband and children shadowing our faces?
Perhaps I was the one who died. Perhaps the boy
who never lived outside my womb was really me,
my tiny male self, the one who wakes when I am
with you, the one who grows into manhood
in your presence. When that baby never lived,
I thought I would lose my mind, but now I see
that I have lost myself instead. Can I live as only
one of my selves, let the other die in my womb?

Part 1

Dear Violet,

Your letter pleads with me to come away with you again, to live in our flowered world where there are no walls, the world in which we do not even try to stay out of the rain, where we can stroll unnoticed except by those who say what a handsome couple we make. I am tempted. I am tempted to throw away all the trappings of civilization, the corset, the assumed delicacies, even motherhood. Then I could live in the wild world with you. I could let my trousered self out of the womb, walk proudly with your gloved hand on my sleeve down the streets of Florence or Monte Carlo.

But your voice is far away. And my two sons' voices rise and fall so sweetly outside my window. I am inside walls, where love and duty have come to rest at my feet.

The maid knocks and asks if I will dress for dinner. I say yes, aware that I can dress only one of my selves here, in skirts and slippers and pearls. My other self must dress elsewhere or not at all.

"Yes," I say to the maid. "I shall come shortly." And still there is no answer for you. Pen and paper mock me—

Dear Violet,

"I shall wear the purple velvet dress," I told the maid, noticing the irony only when I was seated at the long dining table gleaming in lamplight. My dress was the colour of violets, the innermost heart of their curved petals. I smiled at Harold, so comfortable in his suit, born to the head of the table. It comes smoothly to him, being father and husband and diplomat, being who he is. Uneasy in my folds of velvet, in my pearls, I envied his ease, his single self. I envied the deepness of his voice, his seasoned conversation, the clothes that are not trappings but second skin. The boys sat quietly, spoke when they were addressed. How early the walls of civilization have closed them in.

We engaged in lively conversation, Harold and I, and I know there is a self here who loves him, who knows why I married him, who lives beyond duty. He told me stories about his trips to London and Paris, and I am allowed in the smoke-filled rooms that I could never walk into myself—at least not the self who lives here with him. He made me laugh when he imitated Lord Countington, with his blustery words that say nothing, mere wind that fails to deliver the promised storm. The boys laughed, too, part of our inner, secret circle, separate from the rest of the world. Harold and I ended with sherry in the salon while Nanny prepared the boys for bed. He grew serious and told me how happy he is that I have returned home. He told me of his work at Versailles, translating peace into borders, into geography.

France, Austria, Belgium, Poland, Czechoslovakia. My eyes filled with tears. I could not help it—his voice was so vibrant, so present, so sure, his work so much larger than mere boundaries.

But eventually I returned here, to my bedroom, sheltered now from everyone, my attempts to write to you strewn across my desk. Your letter lies in its envelope on the dressing table where I left it. It lies folded and silent, and I realized that for some stretch of time during dinner and afterward, some undetermined length of minutes, whole minutes, I forgot you. And I forgot my other self, dead in its walled womb, born dead into stillness and cold air—

Thomas

1981

I no longer wait for anything. I wake each morning as if for the first time. I dress quickly and go outside to run. I do my stretches luxuriously, taking all the time in the world, because preparation is part of doing, and these muscles are all I have.

And then I run. I run until I stop. Each day I run longer and farther, but there's no plan, or time, or speed. There are no rules. Running is the only rule. I run and run and run, as far and as long as it takes. Sometimes I go past the white church and down the steep hill. Run the dirt road, the main route to Boston in the days when mail was carried by coach. It's a smooth road, well cared for by the county, settled in a hollow between two ridges. I like to run there, where there are no houses, only woods and rock and an occasional stream. When I come to the paved road at the other end, I have choices about where to run next, but I don't make them in my head—my feet carry me past the sheep farm or up the hill to where the old deserted village lies, its remnant stone foundations hidden now by brush and vines and forest.

My feet know all these places, so my head doesn't have to. I run until my legs decide to stop or until they bring me back home or until I find myself looking into the sun, and then I know it's time. I don't decide—it just happens. I'll round a corner into the light, and that's it. My feet move more slowly, cooling me down, and my eyes start their workout. I've developed my regimen enough that I don't have to make it happen anymore. Instead, my eyes and feet take over. Now I can look toward the sun all afternoon, and as the days lengthen into summer, I imagine my eyes will lengthen their looking.

It no longer hurts. My pupils adjust smoothly and immediately. There's no pain when they first find the brightness. I don't waste time anymore. I go right to the opening that lets in all the light.

And so I stare at the sun for hours now, without pain, without any risk of blindness. I know this is impossible, but I do it anyway. I stare at the sun until my eyes stop blinking or closing or looking away. Then I know it's time to return home for food and sleep, so I can run and absorb the sun again the next day. This is the secret of my life now, the way I'll come to the next phase, whatever that might be. I don't think about it. I just know that letting in the sun and running far are important. They are what I do.

I still have dreams. My dreams are about people and places I used to know or have never seen. They roll through my sleep like movies, and I watch them. I don't ask for them—they just come, unbidden. That's what night is for, resting and watching what spins past my eyes after a day of running and sun.

Since I woke that morning, alive, and began running and taking in sunlight, it's rained only in my dreams. Sometimes I dream a storm, and I wake to find a rainbow stretched over the lake, the road outside my house wet, steam rising into the sunny, warming air. But I never see rain when I'm awake.

It must be night spilling into day. I don't question it. I had to give up thinking. I found that I could stare toward the sun for longer and longer periods, but if I started to think about it, I'd get a stabbing pain in my eyes and I'd have to stop. Or I'd be running and a thought would cross my mind, and I'd stumble or get a charley horse. So I gave up thinking. The less I thought, the longer I could look and the farther I could run.

Now the seasons have stopped altogether. I dream of fall and spring and winter and summer, and sometimes I wake to find leaves or snow patches on the ground. But each of my days is sunny, long and warm.

When I woke to find I was still alive, I couldn't go back. Not to my job or my longing or my negativity. I could only go forward into something that didn't exist before. That's the way it was all along, but I didn't know it. Now I do—it's that simple.

So the old fell away. My life became running and sun, food and sleep and dreams. That's what it takes to start over. Take handfuls of pills, wake to life, and then the old will fall away and the new will take its place.

Under all the thinking, once it's brushed away and cleared, you find life. It seems so long ago now. I stopped thought by looking at the sun and running. And underneath it all was life.

Vita

1919

Underneath it all is life. Underneath
the brassiere and underskirt and stockings
and jewelry, the just-so hair, the finely
tailored dress and gloves—underneath it all
am I—naked, revealed—my true nature.
I could throw off these garments and live
as I am meant to live, fiery and bold. My
mother's nature, my father's nature, my own
are woven like a net cast over my body,
tightened—how to undo all the knots? How
to undo all the centuries, the generations
of expectations that come with living
in a great house in a small world?
If I knew, I would be able to heal the sick.
I would be able to fly.

Each night before sleep the knots unravel
by their own will. I slide free into dreaming,
stretch my cramped limbs, beautifully naked.
My movements lengthen, and I dance, faster
and faster, spinning wildly until I lift from earth.
My true nature—I was meant to fly.

The world is a small place. I see that each night
in my spinning flight. The world is a repetition
of green fields, blue lakes, brown tree trunks,
grey buildings. Over and over patterns of expected
colour repeat themselves below me, the manicured
world, the world men have made, each thing
in its own place. But from the air I see, too,
that I have been mistaken. There is not always
each thing in its prescribed place. I see the force
of handiwork. Yes, I see what hands have wrought—
a world bound by walls, fences, neat city streets.

But once in a while a shock of colour shows itself,
a spread of crimson outside a garden wall, or a stable
in sudden flame. Each night in my winged dreams,
I study how flowers escape from their laid-out rows,
reach their tendrils beyond fence or wall, how flames
spread and roar out of control, bursting past organized
life. Last night I flew into a storm, into its pulse, great
bolts of light thrown around me, wind and rain lashing
the air. A night of wild ravings, wild sight. I whipped
and spun with airborne flame, let the wind ravish me.

30 June

Yesterday a poem, today only this diary. This morning I woke in a bed, in a chamber, within walls. The net seemed tighter than ever, cutting into my skin. My day and night selves do not meet. My day and night selves turn their backs on each other, and I am swallowed in the space between. The air is heavy and contained. I wish I had two bodies to live in. One would be the necklaced woman who exchanges witticisms, who notes the glow on the silver serving tray, who smiles with her chin on her son's tousled hair, who knows her place. The other would be the trousered and leathered man, whose strides take him down long city blocks, whose amorous desires translate into slippery love, whose arms and legs are strong and tough, whose laugh is deep and easy.

I wish I could be both and live in two worlds, one I make and one made for me.

I do not wish to live on paper, but that is where my true life seems to be. I watch the ink form across the page, and I wish to give life to it, to weave pigment and paper into breath.

I cannot go to Violet now. She must trust me, not ask too much. I must see myself through Harold's return from Versailles and our fortnight in London. There are things that I must do in this expected life.

But when I go to Violet, I will be a storm at sea. I will sweep her shipwrecked to a hot and fragrant land, and the waiting will turn into sun.

I watched a raven this morning, roosting
in the oak outside my study. I was very still
and the raven very near. He preened himself,
carefully inserting his beak among his feathers.

He was lovely, his blue-black sheen, his sharp,
dark eyes. I wished him to talk to me, to tell me
of the world of flight. I wished to ride his back,
to live inside his body. He arched his supple neck,
spread his wings, fluttered them a few slow times,
and settled. Always his eyes darted everywhere,
keen, watchful, ready. How I loved him. My heart
filled with joy and I admired every inch of him.

He was magnificent, and I longed to know his name,
to be on speaking terms, to let him be my master
and I his wide-eyed pupil. If there is a God, I thought
it must be he, so beautiful and black. I sat watching
him sleep. Then he woke and flew away.

I watched him still, as he grew smaller, a speck
and then nothing, and I was left behind.

6 July

If only Mother understood. She's so absorbed in her own affairs that she doesn't even see me. I have taken her side enough times, even with Father, yet I long hopelessly for her to take mine.

When Violet and I were girls, Mother was delighted with our friendship. She thought Violet flighty but could not resist her family. She loved my stories about Violet and me being swept from the sitting room and hushed when the King's coach arrived outside. Mother could not get enough of it, my glimpses of His Majesty, my descriptions of Violet's mother's complexion. Only later did I come to understand. Violet had to tell me, and I puzzled over what it might be like to be the King's mistress.

For Violet it was nothing extraordinary. It was eating luncheon in the kitchen instead of the dining room. It was quiet, boring afternoons staying hidden and out of the way. But for me it was intrigue and mystery, strapping swords on and off, the feel of fine leather gloves. I would be the King, of course, mounting the steps two at a time to the woman waiting breathless at the top of the staircase.

The first time Violet kissed me I felt strong and lovely, but I brushed it aside. I was so young and taken with Rosamund, and I did not understand then how big the heart can be, how much room it has for love.

This is the morning to face the divided world, to decide, to move into one body and stay there, to withstand the pulling, meddling voices. I mean this. I write it every morning, but this morning I mean it. I shall leave one door open and slam the other closed, locked, nailed shut. This is the morning to erase one world and to inhabit fully the other. Which will it be?

Yet this is where I falter. I contemplate dividing and am exquisitely firm and clear. Yes, I shall. I shall decide. But how? There is the world of this house and my boys and the generations that have come before us and will come after us and our lives sandwiched between. And there is Violet and Monte Carlo and the night air on my face under my man's hat and the early mornings of hysterical love. Both are real. Both are unreal. Both are love. Both are slow death.

This is where I falter each day, when I cannot rise from bed, when I want to go back to my dreams of flying, when I wish for sweet death, sweet peace. I wish I could go to sleep and wake in another century, myself but new.

This is when I pick up my pen. Words slice through dense air, and I take a breath. That is what I manage, words and breathing. I continue to live. I continue to live in this middle, undecided place. Yet this is the place where hope manages to breathe, too, where possibility sits to my right and to my left.

Part 1

The winged child stands in the garden,
head bowed, wings folded. I do not know
whether she has just landed or if she
has not yet taken off. This is how I wish
to live—with the possibility of flight.

She is a girl, with girlish features. I wish
to sculpt a woman, to give her breasts,
elongate her fingers, her face, her limbs.
I want her to stand upright, her eyes
straight ahead, her wings muscular,
poised to lift her from the ground.

Anna

1981

When I first met him, I thought he was really strange. I used to drive the same way to work every day, and some days I'd see him standing along the side of the road looking up. One day it was pouring, and thunder and lightning seemed to be getting closer and more intense. Then I saw him, and I don't know why I did it, but I pulled over and asked him if he needed a ride to get out of the storm. He blinked a few times and then looked at me, his pupils so big that his eyes seemed totally black. He said finally, "No, thank you."

I drove on, a wall of rain flooding over my car so I could barely see, even with the wipers on the fastest setting. I had chills up and down my spine, thinking first that he must be crazy or drugged, but then the chills grew into an uncontrollable shiver when I realized that his clothes had been dry. I shoved my foot down harder on the gas pedal so I could get out of there. But it haunted me. For days it haunted me, so I couldn't concentrate on what I was doing. I kept seeing his image, his dry clothes, his dry hair, in the middle of that violent, crazy storm. I'd go to sleep at night and dream of him in his green running clothes, dry underneath a waterfall, his pupils filling his eyes.

The next time I saw him, he was running along the same road. I couldn't help myself. I pulled over and ran hard until I caught up to him. It wasn't easy in my pantyhose and pumps. He didn't seem to notice I was there, so I said, "Hello. Nice day for running, isn't it?"

"It's always a nice day for running," he answered, without slowing or turning his head. I got winded and my feet hurt, but as I dropped back, I swear I saw the fingers of his right hand ripple a wave to me. I waved back though I knew he couldn't see me behind him. I was a few minutes late to the office that day and somewhat disheveled, but I managed to do my work, even with him stalking it.

I began to look forward to my commute each morning, hoping I'd come across him again. And I found myself exercising more regularly. I wanted to be able to keep up with him. I found myself thinking about him a lot, hoping his form would show itself to me at the movie theater or grocery store or on the shoulder of the road again as I drove.

I continued to exercise faithfully, but months went by before I came upon him again, in the same spot on the side of the road, running. This time he stopped and turned to face me. I pulled the car over. He walked to the passenger door, opened it and got in.

Possibility, I thought, my heart pounding as he got into the car. I could have jumped out, run down the road and away—but there he sat, the one I'd hoped to find again.

I guess I was looking at him too long because he turned to me and said, "Possibility is always on either side. I could open this door and leave," he said, "be away on foot quickly and easily—or there you are, sitting to my left and staring at me."

"I'm sorry," I found myself saying. "It's just that I'd been expecting you, and yet you came as such a surprise." He was young, considerably younger than I. I would say he was in his early thirties. He was slender, with a lean face. His eyes were blue, a shade I hadn't seen before, clear and very light. Now that I had him here, what would I say and do? I had no idea who he was, where we'd go. He had brown hair, longish, and a brown beard. Everything about him seemed lean and stretched, like a figure in an El Greco painting come to life in a jogging suit.

I felt quite strange, as if I'd eaten one of those cakes Alice found in Wonderland, as if I might grow bigger or smaller at the morsel's whim. We sat in the car with the engine running for what seemed like endless minutes.

"I don't have a lot of time," he said, "but I can spend a few hours with you if you like. This is the morning we've met, so we should probably get on with it. My name is Thomas. Where would you like to go?"

I thought about it but had to stop, because thinking would only get me into a senseless realm. I didn't know who he was or where we should go. I just felt compelled. That's all: compelled.

"I don't know," I said, and I really didn't, but he didn't look amused.

"Look," he said, "I'm happy you invited me, and I do have a few hours to spend, but I don't have time to waste. I haven't been with people for quite some time, so the social graces are not my strong point. I need to be back here when the sun hits its peak in the sky, so make up your mind." He didn't say it harshly or unkindly, just straightforwardly, as if he were making an appointment or asking a question about auto insurance. I was used to those questions and wondered what my boss would say if I were late for work, especially today when the quarterly report was already past deadline. At that moment premiums and policy changes seemed foreign, a language I couldn't quite speak. I revved the engine and pulled forward from the shoulder onto the road.

"My name is Anna," I said. I just drove so we'd be going somewhere.

"What was it you wanted to talk about?" he asked, shifting forward in the seat and tilting his face toward the morning sun.

"I don't know," I replied, my voice sounding wavy and little. "I just felt a need to stop."

"That's a good start. It's best not to think or put a name to it too early. The wide approach," he said and smiled a half-smile, a wry smile. "Turn in here," and he pointed to the right with his chin. I turned off onto the side road that followed the river. I kept going and crossed the narrow, one-lane bridge where the river bent to the other side of the road and the woods started. I loved that river, rocky and shallow and fast. I sometimes pulled into this road on the way home from work to sit and hear the water's sounds. It was cool, too, after a cooped-up day without enough air and with too many phone calls and questions and crises.

"Turn in here," he said, gesturing to the left, where a narrow dirt road rose up the slope to the cemetery. I did what he said, but then my heart froze, as I imagined a knife or a gun or a cord at my throat and my body lying awkward in the sun.

It was the only cemetery in town, as old as the settlement and nearly full, but there was one section still open if you could get your name on the list. I knew this because our agency sold life insurance, and people talked about all sorts of things when someone died. It was a part of my job that made me squirm, hearing about bodily secretions, last words, and what someone should wear in the coffin. It seemed like none of my business.

I kept driving up the dirt road, two tire tracks really, with a grass strip in the middle. I inched along slowly. My car was low and there were sharp rocks protruding in some places. Here I was, thinking of my own last rites, somewhere between my murder by strangulation and a client's newly dead husband, dead just the other night from choking on steak. Here I was in the cemetery with a man I didn't know, who sat elongated and thin in green sweats on the other side of the car.

"Stop here," Thomas said. The cemetery was empty and as we got out of the car, I could feel the sun's heat and hear the cascading notes of a robin. It was hard not to think of joy when I heard that robin's song. Thomas and I walked along side by side up the slope to a level place dotted with headstones. He was taller than I, and he walked in an easy, smooth way. We stopped next to a freshly dug grave. From this spot on the hillside, you can see down to the craggy river, to the woods and the tarred road. There's a spaciousness, a sense of expanse.

"I used to think I'd be buried here," Thomas said, and his voice was startling in the quiet. "I imagined a grave like this, though I didn't dwell on that part. It was more of a feeling, a drive, sudden and compelling, and I knew I would end up here." His tone was calm and steady, and I glanced at him out of the corner of my eye, still nervous about his intentions. What if he had some crazy notion that this was my grave? I didn't say anything.

"But I didn't die," he kept on. "I tried to. I did all the right things, the right dosage, the right drug, the right moonless night, but I didn't die."

I still didn't say anything, not knowing my part, divided about being there with the dark, raw earth gaping in front of me. I walked to the grave's other end, and we stood there for some time, he at one end and I at the other, the sun warm, the air windless, the robins singing back and forth to each other. The grave was a deep hole, deeper than I'd imagined when clients called with their trembling needs. I reached down and picked up a handful of the loose, moist dirt, let it fall through my fingers, brushed them clean.

An old woman with a kerchief tied loosely over her hair drove up in a rusty maroon station wagon and parked below us. She took a flat of petunias out of the back and trudged in her rubber boots up the rise.

"Beautiful morning," she said, her face lit by a grin. Thomas nodded and I nodded, and then the woman said, "I have a big jug of water you could carry up here for me if you would be so kind."

Thomas and I both started to move at the same time, so I said, "I'll get it," relieved to break the silence and my visions of impending murder.

The woman kept her slow, steady pace upward, while I loped down to her car and then climbed back up the hill as quickly as I could. The water jug gurgled and made me lopsided. I could see her up ahead, small and bent. When I got up there, she'd set the petunias down and was leaning against a marble marker, supporting her weight by resting her hand on the top.

"My husband," she said, patting the stone. "Been here thirty years. Every spring I come and bring him flowers." She giggled like a young girl and smiled at me, her head cocked coyly to one side. "My son is here, too," she added. "This is the family living room. I come up here and we chat, and I remember each of their faces. I thought I might forget, but I haven't. They were together in the accident and they still are, the first graves when this section opened up. They were here by themselves for quite a time. Someday I'll be here, too, but I'm not in any hurry. You'd think I would be, with both of them gone, but I'm not. I still got things to do. Who are you visiting? I know just about everybody here. I been living in this town all my life."

"No one," I answered. "It's just a beautiful place to come."

"That grave you were looking at is for Anna," and my heart started racing. But then she finished, "Anna Waldrop. She was in the rest home over in Putnam, but they're going to put her here because she lived in this town most her life, too. You live here? I don't seem to know you."

"I live over on the lake road," I said. I could see Thomas walking down toward the car. "I guess I'd better go. My friend needs to get home. I hope you have a nice day."

"Oh, I will, all right, I always do. You, too, Honey. I don't know him either," she said, pointing her chin down toward Thomas, "but he looks okay to me. Maybe a little young for you," and she winked.

I descended the slope to the car, regretting the mistake I'd made, worrying that I should be at work and wondering what Mr. Powell must think of me now. I'd never been this late to work before without a dentist appointment or a power outage. Thomas was sitting in the car when I got down the hill, and he said, "You can just drop me off where you found me. That woman was beautiful, wasn't she? Her smile was contagious."

"Why did we come here?" I asked him.

And he answered, "Don't you know?" His question hung in the air, and then he was quiet. I pulled onto the main road again, heading north, back where we'd started. I didn't speak either. The silence seemed right all of a sudden, and I didn't want to spoil it.

I stopped the car near the spot where I'd picked him up, just beyond the little run-down farm at the bend in the road, and Thomas got out of the car. I backed into a dirt space at the edge of a sprouting hayfield to turn around and head to work again, forming excuses for Mr. Powell. Thomas started to cross the road but then turned and came back toward me.

I rolled down the window, and he leaned his face in, almost touching mine, and he whispered, "Don't you know?" And then he was running.

Vita

1919

12 July

I watch Nigel run, small and steady on his legs, his skinned knee forgotten. My legs do not always feel that they support an adult roving through the world. I take in what is in front of me: my beloved sons and their cascades of laughter, the fragrances of grass and roses, the oaks in full leaf under a hazy sky, nudged by a reluctant wind. The stones in the foundation of this house, laid by hand, laid by hands with broken fingernails, by breaking backs. My back does not feel strong enough to bear the expectations of my ancestors and the needs of my children while my bones try to expand enough for me to breathe.

I live in a house of men. And so I must be my woman here. There is no other way to be. I slip into my woman clothes, button myself into them. There is nothing else to do here. I am the woman and I wear her. It is simple, really, once I get out of bed. But each morning I must be born into her body. I do not wake there. My night flying is without gender, without name. So I must be born into her body each morning. It is not an easy thing.

Sometimes I wish for it to end. Sometimes I wish to lie in a long sleep and dream a long dream. I would not wake for centuries, and then into another body, a body that could bear its load of flesh and longing. I wish for a way to cut myself loose from this collection of bones and blood into the realm of thought, not the messy thoughts among egg cups and silver arranged symmetrically for breakfast, but the pure thoughts that live their sharp and silent lives and then enter me each night as I sleep. I long for the membrane between day and night to disappear and make a way for me to live in the middle, where pure thought and pure sensing meet and entwine their curling fingers around me. I long for a self not divided between thought and sense, but joined, so that a blue sky enters my mind directly and I live in it as much as I live anchored to this earth.

How did I get to this place that is not a place but only longing? How did I arrive nowhere at all, but lost? I am either mind or body, and when I am body, I am two—man and woman. When I am mind, my body exists in some other realm, and it lives like an animal, guided only by instinct and primitive sense, sniffing its way along without me. I am here and not here. And my mind goes on its exquisite way, bedecked with jewels that never grace my slender neck.

Yes, that is what I long for, jeweled thoughts that I can wear around my neck and wrists, thoughts that appear where my body can find them, where I can actually touch their polished edges. I wish to unite everything—

If only I could hold the land of my birth. But I will be torn from it, or rather it will be torn from me because I have breasts, because I cannot record a male name on a deed. I think I must have split long ago, growing up as I have done, Father's only child, knowing I would never own the land of my ancestors—surely a deep divide, so deep it can never be bridged.

Everything is divided: Here is my love for my children. Here is the love for my shrill and notorious mother. Here is the love for Harold. Here is the love for Violet. Here is the love for my benign and distracted father. These are the pieces that can never fit together, a bizarre mosaic from which no picture emerges, only scattered bits cemented to a wall. The wall settles and cracks emerge, so that even a single piece of tile is no longer whole.

Yes, I am cracking. If I were to look in the mirror too closely, I would see brittle lines etched into my skin. Perhaps some morning I will wake in shards, unable even to assemble a body to get out of bed.

I wonder if I can live in cracks. I wonder if I can work star-tipped fingers into the widening cracks, learn to live in the space between pieces, a realm of mind and body that is not flesh or idea. What kind of body do I need to slide into a crack and live there? What kind of mind? A body that is not a body and a mind that is not a mind. The lull between gusts of wind, the silence between sea waves, the pause between night and dawn.

Nigel, in his skinned-knee body, did he enter it when he entered my womb? Did Ben come into those pudgy limbs, that lovely head, in the rounded darkness inside me? And my dead son— the one who never lived outside me, my unnamed son— where did he go?

I do not know how to live in this body. I do not know how to live in my clothes. I do not know how to live in a world that is made and unmade every dawn and dusk. There are no maps here. There are no maps in this wilderness. There is only one wild thing after another.

I keep writing this over and over, in jerking phrases and circular lines. I write this again and again, hating it, hating the way I cannot speak directly about this suffering. There are no words for it.

When Harold is away, I look at him as if through a glass, bring him closer to me as I can the stars, far away but magnified. Harold can make peace for all of Europe, but I cannot seem to create it here. There are worlds I must travel where he cannot follow because even I do not know where they are. Yet he is my home, the place to return, where all is familiar, the chair by the window, the vase of roses on the table. I need to go where there is no map and return to find the furniture in the same place.

Violet wants me to come to her. She writes again, please come to her. And I am compelled to go. With Violet there are glimpses. I go to her for glimpses. With her I step into my male body and enter the world. We stroll. We dine. No one knows that I wear my other body then. It is simply who I am.

I must decide. But tough ropes hold me here, pull me back in this direction. Their fibers would have to stretch and break for me to go. I long for it to be in some other realm than decision. I wish it were easy to slide back and forth between bodies, as easy as dressing.

Is this all foolishness? Some would say so. Some would call me naïve or spoiled. But I am not concerned about escape. I want the full entering. I wish to wake each morning and go about my whole life, not half of it. I feel things seeping from me all the time: thoughts, words, breath, love. I have seams that leak things out into the world, where the press of air carries them to be caught by others. I would like to hold on to it all, just once hold on to it all and rise into nothing, suspended over earth, lifted higher and higher, full of everything but weightless.

The whole of life: seamless and smooth, a polished globe that captures the sun and casts its light in focused streams that blind and burn. I would be the sun itself, my own heat and light reaching everywhere, resting only at night with the moon as my memory. Yet there are dangers. The sun is farther away than it seems. And there is the danger of flying too close to my own flame and falling back to earth broken. I must be ready. I must be ready to look into my own light without being blinded, without burning away.

❧☙

"Agnes, what do you say of love?" Vita asked, as her maid fastened a string of pearls around Vita's neck and stood back to admire her in the mirror.

"Oh, Madam, I love putting me feet up at the end of the day." Agnes brought her hand to her mouth, but in the mirror her twinkling eyes belied her propriety. Both women laughed.

"We have conversed often in this mirror, Agnes. You know me better than anyone."

"Those are sad words, Madam. You have a handsome husband and such pretty little boys, so many grand friends and parents what dote on you. I hope I haven't taken liberties to say it."

"The mirror welcomes liberties, Agnes. Please—say something about love."

"Madam, pardon my words, but love is for those of your station what has the time for it. What could the likes of me know about love?"

"Haven't you loved someone, Agnes? Surely you have."

"I loved me mum, but she were taken early by the consumption. I loved me brothers and sisters, but being the eldest, I went into service young. You knew these things when I come here, Madam. What more should I be telling you?"

"Was there ever a time when you did something wild, without regret, when your heart spoke more loudly than duty?"

"I have not liberty to be wild, Madam. Surely you understand what divides us."

"Of course, Agnes, but I speak of the heart."

"Some things is best unspoken, Madam, the heart being one of them."

"That sounds harsh, Agnes, when I know your heart to be kind."

"I cannot afford it, Madam."

"Afford what, Agnes?"

"Please Madam, do not force me to speak of it."

"I do not wish to force anything. I ask you to speak of your heart only because my heart needs a friend. In the mirror we have been friends many times, have we not?"

"I have loved, Madam, foolish and wise." The words tumbled out, as if Agnes had been waiting to release them. "But he fell at Ypres."

"Oh, no, Agnes—where the Germans used poison gas." Vita turned away from the mirror, toward her.

"No, Madam, keep the mirror between us. I cannot bear it otherwise."

"Tell me about him," Vita whispered, obeying.

"A tailor he were. He come to measure the master of my last great house, where I were housemaid, before I come here to be lady's maid to you. He laid out his fine woolens and silks, his buttons and threads, while I tended the fire and lit the lamps. His fingers was slender, his smile so handsome. He visited again and again—the master were fussy and a clotheshorse. My man were always joking and lifting the spirit, he were, and always he had the latest fancies to show the master. He asked for my hand, and I did not refuse him." Vita fought her inclination to turn, met Agnes's eyes in the mirror instead. Agnes swiped at her tears with her fists.

"I am so sorry to know that you lost him."

"Oh, that weren't all I—" Agnes looked away. Vita waited, but Agnes remained silent.

"Is there more?" Vita finally asked.

"I cannot speak of it, for your sake."

"Whatever do you mean?"

"Madam, I do not wish to make you cry."

"I do not understand you. Why should I cry?"

"Because you lost ... oh, no, Madam, I cannot say it."

"Lost what, Agnes? Whatever do you mean? Now you must say it."

"The babe," Agnes whispered. Vita stiffened, then took an audible breath.

"You must say it. Please, Agnes."

"Madam, when you lost your babe, I could not help you. I were thinking only of mine. I lost my babe, too, you see. Not like you—mine lived—but I lost him. I gave him away." Agnes began to cry again.

"What are you saying, Agnes?"

"I could not keep him, I could not. My man and I never married. He had to go too long to his father's sickbed and then make his father's funeral, and then he went for the soldiering, and I never did see him again. He were a good man, but he did not know of the child. I were afraid to tell him, for fear he would not go to his father or to the war as he should. I did not want to spoil his conscience, you see, to make him feel split in two."

"How did you manage, Agnes?"

"I told Mrs. Stiles, the housekeeper, and she sent me to her sister in the North. It was all arranged. I gave the babe away the day he was born. I do not even know who took him, but I have to think them kind because Mrs. Stiles and her sister was so kind. I could not go back to the great house then, but Mrs. Stiles give me a letter of introductory, bless her, and I come to you. I were grateful, you see. There were naught else to do. I had no prospects otherwise."

"How awful for you. I cannot imagine it," Vita said after a moment, tears filling her eyes. "Oh, Agnes, you did help me. You helped me more than anyone. I am able to say it aloud: the stillbirth of my middle son. Afterwards, without you, I shan't have risen from my bed, morning after morning." Vita's shoulders shook with sobs, though she made no sound. Agnes stood behind her, resting her hands on Vita's shoulders until the shaking stopped and Vita raised her head.

"I need you now, Agnes. There is something I think you know, which divides me, and I cannot put myself back together. Do you understand what I mean? I have no one else to tell, no one but you. Many would say it is mere wildness, but I know you will not judge me, because truly, Agnes, it is love. Real and honest love has torn me into pieces the way you did not want your man divided. You protected him, but I have no protection. It is too late for me. Do you understand? I love Harold and my sons, and I love Violet equally. I cannot live without any of them. I have tried, but I cannot. What am I to do?" Vita looked to the mirror as more tears came, but Agnes did not meet her eyes.

"If I may say so, Madam, this crimson gown and these pearls suits you. Far more than them trousers in the wardrobe, no matter how fine the wool and stitching and how sharp the crease. I will take my leave now. Your husband will be waiting in the dining room, Madam, and you are looking so well."

Bill

1945

I'm in snow. It's white everywhere. Only stick trees break it up, cutting into milky sky. There are so many of us, hundreds or thousands. We're lost in a white, blinding hollow.

My feet are still in my boots. I move one boot at a time, heavy and wet. The snow is deep. I follow the feet of the man ahead of me, step with the man beside me. We are a long column of dim men in ice. I can't look behind me, can't risk it, but I know I'm in the middle of an endless line of stumbling men, walking and thinking. It's impossible not to think. I've been trying to turn it off, just watch my feet, let the rhythm of so many feet quiet me. But they keep sliding in, thoughts.

I wonder what the others think under their rock faces. I don't dare go beyond what will keep me going. To think or feel more than that—I might as well turn and run and get a bullet in my back.

I still have my boots. It's lucky. When I got wind the Germans were taking boots, I sliced mine up, the tops flapping like crows. A lucky thing to think fast. Now I have to think slow. Slow. They got my knife. They got my gun. But I got to keep my boots. So far. It doesn't do any good to wonder where we're going. It won't be a good place to come to. This walking in snow, marching in a line of dying men—this is the best I've got.

A handful of snow, quick, in step, the only food. It's grainy, something to chew on and swallow. I got to keep my wedding ring, too, under my tongue. Everything else they can have. Boots on my feet. Ring in my mouth. This is how to stay alive. Watch my feet. Watch the white ground, the packed trail. Other men marching in socks, wet, matted socks. Or bare feet.

This is about keeping. Keeping boots, ring. Keeping quiet. Keeping hope. Keeping alive. Keeping going, one foot in front of the other.

※

I can't get warm. Hot, but icy cold. I don't know if it's morning or night. They merge in this fever, this sweat. This is the time I could die. It's come to this.

There's a white light inside my head. I make myself look at it. I look long and hard, and everything else burns away. Everything except me. If only there was water. Water to drink. A drop on my lips.

※

We're here now, arrived I don't know where. Days in snow, in cattle cars, to get here— dingy barracks on some damn German map.

Tea in the morning. Lukewarm tea. A hunk of bread. Lucky when it's not green. I don't drink the tea. My buddy taught me that. I wash with it, let it clean the bed bug sores. The bread is hard. I chew and chew, trick my stomach into thinking it's getting something good. A turkey dinner with gravy and all the fixings. I chew and chew, try to fool my stomach. It doesn't last long.

I write Madeline letters in my head. *Darling—I'll be home soon.* I'll get off a ship and be on solid ground. The other side of the ocean. A train, and home. Everything is monumental. The sofa we saved up for. A Sunday drive in the car we saved up for. They're like movies in the theater. Big and dramatic. The soldier always comes home to the girl. It ends with a close-up, a kiss.

I used to play basketball. I was pretty good, had a pretty good lay-up. I never went to high school because I had to work, but we had a town team that played all over. Once I got carried off the court on the guys' shoulders. A lucky shot that won the game.

Luck. The right place at the right time. The right thought at the right time can save your boots and your life.

They killed someone this morning. I heard they caught him in the kitchen stealing food. He was a kid, just a kid. Eighteen, nineteen at the most. They shot him.

This goes on forever. Each day a few more minutes of light.

Minutes make a difference. Each minute is more time, more light. A hair's breadth of warmth. One blanket is all, one blanket on a mat stuffed with hay, full of bugs. One minute makes a difference. We're counted. Each morning and night we're counted. Tonight there was one less.

They gave each of us a postcard to write home on. A red cross at the top, a blank for each word, twelve:

Darling. Alive. Prisoner Germany. Fine. Send peanut butter, cigarettes. A baby! Love.

Madeline goes to the post office after work and it's there. Real words from me. I still have her letter, here in my pocket, the one I carried on the ship, through the nightmare, still here. I didn't get to answer it. We're going to have a child. Next summer. I hope he has a father. Words are all there is. There are words on paper, and a world closes and another one opens.

∽⟁∾

From a distance you couldn't be sure it was human, a heavy thing, limp, turning. You imagined a sound, rope creaking, strained. You imagined a last thought, a last word. What would it be, a last anything?

The last time I saw Madeline, I knew it was the last time, so it was awkward. There was a hanging together, a reluctance to let go, one more minute, thirty more seconds. It's different when you don't know. It's different when you go along not savoring, not holding, because you don't know it's the last time. Then when you look back, you see how everything was charged with an urgency you didn't recognize.

I shouldn't spend my time thinking. But thinking is what gives my time no end. Otherwise it's hemmed in by four walls and mud, a tiny world with no past or future. I can't live like that, suspended, with nothing behind me and nothing ahead.

I saw the edge of the woods. I saw a leaf, a small, shriveled leaf, suspended in the air on a length of spider web. The air was still, but the leaf moved, turning slightly. It hung there, a remnant, turning just a trifle in quiet air.

Another young one, another kid, probably foolish or maybe too brave. They made us watch it, like they make us watch everything meant to maim us, meant to make us not think.

They made us watch while they checked and rechecked the sturdiness of the structure, while they tied the knot and checked its hold. They made him watch, too, his hands bound so tight behind him that his chest was pushed forward. They made him hold his head up, his neck bent back at an odd angle. If his chin sunk down or his eyes dropped, they'd prod him with a bayonet until he looked up again.

I didn't know him. I only knew his age, twenty, and his crime, attempt to escape. I knew how some of the men around me reacted, either shaking their heads at his foolishness, or nodding in thanks that it wasn't them. Or muttering praise under their breath that made him a hero for just a minute. I was all three, muddled about whether to laugh or cry, knowing either was dangerous.

They stretched it out. They made it stink. They made a show of checking and rechecking, prodding him to bent-back attention. Each minute they took made his life a little longer. All of us watched him have his last thoughts. All of us watched, lined up and counted, counted more fiercely than the day before.

Finally they poked him forward, made him step up on a stool, made a big show of putting the rope around his neck, tightening it. We stood there in our rows. They made him wait on that stool, made us wait. Then they kicked the stool out from under him, hard, made us watch until the swinging gradually stopped and he just hung there, a dead weight.

In the movies they make a big show out of people being unsuspecting. They don't know this is the last time they'll be in one piece, the last time the lover will be there, the last time they'll ever see home.

I used to sit in the dark theater with my warm popcorn and watch them not suspecting a thing. I used to be one of them, living minute to minute, with time stretching everywhere, never thinking about what a minute meant. That ended abruptly with a draft notice. Suddenly everything had weight. Suddenly everything was worth holding on to.

Here each minute draws itself out, long and grim. Each minute is a double-edged sword, the edge of a bayonet. It exists only here and now, where it could be my last. There's an odd sense of savoring, holding. But there's a whole other side to it, an animal side, saving up crumbled, stale bread to space through the day, calculating to the minute when the watery soup will come, desperate gratitude if there's a rotting piece of meat floating in it. Thinking, not thinking, thinking, not thinking.

This could be the last place I ever live in, the last faces I ever see. This could be the last thought I have.

A few men have gone crazy, sitting still like gravestones, not responding to anything. We pick them up and walk them to the morning count and back again, their feet stumbling along, their legs somehow holding them up. We take turns trying to feed them, but most of it ends up dribbling down their chins, so someone else eats the rest.

They'll die here, I think, the crazy ones. They'll starve before the rest of us. But they won't have last thoughts, only blankness, nothing, before the end.

Sometimes I dream about snow. It's falling around me, thick and blinding. I'm standing in it, my legs buried to my knees. I try to lift my feet, one at a time, but they're frozen to the ground. They burn hot, searing hot, but they're too frozen to move. I stand there, the snow mounting around me, higher and higher. I can't move at all, my arms pinned to my sides. The snow piles deeper and deeper until only my head sticks out and my whole body burns with frozen heat. I look to the right and left, but soon the snow is up over my chin, then my mouth and nose. The world goes completely white and then completely dark. I fight for breath, but my mouth is full of snow. The snow piles higher and higher over me, and then I can't feel anything.

Anna

1981

I won't feel anything. It was an old refrain, one that sung itself so regularly it had become like breathing. Each day Anna answered the phone dutifully and evenly, listening to stories of other people's tragedies. Some of them were small ones, clients unable to pay their premiums and asking for a grace period. Some were much larger, a tree crushing a car or a house burned to the ground. People on the other end of the line sounded either panicky or like zombies, rarely in between, unless they had a simple change of address. Anna prided herself on not feeling any of the ups and downs of people's lives, on not becoming personally connected in any way to the vagaries of cars and houses or to the dramas of people's disasters. She could do her job better that way, meet their needs with facts. Often people tried to pull her in with tears or tirades, but Anna used her workday voice, a voice that was steady, friendly, and above all, nice. In the early days of her job at the agency, she'd consciously practiced the voice, but after twenty-five years it was automatic, and she no longer had to put it on like pantyhose every morning. In the evening she used the same voice with the telephone solicitors who tried to sell her sides of beef and rug shampoo.

But now there was a crack in the voice and a skip on the tape that usually played so smoothly. She kept seeing the open grave and hearing the voices of Thomas and the old woman slipping through.

Don't you know? The phrase now repeated itself over and over like a pop song she couldn't shake. She sat at her desk with her work in its usual piles, her typewriter making its usual hum and her hand reaching toward the ringing phone. But when she lifted the receiver, she held it against her ear and didn't say anything. She was too startled by the image that kept appearing—she was lying on her back in the freshly dug grave, dressed for work, with her arms by her sides and her eyes wide open.

"Hello?" said the voice on the phone. "Is this Hardin and Powell Insurance? Hello?" The voice was a woman's, deep and raspy, and the words were punched in staccato.

"Yes, yes it is," Anna found herself saying, and her desk came into focus, along with the renewal form in her typewriter and the picture on the wall of a sunlit path checkered with leaf shadows and winding through the forest. "Can I help you?"

The client spoke haltingly, punctuating her words with drags on a cigarette and long exhales followed by silences. In the middle of the story Anna was engulfed by emotions so strong she could hardly remain upright. She felt as if she'd been smacked by a huge wave and sucked out to sea. Struggling for breath, Anna couldn't understand what was happening to her. With each detail the woman offered, Anna was pulled farther and farther away, losing sight of land. She clutched her desk with her free hand, trying to steady herself. She felt seasick, cold, and she put her head down as if the solid wood of her desk could keep her afloat. On and on the woman described the hideous car accident that had claimed her daughter.

Anna stifled a moan, managed to whisper, "I'll call you right back," and hung up. She was frightened and scribbled a few words on a message pad, stumbled to Mr. Powell's door.

"I'm sick," she whispered hoarsely. "I have to leave." She lurched toward his desk, and he took the note from her shaking hand.

"All right, Anna," Mr. Powell answered, looking as if he'd opened the restroom door with someone in there.

Anna managed to get her purse and reach her car. She wasn't thinking, and this made her feel like an animal, moving by instinct rather than her usual logic. She turned the key in the ignition and backed out of her parking stall, her knuckles turning white from the force of gripping the steering wheel. She didn't know where she was going.

Driving toward home, Anna didn't see the trees or other cars. As she crested the last hill before the road descended to the lake, she pulled over, realizing all at once that she didn't know how she'd gotten where she was, unable to go on in the danger that overwhelmed her. She held on to the steering wheel and leaned her head back against the headrest, drawing in a deep breath. The realization that she could breathe seemed to comfort her. Anna's eyes lifted to the rearview mirror and there he was, running toward her car, growing bigger and bigger in his green sweats. She watched him come closer and closer, until he disappeared and then reappeared in the window next to her. He was breathing hard, and his eyes flashed something that made her raise her head and relax her grip on the steering wheel. Thomas rounded the car and climbed into the passenger seat.

"You're here," was all he said. They sat there quietly for some minutes, his breathing slowing down and hers deepening to match it. Finally he said, "Where would you like to go?"

She said back, "I don't know. I've just come this far." Thomas gave her a smile that made his face look even younger. Anna trusted his face; everything on it seemed real and sincere. She leaned back far enough to look at her own face in the side mirror and it looked odd to her, like a mask, and she wished she could take it off.

"What if you could go anywhere?" Thomas's voice seemed round, a voice that could fill a huge space and then roll to fill more. "Where would you go?"

"I'd go to a high place—where I could see a long way," she answered, her voice not flat like on the telephone but growing rounder like his.

"Good," he said. "Then do a U-turn and I'll take you there." Anna turned the car around, and Thomas directed her down the hill, then left, straight past the tall white church and down the curving road that led into a narrow, forested valley. At the fork they went left again, where the road turned from pavement into dirt, a thin road etched in the hollow between two ridges. It was very green, a forest of birches and pines creating spotted light and shadow. Anna drove slowly, barely raising any dust. To the left among the trees there were some huge, scattered boulders, the largest of which had a pine growing from its flat top. Thomas told her to pull over at the opening to an overgrown side road.

"Now we'll do a little climbing," he said softly. They walked into the narrow lane, each of them following a dirt wheel track, separated by a grassy middle. Brush had begun to fill in from the sides of the old road, and eventually they had to climb over a fallen hemlock, where the lane disappeared and became a simple path. Anna let Thomas go ahead of her on the trail, his green clothes seeming part of the woods, his back rising and falling slightly with each step. Feeling less shaky and more settled into her arms and legs, Anna began to relax into her steps, grateful she'd worn sensible shoes and a flared skirt. She found herself taking bigger steps and swinging her arms, falling into Thomas's rhythm, yet growing more and more aware of her own feet on the ground.

They came to an intersection of trails, and she could see to the left a patch of blue paint on a tree trunk and then another on a tree beyond it. Thomas turned in that direction, briefly catching her eye and smiling as he rounded the corner. The new path began to rise, first gradually and then more steeply, and in some places they climbed up fat roots like stairs. Anna noticed how green the moss was, how many greens there were, and how red and silver lichens spread over rocks. She looked up to see a mountain laurel leaf glint in sunlight and felt her eyes moisten and then clear. Everywhere she looked there was some exquisite little still life.

They kept climbing, and she took a few deep breaths, with the sensation that the air was washing out her lungs so she could breathe even better. Reaching to touch a mound of moss growing on a stump at waist level, Anna trailed her fingers over its cool, wet surface. They came to a rock ledge where they could look down and see the dirt road below them. A car crept past, small and distant.

"Let's rest here a little," Thomas suggested, and they sat down on the wide shelf of rock. The sound of the car faded, and Anna became aware of wind lifting the leaves around her and sparrows calling softly and unseen. She wanted to talk to Thomas but felt shy, so she sat quietly a few feet away from him. She glanced out of the corner of her eye, and he had his eyes closed with his hands resting lightly on his knees.

"This is the place to begin," he said, his voice clear and lovely as birdsong. "I have as much time as you have today," he continued. Again Anna felt shy and said nothing.

"I've been looking straight at the sun, and I can tell you it isn't blinding if you're ready. I've been clearing my eyes and mind enough to do it and preparing my body for it." Anna felt herself tense. A voice inside her head pointed out that she was in the middle of nowhere with a man she didn't really know. This time no old woman was likely to happen along to protect her, and now this man Anna didn't know was talking in riddles. She ought to be at work where she belonged. She imagined herself saying, *That's nice,* or, *Isn't that interesting,* slipping into her telephone voice. But she continued to say nothing, calculating how she might fight him off and how long it would take her to get back to the car.

"I think I should go," she said finally, leaning her weight back on her hands to push herself up.

"Yes, you could go," Thomas said in reply. "You could go, and then you would never know what I have to say, and you could rely on your telephone voice forever." Anna looked at him hard, and swallowed. "There are always choices," he said simply, and he rose and continued up the path. Anna looked at her fingernails and at his receding back. Her heart began to race, and she heard spinning voices inside her head: Mr. Powell's, the woman on the telephone, the old woman at the cemetery, Thomas's, and then finally her own.

"Wait," she heard herself saying, "I'm coming," and she scrambled off the rock to follow him.

Vita

1919

"Wait," she said, "I'm coming," and Eve scrambled off the rock, as Julian strode away quickly, his long legs carrying him without hesitation. His boots were dark rods leading the way, and she gathered her skirts high enough to be able to match her strides to his.

"Wait," she called out, but the surf drowned out her voice. She wished she could follow Julian's thoughts as swiftly as his gait. She began to run, laughing hard as she went, her legs freed from her skirts, her voice freed by the laughter. Finally he heard her and turned, and they fell into each other's arms, tumultuously, as wild as the waves that dashed over the scattered rocks. They kissed as if they had been starved of food and a heavenly table appeared before them. They wished for nothing but each other, and they received all they wished for.

Dear Violet, my Lushka,

I have begun our novel. We shall not be Mitya and Lushka in its pages as we are in life. You shall be Eve, the one God created first—I think God should have started with woman, her creases and folds, her soft and luscious flesh. If he had, the world would have been happy. I will be Julian, after the great Caesar, after Julian of Norwich, who dared speak in her own holy voice.

Eve and Julian will live in Greece, where the climate has passion. There will be a revolution, and they will meet their destiny. I'll not tell you more now—I'll wait until we are together, when life will follow art.

Today I believe all things are possible. And so I make plans to come to you, to shed my life here swiftly and take you away to a place where we can be ourselves. How can I go on merely admiring the flowers at the forest's edge, my dearest, your namesakes? I wish to lie among them in my naked skin, to feel their fragrant delicacy, to crush them with my weight and watch them spring back again, alive. It is in my lineage to be untrue. I have my grandmother's impetuous blood flowing in my veins—her flamenco blood—and I have kept it cold until today. Now I apply heat, and I can feel her pulse beneath mine, her dancer's limbs moving in me. She sends me to you. She in her great illegitimate love sends me to you. And you, with your open lips and honeyed eyes, with swinging, swaying skirts that show your calves—you were taught how to walk by the King's mistress and made for sheer, unbridled love.

We shall blaze through the Continent. You shall be my flame and I your taper. This is how it must be or I cannot go on. Ah, this reads so sentimentally, so garishly. But how to write my thoughts without excess when they are so excessive? I built a rough dam and now I spill.

My boots bring me a new walk, a new name. My man body covers ground, owns itself, seeks its own level. This is the day I step into it. I take off my other self, hang it in the closet among the underskirts and dresses. I cannot reconcile boots with shawls.

We will ride the train, anonymous. You and I will move relentlessly to port. A ship awaits us, stately and calm, and then you and I shall lie pressed together in the night, breathing each other's breath, kissing each other's kisses. You are mine. I have never really doubted it, Violet.

Water is the substance of life. Thin and clear, it tells the truth about all it flows over: rocks, sand, rough road. Nothing can hide from it. No imperfection or perfection remains hidden from its touch.

This is how I want to be, to run freely over you, to moisten, to flood. I wish no part of you to escape from me. I will be the water, not the riverbed, not the hollowed earth. Unyielding force: endless surf, hitting and receding, taking rocks and bones out to sea.

Come with me, Lushka. Come with me, Eve, as you promised. Look into my sun and be blinded, and be grateful for the blindness. See only with your fingertips. Let me rise each day and blind you. Let me leave you each night in darkness. Over and over, let me be midnight and dawn. There are only excesses now. There are no restraints, no voices but our own. There are only longing and its answer. Come with me.

Your Vita, your Mitya, your Julian

6 August

They are my brave boys. I leave them now because I must walk through another life. I must change my clothes for some that fit differently. Nigel and Ben are my soul and breath. But I am my own blood, and where I flow is to a new world, a different world of longing made manifest. There may be a day when they will understand, at least that I love them with my grandest heart. I carry them always. There is room enough.

Now I must make room for myself in a wider realm. This is a story that has no ending.

Dear Harold,

What is love? Duty, care, legality—or the nurture of the soul, to be reborn, to live? There is blue sky breaking over the hawthorn grove, and today I can no longer do what ought to be done, only what will be done. On earth as it is in heaven. My Hadji, we have been happy, you and I. We are the ones who buy a house and plant a garden. We harvest boys from our careful tending. I wish only to respect you, and so I must go.

I can no longer keep myself shut away in my tower room like Rapunzel, day after day creating another me on paper. No, I keep my hair short on purpose. And now I must close the wardrobe doors on all those dresses and walk away on my own two legs, take the fierce strides I was meant for.

Part 1

But my absence has nothing to do with you. You are its recipient and not its cause. You see, my male body is untested. I wish to know if it is real without having to go to war. I wish to know if it is mere garment or if it is made of skin and bone and muscle. You cannot tell me. You see only what you can see. But I seek a good coating of dust on my boots. It is the only way I can know if I am real.

We are born into bodies in order to visit the earth, our wings pinned into the display case. Our colours fade, and we retain only reminders of the cocoon, the flight, the quick death at the collector's hand. We are mounted and displayed, and the world admires us. But it is only our bodies they see, not our fluttering memory, not our sipping from the flower's center.

Yours,
Vita

10 August

    It is night, a soft Monte Carlo night, and I am awakened by silence again, by the wide Mediterranean emptiness. I do not wish to fill it, only to live in it, in the endless possibility that light will come. There is no moon yet, only the utter darkness with its secrets kept pure and its colours hidden. My love's breath is as gentle and steady as her sleep. She does not hear my pen scratch along the page.

Oh Violet, what if we never went back? What if we stayed in each other's arms and talked gently forever, forgetting our addresses, forgetting our names? What if nothing exists but this room, if the worlds we left behind have disappeared, burned to ash and blown away? There is only now, this moment, and no other moment exists, even in memory. Can we not remake ourselves, minute by minute, remake the world, no broader than what we can see? What if this is our only home and we its only inhabitants? There is no need to expand, only to collapse in on ourselves, to fold and enfold, deep and deeper.

Anna

1981

By the time Anna and Thomas reached the top of the ridge, it was almost dark.

"You wanted to be somewhere high so you could see in all directions," he reminded her. They sat on a broad slab of rock, exposed, the woods behind them.

"But it's too dark," Anna objected. "I can hardly see anything." She realized that she felt panicky, a little undone by the long climb, the diminishing light, the lack of recognizable scenery. She was intrigued by Thomas but afraid of him at the same time. She wasn't sure why she'd come, why she'd gotten up from that first rock and followed him. He was so intense, so no-nonsense, so clear, harsh almost, in his exchanges with her. He seemed to be obsessed, yet without goals or direction. Anna wavered between fear and curiosity, hoping her mace was still in her purse, then realizing she'd left her purse—and her keys—locked in her car far below.

"There's no need to be afraid," Thomas said quietly. Even his soft voice bore an intensity that startled her. "Consider the opposite view. I'm not here to hurt you. You found me because it was the right time for us to meet. I have some things to tell you, and when I'm finished, you won't need me again. You'll most likely forget what I look like."

Anna said nothing. What was there to say to him? For all she knew he was a serial killer and these were her last moments. She tried to breathe without gasping.

"Look over there, and in a few minutes you'll see the first sliver of moon appear," Thomas said, and Anna could feel goose bumps crawl up her arms. "I thought we'd start with the moon because it's easier to get used to, easier on the eyes. Watch it come over the horizon, how at first there's a dim glow like the lights from a distant, unseen city, and then the edge of the moon itself comes over, so bright your eyes aren't ready for it. Watch it. Just keep watching it." Anna felt distracted, saw lights going on below, one by one, scattered across the valley like stars.

"The horizon," he said. "Let yourself have the horizon. Look." Just as he'd predicted, a glow appeared in the east, a luminous layer above the edge of the earth. The light was clear, white, a contrast to the deepening sky. "The moon gives remembered light," Thomas said. "You can tune your eyes to read it in preparation for what the sun will bring."

Anna tried to concentrate, feeling herself relax a little as Thomas kept his distance several feet away. She'd made her decision to follow him, and now she must endure the consequences. She wondered if she'd be alive by morning. Though he frightened her, Anna felt a strange, contradictory trust in Thomas, as if he carried something she knew but couldn't put her finger on, and he kept turning up at times when she was uneasy or downright confused. He held some kind of promise—or was it just adventure? She'd felt herself pushed to follow him. If this were her last night to live, she might as well enjoy it. Yet she imagined the rock ledge covered with her blood, her body lying still, her arms and legs bent at odd angles.

"See it now, how the edge of the moon is breaking over the horizon. Moonbreak. It's an amazing time of day. Watch what happens to the world in front of us." Thomas whispered now, coaxing her away from her bloody thoughts. She saw the sliver of orange moon curve over the horizon. She'd never seen it quite like that before, never stopped long enough to see its slow rise.

"The moon is full tonight," he said, "and this is its first edge." The voice was the same earnest whisper, asking to be heard, careful not to disturb, an even whisper that soothed Anna. "Now you're on your own," he added. "Watch it rise. Watch every second of its rise, and when it's fully up, study it. Study its surface. Study its light, how it changes the earth. I'll be back in the morning."

"What?" Anna cried. "You're going to leave me here?" Her voice came out in a whine, a small voice. "I'm afraid."

"There's nothing to be afraid of. This is the place of the moon," Thomas replied matter-of-factly, and then he disappeared into the woods where the trail had come out. Anna heard her own heart thumping and then a far-off voice: "Watch it closely. Don't miss anything. It's all important."

Anna flashed back to the edge of the moon. More of it was

showing now, an orange arc that hurt her eyes briefly until they adjusted. She took a deep breath, felt the cold, hard rock beneath her.

"Well, now you've gotten yourself into it," she said out loud. The words from an old song, "Shine on, Harvest Moon," came next, half-sung and half-hummed. Then, "By the Light of the Silvery Moon" whistled out thinly, and Anna laughed. She laughed and laughed until tears filled her eyes and spilled down her cheeks, and then she found herself sobbing uncontrollably. By the time she recovered enough to look, the moon was a third of the way over the horizon, and Anna began to notice how beautiful it was, huge and orange and round. This was not a flat moon hung in the sky, but a three-dimensional globe glowing wildly in front of her. She was astounded by it and sat back on her hands with her legs out wide in front of her under her flared skirt.

The moon continued to rise, gradually and deliberately. Anna marveled at how she could actually see it move, watched it backlight a cloud and then pop up above it. When the whole orb of the moon was finally free of the horizon, she felt a stab of joy, and she didn't know what to make of it. It was a feeling she couldn't relate to, yet it was familiar, something she could almost remember but not quite identify. She felt slightly out of focus though her eyesight was sharp and her hearing keen. A dog barked far below in the valley.

Anna looked at the maples behind her and thought it amazing that they had no color. They were silvery gray like an image from an old black-and-white movie. She wondered whether they were really green or if they had actually changed color in the orange-white light, whether color was just a whim of the light, a thing it allowed her to imagine. Turning back to the moon, Anna watched its slow-motion rise, its slow transformation from orange to yellow to white. She noticed the color drained from the whole world, not only the trees, but the rock she sat on, her skin, her clothes, the valley below her. She was sitting in a negative world as if she were inside a photographer's darkroom or inside the film itself.

The moon was straight in front of her now, big and shining,

ready to swallow her. Anna fought to keep her distance and began to notice its surface, valleyed and hilled, pocked. She saw shadows on it, then focused on patches of clear, unbroken light. The more she looked, the more she could see. A glow ringed the moon, as if it had a shadow made of light.

It was high above her now, and Anna lay back with her arms folded under her head and watched it ride over her. She closed her eyes and swore she could feel its light. Anna couldn't get enough of it. She wanted to close the distance, to absorb it, to breathe it. Without thought, with only the moon's power pulling her tide, Anna quickly undressed and lay below the moon naked, nothing between her and the light, let it enter through her skin.

They were the hours that belonged to the moon, waxing and waning, growing round-faced, disappearing altogether. Anna didn't know how to count them because they melted into each other. Was this dawn or dusk, midnight or day? She'd lost her bearings as if flying in a snowstorm and not knowing up from down. She'd lost all sense of anything beyond herself and the immediate surroundings she found herself in. Forgetting how to think, she knew only how to take in, how to release.
Gone was everything she'd known: her tidy desk, Mr. Powell's formal, "Good morning, Anna," and "Good evening, Anna," the ringing telephones, her small, cluttered house, her memories. They all fell from her like old, shed skin. Underneath was moist, golden-pink new skin, sensitive and warm. All Anna had was skin.

Vita & Violet

1919

"Lushka, let's tell a story, a story for the middle of the night," Vita said. The full moon through the open shutters had coaxed them both awake. "I'll go first, shall I?" Vita traced the outline of Violet's lips with her finger. Violet sighed, then nodded, and Vita began. "At dusk the night grew sultry and warm. Cicadas sang in the dripping palms, rising to a hot crescendo. The very air buzzed with heat and split wide open. Everything was full. Bushes were swollen with birds, trees were weighted with fruit, and all the winged and legged creatures pulsed in a steady, quick rhythm. It was time. It was time for the great awakening. As the last daylight faded and darkness deepened, the fullness reached its great good climax, and all the night flowers burst into blossom, all the night fruit ran with sweet juice, and the night beings fluttered and sang."

"I like this place. Very much," Violet murmured, rolling onto her side to face Vita and then taking her turn with the story. "They were alone in this wide, untamed garden. They were the human witnesses to all the earth's abundance. They, too, were full and ripe, ready for the moon. This was their night. All their longing had come to this moment, and they would soon explode into bloom as wildly as the lush garden in which they'd arrived. They had come from the flat, dry place where rain never fell and nights were chill. They had walked unaided through endless desert, drawn by the idea of fruit, by the dream of colour, by the possibility that not all the earth was arid and barren. They were shy with each other in the desert, barely touching in daylight but holding each other through the night cold. They never spoke the whole way, except the last few days when they could see a river far in the distance at the horizon's edge, a river of blue so rich it was almost purple. Now it's your turn, Mitya."

"Yes, I believe so," Vita replied, yawning luxuriously. "*Pomegranate,* said one to the other. And they smiled knowing smiles, traded them with one another. They actually exchanged lips and could feel the insides of each other's mouths with their tongues.

Plum, said the other to the one, and they licked their exchanged lips slowly, imagining the juice running down their chins. They had never had fruit but always had been able to imagine it, across the long, sandy plains through the searing days and frozen nights. Now they knew the names of what they had imagined and could taste on each other's lips the sweetness they had dreamt of. Once they came to the river, they were astonished. They walked into the cool, clear, blue water and marveled to feel it all over their skin. They both laughed, deep and raucous laughter, as they felt the cool wetness envelop them. They moved through the water like fish, like lovely, liquid fish, shimmering blue and magenta and phosphorescent green. *Anemone,* one said to the other, and they laughed fluid laughter, letting the water touch every part of them. They exchanged their melodious laughter and then their melodious skins that the water played so beautifully, and each could feel inside the other's skin what it was like to play and be played like harps by the river's wet fingers. Now you, Lushka."

Violet slid closer to Vita. "A great wave roared down the river's length, pushing under them, heaving them up on land, and they found themselves in the magnificent garden they had always believed was there. The moon rose over the sheltering leaves of the plentiful trees, and the moon pulled on them and loosened their tides. They embraced each other in their borrowed skins and kissed each other with their borrowed lips, and then gave back to each other their own. Along with the newness of their returned lips and skins, warm and wet from the river's blue water, each kept a memory of being inside the other. The moon pulled them together, and they rose and fell like the earth's tides, rose and fell together, kissing with lips and skin that remembered the other and yet were fully their own. They harbored each other through the great waves the moon created inside them, and—"

As Violet paused for a breath, Vita took over. "They were neither male nor female but both. Each gave to the other the greatest desire of the moment, and each received from the other the greatest bliss. Each offered all that the other asked, over and over and over. This was their garden and their life and their skin, and the moon bid them rise and fall, rise and fall endlessly. When morning came, they knew they would live forever. They knew they would never have to leave the garden. The apple was theirs. The snake was theirs. The round, red apple and the long, supple snake were both theirs. Alone, each took a long walk deep into the garden and ate of the fruit of the trees and picked the fruit of the vine. And they came together and shared their harvest. They draped each other's bodies with flowers and woven vines, and they rubbed each other with the juice of pomegranate and plum. They danced in their own skins and gave praise from their own lips for their beautiful, perfect garden and for the moon."

"And then they acted out their story," Violet said, as she reached for Vita.

Dear Mitya,
    It is perhaps the opposite view we wish to consider. What if the world is ready for us? What if the world opens its wide arms and embraces us so wholly that we can be anything we wish?
    I have gone walking by the cliffside on this, a new day.

Your Lushka

Vita held the note in her hand, trembling with the truth of it. She lay alone in the morning light, the other side of the bed still holding the warm echo of Violet's body. But Violet was gone, leaving behind the hollowed bed and the note. Vita reached for her pen and ink, tore a few pages from her diary and began to write.

Dear Lushka,

I wish to consider the opposite view. This is what I have wanted all along. I wish to cross over, to release the view that has pinned me, to take on its opposite, to live the truth that all things are possible. I've lived too long on an abstract plane, a plane created in my mind. Now I have no choice but to live in a concrete, passionate, immediate world, the real world, with you.

In the early morning landscape between sleep and wakefulness I walked on a cliff over the water. Below me, waves tore at the rocks, and the rocks gave themselves up, grains and chips at a time. I stood on the edge, or did I lean over, daring myself to fall? I could not tell, knew only that the land was behind and the sea below. I could feel myself sliding, feel the rocks and roots giving way under my feet. I was capsized, hovering like a dark angel.

Then I found myself in the hollow under a wide oak, a storm whirling around me, branches sweeping low over my head. I waited for the lightning, the lightning that would strike the tree and travel through its roots to singe the ground beneath me. The electric shock would bring me to life, as Mary Shelley's man was brought to life. I felt the jolt, the burning.

Then I dreamt of my journal, the one you gave me. I ran my finger over the embossed cover, over the single leather violet raised from the smooth background, tooled and stained by a careful hand. I sniffed my fingertip, startled by the delicate fragrance of a fresh blossom. I opened the cover, revealing the first white page, then fingered through them one by one. They were all empty, waiting.

I wondered where I was. Outside the window the city lay, but which city? The air was balmy, fragrant and full. Yet it gave me no hints I could use to place myself. I wondered if there were maps I could consult, and I looked in the desk drawer and under the bed. I wanted to ring the servant's bell, but there was none. There was no way to navigate, no instrument to use, just a sky above riddled with stars, and no moon—

Vita put down her pen and paper when she heard the door open and close. As Violet returned to the bed beside her, Vita listened to her soft breathing, felt her scented warmth. Vita closed her eyes, watched the colours inside her eyelids: purple, blue, red. She squinted the muscles around her eyes, and the colours broke into sparkles of gold, whirling in spiral patterns.

When she opened her eyes to the glaring sky, the white light overtook her, and she lay absolutely still, staring as near the flaming sun as she dared. She could not move. The light held her, and she welcomed it. She let the light stun her, let the white light penetrate her whole body through her eyes. This she did gladly, freely, and she was utterly dazzled.

Anna

1981

Consider the opposite view. The words spun in Anna's mind as the early sun warmed her skin. These were the words she woke to. They repeated themselves behind her closed eyes as she became aware of the earth beneath her, the shelf of rock on which she lay, curled on her side. Anna felt the cool, rough surface of the rock beneath her skin, the unforgiving hardness. *Skin and rock,* she thought, and still her eyes remained closed, still she lay in the limbo between sleep and wakefulness.

It was morning. Anna came to know that as slowly as she came to know the rock, solid and unrelenting. She had the brief sensation of not knowing where she was, but it quickly gave way to the certainty of the rock. She remembered her aloneness, the solitary night coming on, darkness masking all the trees and rendering them colorless. She remembered the silence Thomas had left behind, the desolation that had given way to something else. She remembered the clothes cast aside, her nakedness.

She remembered it all as one might play back a shocking event, the police coming to tell of death, sudden and absolute, the forgetfulness of sleep and then the renewed, alien shock at dawn. This couldn't possibly be her skin, her body, layered on the rock like snow. She couldn't possibly be where she was, utterly alone and naked. No, this must be some other body she was waking in. These must be someone else's words stuck inside her head.

She willed herself to open her eyes, but they remained shut. She willed herself to speak so she could hear the sound of a voice, but she was silent. She lay quiet and still, slowly trying to accept what made no sense to her. Finally the sun broke over the trees, and in that moment Anna opened her eyes.

The sky above her was dazzling, blue made white by the force of the sun. It was all she could see, white light that took up the whole sky. Anna wondered for an instant whether she might be dead, whether her body was actually becoming stone. She tried to lift her hand, then her foot, but they seemed paralyzed. Only her eyelids seemed to work, and she closed and opened them rhythmically like a china doll. No other part of her body seemed able to move. She gave in and lay motionless, opened her eyes and looked.

Over her head branches and leaves were silhouetted against the white sky. She noticed them dipping and shaking, moved by air. That was when she realized she could feel the wind on her skin, just as she could feel the rock beneath her. If these things could touch her, she wondered why she couldn't move. She wondered whether she should feel afraid. But Anna didn't feel much of anything, a mild curiosity perhaps, nothing more. She didn't know what to make of it, this lack of feeling, this inability to move. Yet she knew she was alive, able to sense earth and see sky. She seemed to accept her state without resistance, to be content to lie and look.

"What do you see?" It came like morning, Thomas's voice from somewhere, from among the trees or from the sky. She couldn't tell where. Anna noticed that she didn't react, didn't jump or scream or try to cover her exposed skin.

"I see the light, the shapes of the branches against the light." She heard a voice she quickly realized was her own, sounding clear and even, without fear or unease.

"What else do you see?" he asked. "Keep looking until you see something else. Focus on what you see." She did as he said, stared unblinking into the harsh sky. "Keep looking," Thomas added, his voice earnest and comforting.

Anna saw a day many years before when her father had taken her to an open field near their house. They had packed sandwiches and a thermos of lemonade into a basket and sat on an old faded beach blanket in the middle of the tall grass. She ate her sandwich slowly, chewing each bite twenty times as her father had instructed her.

"When it starts," her father had said, "you have to remember to look through your viewer." She held the cardboard contraption her father had made, fingering it in the same spot over and over until it grew soft and limp. "Otherwise you'll go blind."

Anna sat next to her father for hours as the sun became its own ghost, masked inch by inch, and midday turned to silvered dusk. She looked through her viewer at the vanishing sun, watched as the giant shadow took it over. Her father had told her it was a once-in-a-lifetime thing, that it would never happen again.

Anna sat trying to eat her sandwich and her apple, chewing hard and trying to swallow. It all seemed to stick in her throat, next to all the miracles and Amens and prayers for salvation that lodged there each week when her mother dropped her off for Sunday School at the church on the corner of their street. The bread tasted like the flat figures of Jesus and his disciples that stuck smiling on the felt board over her head while the teacher listed sins. One Sunday the teacher let Anna rearrange the figures on the board. They'd been in their places for so long that the sun had faded the color around them, leaving behind their shadows.

Anna didn't know what salvation was, only that it was a dark thing, as dark as the negative world in which she and her father now sat. She knew she was supposed to want this thing salvation, but she couldn't seem to, just as she couldn't notice any difference when she invited Jesus into her heart each week with the words the Sunday School teacher told her to use.

Anna had always done what she was told, but this day on the blanket under the miracle sun, she'd defied her father. She let the viewer drop down her cheek enough that she glimpsed the sun as it began to reconstruct itself, to emerge inch by fiery inch from the other side of the great shadow. For days afterward Anna looked at the world through a dark haze, a negative image of the sun, but she never told her father.

Bill

1945

The light hit my forehead and left something behind. It wasn't something I could get hold of all at once. I had to let it dig into me, under skin and bone, let it drill deeper and deeper until I lost all sense of it. And then I understood.

I understood what I'd seen looking out the narrow ventilation hole we take turns using, to get a gulp of fresh air, a glimpse of cloud, something to guarantee that earth and sky are still there. We each climb on a makeshift stair we put together, a step that grants a small slit into the world. I take my turn each day along with everyone else, sniffing clean air, feasting on the world outside, mud and faraway trees.

But yesterday my turn was lined up with the sun. I stepped into a ray of light that drove itself into my forehead like a nail. I could feel its steel strike my skin, then penetrate my skull and go way inside my head. I felt stunned. The sun was in all its glory, and it hit me on the head. Just as quickly it was gone, replaced by cool, filtered light. I stepped down to give the next guy a chance, lay in my bunk on the straw mat full of lice. There was a nail in my head, left by the sun.

I'd forgotten what it's like to think. It's not wise to think here anymore, to remember. But my brain congealed around this spike, and I remembered everything. Memories ran together like stories in a newsreel at the picture show, pieces of my life playing one after another. I lived my whole life over, as if the sun had flipped a switch and I was powerless to stop it.

The guard pounded on the door with his rifle for the evening count, unbolted the heavy lock, and yelled his chiseled command. But I was busy fishing the stream in Peoples State Forest and I had a bite. The trout was putting up a good fight and I needed just a few more minutes. Everyone shuffled out, but then the fish took a big dive, ran my line, and the fight was on even harder. That was when the rifle butt struck me in the ribs, and I sat up moaning and holding my head.

"Sick—*krank*," I yelled, one of the few German words I knew, enough to keep him from butting me again. I stumbled out into the biting air and took my place in line. Still, I could see the glistening trout, its rainbow side shimmering in the sunlight, the water clear and cold around my feet. I stood there in the freezing line among ragged men with chattering teeth and caught the most magnificent trout of my fishing career, all the while with my eyes on the ground and my hands tight by my sides like every other guy standing there.

The sun left something behind, something dangerous. There's danger here in the rifle butts and leering grins, in the draining cold, in the water they call soup and the mold they call bread, in the wrestling they call sleep. But there's a bigger danger inside me. No matter how skinny I am, how sunken, no matter how much my hair falls out in clumps, there are worse things inside my head. Things old and forgotten can rear themselves, make me weak, make me fall quivering at their feet. I'm afraid of myself. I have more deadly means than they do. It's good to keep it all locked up. But now the sun has driven through my skull and there's an open wound, memories shooting out like blood from a severed artery. I've tried not to think about whether there's hope or not, whether the world really exists outside these four walls and this muddy yard with the forest beyond. Here hope is a fatal thing.

My body has taken over my life, keeps itself going. I eat the crumbs, sleep in fits, hold my burning sides over the stinking pit they call the latrine. Everything outside the high fence and guard towers has been flat like a photograph, torn and bent from too much handling.

But the sun changed it all. The hole in my head can't be stopped up, and memories are leaking everywhere, spilling all over the ground.

Things whirl by like horses on a carousel. My father crying in the night. My mother's coffin at the church. Everyone telling me to be a big boy.

My car, that long and lovely Studebaker I drove when I could afford to. I could drive it right through these bolted gates to the edge of the earth.

My first job, shoveling manure out of cows' and horses' stalls, loading the hay wagon, mending fences. Followed by more jobs wherever I could get them. I loved the feel of a little money in my pocket when I knocked on her door.

There she is in her new dress and beaming smile, her face nearly touching mine, her breath grazing my chin. We dance like satin, the packed hall spinning with couples. Most Saturday nights we'd go to the site of the Old Newgate Prison, a park now with a new dance hall, the varnished floorboards and clean walls bouncing music all around us. The Savoy Springs Broadcasting Orchestra—that's the last group that played, fresh from New York, and they were hot.

Outside, the old prison buildings left from the Revolutionary War were crumbling to the ground, their pieces scattered like bones. The men would dare each other to descend into the mine the prisoners had worked and slept in, a thin flashlight beam hardly enough to light our way. We'd duck, unable to stand upright, the stone ceiling of the cave pressing cold, damp air around us. Some of the women would follow, whispering or shrieking their way. We'd walk on the stone trail of those prisoners whose lungs killed them little by little, long before they could ever get out of there.

There's this hole in my head now. It must mean something. It must have come for some reason or I wouldn't have been struck. Sunstruck. Nothing to live for but light.

I'm failing. What they call food runs straight through. I can't keep it inside. I wobble my teeth with my tongue. Each day it's harder to get outside for the counting.

But I've seen spring come. It entered through the hole the sun left, and I could smell it on the air. Underneath the odor of unclean flesh there came spring, riding high on the wind and passing straight into my head.

I've watched the same bud on the same elm through the ventilation slit, and it changed, it swelled, ready to burst. I've tasted it on my tongue and swallowed it, spring in all its green, filling my head to busting.

❧❧❧

I walked away on my own two legs.

That day was different than I ever could've imagined. It followed a series of unimaginable days. I'd drifted into a small, caged world, smaller than the barracks that held us. It came slowly, a little shrinking day by day, just as the nights shrunk facing spring.

My days consisted of washing with weak tea, lying still to conserve my strength, struggling to get up when the guards crashed in and pushed us out to work—*arbeit, arbeit,* they yelled—and stumbling out to the shovels and pails that awaited us on the rail line. I drank my gruel, felt it run right out of me into the latrine, did my best to let the light in through the hole in my head. Day after day my body grew skinnier and frail, my thinking dull and repetitive. I thought only simple things: up, down, in, out, here, there.

I saw men go crazy and die. I saw dogs fed good meat under the thin-lipped smiles of the guards. I heard men around me talk about nothing but food and how they wanted it cooked, potatoes and pot roast smothered in gravy just like their mothers made it. Liver and onions. Eggs fried in bacon grease, sunny side up. Pumpkin pie. The lists went on and on, the menus more and more elaborate. They weren't just dinners but holiday feasts. I dreamed of food, night after night, nightmares that I was being force-fed until I was bloated and sick. I was made to lick the cream from the top of a bottle of milk, bottle after bottle, the thick stuff gagging me. I was made to eat until I threw up, night after night, and then I'd wake to the same lukewarm tea and hard bread.

There was never any end to it, talk of food, lack of food. And one day the guy in the bunk next to me said we'd all starve to death, die in our own dysentery, rot in our matted straw, our blackened teeth circling our skulls. I told him to shut up, and then I could picture it myself, my skull with the hole the light made, my eyes hollow sockets, my teeth like black piano keys against the white of my skull. I dreamed that night of bones, scattered bones that didn't look human. It was then that I believed I wouldn't get out of there alive, and I stopped washing, stopped eating, and slept.

The last day dawned early, it seemed, and woke me when men stirred in nearby bunks. Some men didn't stir, but we no longer saw much difference between waking and dying, so their stillness didn't bother us. I closed my eyes again as I did each morning, but I couldn't sleep. I just couldn't sleep.

All of a sudden there was a huge ruckus outside. I heard shouting in German, the guards' clipped tones louder and louder, with a growing edge of desperation under the halting words. I tried to get up, thinking I could reach the ventilation slit, but I got dizzy and laid my head back down.

"What's that?" Voices nearby whispered the same thing over and over. And I broke through their hissing to sit up, this time holding my head to keep things from spinning. I dropped to my knees and crawled to the ventilation hole, and using each other liked knotted ropes, another guy and I managed to stand. We held ourselves up, each bracing a hand against the wall.

"You first," he said, and I lifted my foot onto the block. We both gave it all we had, and I kept my balance, even when I brought my other foot up beside the first. We were breathing hard, and it was a long time before I could completely straighten and look out the hole. What I saw I still can't believe.

My voice came out harsh and choked as I gulped air. "They're running around like chickens with their heads cut off. The gates are open. The gates are—open. They're running out. Guards—dogs—running out."

The chaos continued for some time, and my buddy and I stood there holding each other up until it slowed and dimmed and finally faded away.

"They're gone," I said. "Gone." My words came out low and even. There was stunned silence in the barracks. No one moved. I wasn't sure anyone was breathing. Time went by, whole minutes.

"What are we waiting for?" my buddy finally said. His voice was thin, like a ghost's. His face seemed odd, unfamiliar.

"I heard something about Russian troops, something I couldn't quite make out," a quiet voice from the bunk behind us said, causing men to stir around it, and those who could get up began to shuffle toward us and the door. We exchanged looks—I can only call them bewildered—like we were searching, trying to remember something.

I found myself on the outside . . . in the air . . . in the air that smelled of spring—I could smell it. I'm not sure how I got there, but the swinging door was behind me. The light was so bright I had to cover my eyes. It seemed to go right through the hole in my head and make my brain hurt. We walked here and there, my buddy and me still hanging on to each other to keep our balance. Finally there was a sense of slow, trickling movement in one direction, so we followed it. My brain began to adjust to the light, and I could make out the gate, the layers of barbed wire. I could make out the gate, still wide open.

The counting yard looked strange. We were all there, dragging each other along. We weren't in lines, didn't look at the ground. Our eyes met, and we saw each other, like looking into mirrors. We were skeletons with skin, what was left of our uniforms flapping in the breeze. There were a few guys with a ragged two-by-four ramming the barracks door across the way, stopping to gasp air, and then giving it their all. Other guys took their places until the door cracked and swung in, and more scarecrow men shuffled out into the sunlight.

Now I know there are two places on earth: there is in and there is out. That day I passed from one to the other. I entered one and left the other behind. I stopped briefly on the in side of the gate and looked out. The world was there, a field with the beginnings of grass and at the end of it real trees. These were not the trees inside my head. They bent in the wind I could actually feel. And it came back to me in a rush, like water over rock, the feel of wind. My buddy urged me on, and we went through the gate. I didn't look back.

We walked on our own feet, our own legs. Some men stumbled and fell. Others helped them up. Some didn't get up.

I remember now that a wave of fear swept through the group when one guy said, "What if they're waiting in the trees to shoot us?" Another guy told him to shut up, and we pressed on, a mass of arms and legs, bones held together by clothes.

My buddy, Tom, and I stayed together. Once we all got to the woods, it was hard to see the others in the gullies and hills. We scattered like fans after a basketball game, only we were silent and walked like sticks. Tom and I stayed together, so we had four legs and four arms to make our way. We walked like some odd animal, a newborn deer maybe, all skinny and wobbly on bony, long legs. The point is we walked. One foot in front of the other. We left behind what had been our world and entered the new one, the one that had existed only in my head, now tall and wide around us. We walked, step by step by step.

Vita

1919

13 August

    We walked together, one foot in front of the other, step by step. It was such an odd sensation, though we had done it before, this promenade, at precisely this time of day, Violet's gloved hand resting lightly on my arm. But this time was different. We had a sense, not of stolen time and place, but of our rightful presence, together, moving down the broad avenue in the heart of Monte Carlo. This time the street was our own, we the lord and lady of our inherited kingdom. We held ourselves tall, our chins at a royal tilt, our steps matching and courtly. This was our city, our street, our time.

    We made a lovely couple, a couple to turn heads. Such a handsome gentleman and so fine a lady we were, and this our nuptial night, tomorrow our first married day. Oh, we were one, our eyes only for each other, our ears tuned to the music of each other's voices, hers delicate and clear, mine deep and certain. Yes, we talked and strolled and admired the evening sky, the glowing city. We walked side by side, aligned with each other, matched, complementary, following each other's orbit like the moon and the sun.

    Our villa overlooks the city and the water, over the sparkling city and under the sparkling sky. We left the shutters open to the sea, so that the sound of its roaring could carry to our bed. We lay skin to skin, the curves of one filling the hollows of the other. This was our honeyed night, our fragrant, rolling night, and we belonged to each other, and finally, to ourselves.

    Morning presented itself as a gift, one we opened with our full appetites, the blue air blowing through the window and bidding us rise. This was the first of the splendid days, and we were just beginning to remember the importance of sky, wind, sea and sun. We changed into our bathing clothes on a dare from each other, having descended down the steep stairs to the bathhouses, Violet with her parasol and I with my cane. We emerged a mermaid and a sailor, captivated by each other, and I swam my long strokes just beyond the cresting waves while Violet splashed in the shallows where she could still reach bottom. But this was not enough, for we dared each other further with our joined, lingering glance. Soon Violet threw all caution and convention aside and swam out to me, and we delivered salty kisses to each other's waiting lips. We could see the distant faces along the water's edge, imagined the wagging tongues and averted eyes, and kept swimming. We raced each other into deeper water and then rested on our backs, floating side by side on our seabed, our arms locked, the sky our canopy, this our home.

23 August

    Violet grows more beautiful each day and I more dashing. The sun and sea air become us. Each day we swim recklessly and far, and then join on our floating bed together.
    Our nights are fragrant. We have added hours to the clock and days to the calendar. There is always more of everything now, never less.
    Sometimes on quiet afternoons we separate, each to our own thoughts, our own wills, our own restless wanderings. These we write to each other in letters left on the bedside table, to be savored in the evening by lamplight and then burned. We watch the moments of our lives go up in smoke, rise up the chimney and out into the night, knowing we no longer have to hoard them.

    It is a revelation to know there is no end, no limit, no forsaking one world for another. There is only endless time and this eternal place. Each limit exists only to be broken, and each day we swim farther and farther out to sea, swept along by our own currents. We shed our respectability to swim side by side like fish, leaving land far behind. Each stroke is a measure of our singular and joined daring.

Yes, Shelley died in this same sea, poems in his pocket and his love on shore. But Violet and I swim our poems, aloud and wide, love beating wildly in our breasts, and each day we survive. Each day we come back to swim again—because there is no need to die here.

❧☙

The sea is churning, the colour of my lover's
name. The sky is dark and roiling, quaking

the earth with its winds. Everyone is safe
inside their shuttered villas, in their couched
salons, at their predictable gaming tables.

But Violet and I walk our high cliff
above the water, her gown whipping
and flying, my jacket sailing behind me.

Part 2

That was not how people changed; they didn't change themselves: you got changed by being made to live through something, and then you found yourself changed.

Doris Lessing

Madeline

1945

Mornings have always offered a fresh start. It's been true since I was a little girl. The night's loneliness always gave way in the light, and I came to worship dawn, to hang on it all rightness and good. But that's no longer true. After the two army officers delivered the telegram, dawn became a big hammer that strikes me day after day. I welcome sleep when I can get it, the dreamless kind that wipes away my life, the kind of sleep that's next to the grave, deep and empty, nothing.

But sleep means dawn will come, the first rays creeping in under the curtains, spreading like mud across the floor and onto my bed. I bury my head beneath the covers, but it's useless. I still wake, slide immediately into pain, dull and complete. It makes my limbs heavy and my head ache. I can hardly lift myself enough to move from the bed to the bathroom in time to vomit into the commode. This is the beginning of each day now, inevitable and relentless, the unwelcome ending to the night.

More and more, sleep barely comes at all, and so the nights and days are running together. I try to will myself to sleep for the sake of this baby I carry, but no amount of guilt or duty can make the images go away when I close my eyes.

First come the matching officers with their twelve words: *We regret to inform you that your husband is missing in action.* The sentence was interrupted by Bill's name, so alien, a combination of letters that could not come close to being human, and his rank and service number. This is what Bill has been reduced to, letters and numbers on a flimsy piece of paper. I wanted to punch the twin officers, to pound my fists into their eyes as they took off their hats in unison and spoke in calm and even tones, alternating their parts as if they'd rehearsed them for the stage. They had nothing to offer beyond the piece of paper, their words of condolence thudding at my feet. I wanted to shove them back out of the doorway and slam the door in their faces, but instead I did the proper thing and thanked them. Thanked them, for what, I didn't know because they had come to ruin everything, and I hated them with a fury that burned through me and threatened to level the house.

This scene plays itself over and over each night as I lie down and long for sleep. And if sleep does come, the scene plays itself again each morning when light comes like a bully. It's followed again and again by the image of Bill lying in the snow, completely still, with his limbs splayed awkwardly and his eyes open. All around his head the snow is red, and it keeps getting redder. I never knew a human body could hold so much blood. His body is still warm, his skin the skin I know, but then he turns hard and cold like the columns in the front of the town hall, so cold he could splinter with a touch.

Then there's the endless variety of the ways Bill could have died, all of them bloody and frozen. I try to turn them off, this eternal reel of pictures, to feel the warm place where this baby grows. I think it's a boy. I've thought it from the moment I discovered I was pregnant. But I keep picturing him as a forlorn and tiny crying thing. I try to tell myself a story about holding him, rocking him, try to imagine lullabies and stuffed bears, but I just can't. I want to love him, but he keeps slipping away, as if he's lost, kidnapped, and I can't afford the ransom.

Each morning I hold on to the pain. Maybe it will keep Bill alive. Since the telegram arrived, my girlfriends don't let me stay alone, take turns here for the night, help me get ready for work after the morning sickness has passed. I'm grateful, and yet I've come to hate them, too, just like the two officers. I hate their smiles and tears, their quiet sleep, their living husbands and boyfriends, their sitting comfortably on my sofa, legs crossed, relaxed. I hate everyone and everything most of the time, but I'm trying not to hate this baby.

Each morning I manage to get myself to work. I try to keep down a few crackers or a slice of dry toast, even though they taste like sawdust. I have a few sips of coffee when I can get it or plain hot water when I can't. Each morning whatever friend is here tries to cheer me up, but gradually over the days and weeks, they've all gotten quieter in the face of my quiet. What is there to say? Whatever friend and I walk up the steep hill to Main Street, where we wait for the bus. I had to sell the car that Bill and I scrimped and saved for, the car that Bill had washed and buffed faithfully each Saturday. I needed the money for the rent, though I got only a fraction of what the car was worth. I try not to think of it, shiny and sleek, when I stand at the bus stop surrounded by brown slush that used to be snow.

Each day is the same, each morning and each night, everlasting and uneventful. I feel like I'm riding on a conveyor belt, moving forward, but not by my own will. At the end of the day, I get off at the stop nearest the post office, and I know there's no letter as soon as I see the postmistress's face. Then I walk home, with whichever friend is by my side, to my apartment. I turn the key in the lock and step into the hollow, familiar rooms.

My landlady soon climbs the stairs from her apartment below with a pot of hot tea, her old face drooping and her brow wrinkled with concern. Marta's dark eyes are deep and watery, and each time I see them I melt a little. I sit with Marta and my friend, sipping the hot, sweet tea—Marta knows how to make her sugar last—and there's comfort in the steam and the clinks of cups against saucers.

The first time I felt the baby kick, I was sitting like this with Marta and my friend Irma, and I was startled upright by the odd sensation.

"What's wrong?" Marta and Irma spoke in harmony.

"He's alive," I said softly. "He's alive!"

Part 2

Vita & Violet

1919

"You're alive!" Eve screamed, her words flying toward Julian on the hot wind. Then she flew into his arms.

When they finally loosened their embrace, they stood face to face at the edge of the cliff, their hands clasped across the air—the only thing between them.

"I thought you were dead," Eve said, her voice husky with tears. "The messenger Stavridis spoke your name before he died of his wounds. I thought his message meant your death."

The wind pushed against Julian, yet he felt the power in Eve's arms that kept him standing in spite of his wounds. Eve was small and slight, but Julian could see her toughness, as the wind tossed her skirts into sails that aimed to sweep her inland, as Eve stood firmly enough for both of them.

"Here you are in all your magnificent glory, as glorious as the sun, burning and beautiful," Eve shouted into the gale. But Julian could no longer hear her. Eve managed to catch him as he slumped forward, managed to lower him to the ground.

30 August

This morning I wrote a new scene for the novel, a scene in which Julian has been wounded. I had thought he would return to Eve triumphant, after he led the rebel force to its first victory. So certain had I been about his invincibility that I had picked up my pen with a flourish. Yet things were not as I'd thought. The rebels could not outlast the government troops of Aphros, and he was struck down. I do hope that his wounds will not turn out to be fatal.

I am startled by the turn of events. In this homecoming,

Julian is weak and vulnerable. Eve is the strong one, keeping both of them on their feet. I find this to be a revelation. I have always believed that I could bend Violet to my will, could ask anything of her and receive it. But Eve gives me a truer Violet, not a weakling blown about by passion and need, but a fiery candle that cannot be extinguished by any force of wind. Eve is Violet stripped of convention, freed by the force of her own will.

I see now that I have used Violet's strength of will to step out of convention myself. And not just to step, but to walk with a long, booted gait into a new body, a truer body. Yes, I have depended on Violet's strength to take on my own stride and my own true nature. It is Violet whose glory rivals the sun's.

13 September

Violet has taken up painting with the same passion she gives to everything. We venture out on lengthy excursions along the cliff or along the beach below, where she paints what she sees, not like the great masters, but with her own sense of colour and shape, she creates landscapes of rock and sea and air.

And I write my own inner landscape, the daylight crags and gardens and the silver night, the positive and negative worlds that reflect and focus each other.

When we return to our airy rooms, I read aloud against the backdrop of Violet's paintings. I have become increasingly astonished by her work, the unselfconscious, flaring brushstrokes, the layered, piled textures, the startling colours, the physical, visual landscape of Violet's heart. I am in love with her paintings and feel a host of new sensations toward Violet herself. I see that she was not named for a flower at all, but for a pigment so vibrant and deep it makes the earth seem pale and colourless.

The ink from my pen dries instantly in the warm sunlight. I watch the letters form, round and sensuous, slim and straight. I have found unexpected places in myself that are translated through my arm into my hand, through the pen and onto paper, surprise after surprise. I am sometimes taken with the wonder of it, watching my hand move rhythmically, watching the liquid letters form and then dry into permanence. There are words I hadn't known I possessed, people I hadn't known I knew, scenes that appear and slide into the wet ink. I am creating a life on the page, a world Violet and I can live in, where we are Eve and Julian at Aphros, our forbidden love as real and as impetuous as the Aegean sun, where Eve nurses Julian back to splendid health and he conquers the opposition, fashions a new government.

I write day after day, the pace of my pen matching the beat of my heart. I can feel Violet's presence in the air, hear the glistening slide of the brush against canvas. The pounding of the sea plays to us as we work in our solitary companionship. Our joined daring emerges in paint and in words day after day as we work, separate, side by side.

20 October

Next month Violet and I shall move to the south of France, pawn our jewelry, find cheaper, smaller rooms that can sustain us in the cold. We will no longer need large spaces to live in, nor elaborate furniture, nor elegant wardrobes. We will live and eat simply, sleep warmly together, and wake always to new, raw light.

Our work will become our ballrooms, our cathedrals, our endless horizon. Violet's canvases will cover our walls, a chaos of colour and shadow, light and texture. My pages will grow into stacks, filling the corners, softening the edges of our sitting room.

We have learned each morning that there will be more. We have learned not to fear the blank or the void, knowing that on the other side are startling words, stunning colours. We have learned that silence and emptiness are thresholds to cross, doorways to enter. We are stripping away what our lives have been, moving toward one purpose, and we will give ourselves wholly to it. We wish only to live truly and free, to watch what comes from brush and pen, to uncover what each of us has known forever, what waits for discovery.

Each morning we rededicate ourselves to our work, to our

life, to each other, not through elaborate rituals or vows, but by picking up the instruments of our playing, and over and over, we let ourselves be played.

Anna

1981

Over and over she let herself be played by the light. There was nothing to see, only to feel, the heat on her skin, the instant narrowing of her pupils. Anna had the sensation that the sky entered her whole body at once. She could feel a tingling descend from her head to her chest, through her arms, her abdomen and into her legs. She had the thought that someone looking down on her would be able to see her bones the way she'd seen her mother's ribs behind the doctor's fluoroscope when she was a little girl. She felt outlined on the rock and imagined the shadow of her skeleton left behind if she were to get up and walk away.

Thomas came and sat near her. Anna sensed his presence there, not right next to her but off several feet. She became aware of her nakedness, but before she could lift her hands to cover herself, Thomas spoke in an even, soothing voice.

"There's no need. I'm interested only in what you see."

"Nothing." Anna's voice seemed disembodied to her, as if it came from the rock or the dirt. "I don't see anything."

"Keep looking." Thomas's voice was flat, as if he, too, spoke out from the rock.

"When I was a child, I glimpsed the edge of the sun during an eclipse," Anna went on. "I sat beside my father and pretended to use a shield he'd made for me."

"And what did you see then?"

"I saw the sun just beginning to reform itself."

"And did that change you?"

"It was the beginning of my separation from my father. We became like the eclipsed sun, shadow and light resisting each other. I broke his heart."

"And what about you?"

"I became free inside. Not outside—I still did as I was told. But inside there was no end to the ways I could defy him. I became a secret person, real only inside, and no one—no one—knew me. I lived utterly alone. My outside matched everyone else's. I said 'please' and 'thank you.' I did my homework. I was never any trouble. But I was free and alone." Tears welled up in Anna's eyes and spilled over, running into her hair. Thomas was quiet. "I loved my father, but I couldn't reach him because he lived in another world, where he thought I lived, too. There was no way to talk about it, so we didn't talk. As I grew older, I asked him for permission to do things, go to the movies or stay at a friend's house, but none of it was real, not the asking and not the doing. Those were just things I did on the outside." Anna continued to cry, and small dark patches formed on the rock on either side of her head.

"Why does that cause you pain?" Thomas asked, and Anna realized that this was the question she needed.

"Because I had to let my father go, because I was two people, pretend and real, and I wanted to be only one. Because my father grew ill, had a heart attack, a heart attack, do you understand?"

"Why does that cause you pain?" Again, Thomas's voice was emotionless and even. Anna described the scene to him, told him of the walks she and her father took day after day when he was recovering from his heart attack.

"Everyone lives alone," Thomas said. "Everyone lives inside. Sometimes it's possible to join together, to walk holding hands like you did. But you do it alone, together and alone. Do you see? Your father was as lonely as you were. You wanted each other—and you had each other—by the hand. Words don't matter, but hands do."

Anna could feel a hand, warm and big, wrap around hers. She lay still, feeling its comfortable heat and strength. Then she saw herself home from college telling her mother and father she was going away to Florida for spring break with her boyfriend and some of his friends. This time she didn't ask permission. She made an announcement, stark and cold. Her father gave her a look, and then tears were running down his face, and he didn't wipe them away. She fled to her room, closed the door behind her, slumped onto her bed. A few hours later there was a knock on her door.

"It's me," her father said. She opened the door, facing him, and he handed her two hundred dollars. "For your trip."

Images piled up and pushed against each other, images she barely knew, as if she were watching someone else's life on film:

Part 2

her father's angry shouting that she was a Communist when they talked about politics. The one spanking he gave her when she was seven, which was never repeated, for telling some family business to the girl next door. His snoring on the other side of her bedroom wall, his falling asleep on the couch each night after three Manhattans. His harping about driving slowly on wet leaves. The buzz of the monitors in his hospital room, the tubes in his arms held stiff with tape. He showed her how to wet-sand her car so he could repaint it metallic blue. Called her before dawn on a Sunday morning, drunk, mistaking the time for evening, and she hung up on him. He lay beside her when she was little and afraid of the dark, falling asleep before she did. His Santa Claus hat drooped crookedly over his left eye.

"But he died." The words fell out of her mouth, and she could feel the hand slipping away.

"But he lived," said Thomas, this time his voice intense, almost angry. Anna could feel the hand again. She squeezed and felt it squeeze back.

"He lived," repeated Anna, and she lay there, quiet, holding on.

Madeline

1945

I'd been kidding myself. I can see that now. Just months ago I thought I had everything: my looks, my husband still home, and years ahead of us, in spite of the men around us disappearing one by one.

That afternoon six months ago seemed ordinary enough. I'd always felt grateful at work because my boss, Old Man Reynolds as my friends and I called him to his face, liked me so much he'd let me keep my job even after I'd gotten married. So I sat at my desk happily with the ledgers in front of me, even though I was preparing notices of delinquent accounts. I couldn't help smiling a little to myself about my good luck as I sealed the envelopes, all addressed to men, in spite of the fact that I knew who would really open them, the women with brand new creases in their foreheads, the women left behind to deal with all the bits and pieces.

That afternoon, the sound entered slowly, so slowly I didn't recognize it at first, but as it grew louder and more insistent, I looked around me, met the other women's eyes. The noise became more chaotic, more demanding, and we rose from our chairs as if we were a congregation after the benediction. We spilled down the stairs to the sidewalk, puzzled, and together we looked up, trying to understand.

"Maybe we should go to the basement," said Enid, who was always cautious, her suggestion a response to the only reasonable explanation. The sky was full of smoke, so much smoke I could feel it in my throat, yet there had been no high-pitched whine, no roar of bombers overhead, no explosions. It was all just sirens and smoke.

Only later, after we returned to our desks, perching on the edges of our chairs and shuffling the same papers over and over, did the details come. A customer on the other end of the phone told the story, as far as it was known—and the story was unbelievable.

I listened to the voice but even in my wildest nightmares couldn't imagine the scene, couldn't comprehend that the circus tent full of women and children, all just trying to have a moment's peace, had caught fire, that there weren't enough fire engines, enough ambulances, that there wasn't enough water to turn back the minutes that were all it took. And that my friend Muriel might be among them.

I put down the receiver, then lifted it again and dialed Muriel's house, let it ring and ring, finally gave up. I decided I had to call her husband at work. He was another of the lucky ones like Bill, still working in a munitions factory back then. My hand shook so much that it took three tries to get the numbers right. I waited and waited while the company operator connected me to his boss, while his boss went to find him in the shop.

"Hello?" Jerry yelled, the machines in the background overwhelming his voice.

"It's Madeline," I shouted.

"WHO?"

"MADELINE! Wasn't Muriel going to the circus today?" He had such a hard time hearing me that I had to ask him twice. I couldn't get enough air, as if I were running for a bus that was pulling away. "Did MURIEL take IRIS to the CIRCUS?"

"I don't know. She talked about it."

"There's a FIRE." I spoke the word as calmly as I could, as if I might be reporting the chance for rain, as if I could keep him from the real possibility, that Muriel was inside that tent with her sister's only child. "I called your house and there was no answer. Maybe you could try the hospitals."

"No. NO!" His voice sounded like a howl, and he hung up, leaving me to all the smoke and the terrible din outside the windows.

It took all afternoon and evening to find her. Bill and I discovered Jerry standing by a gurney in a hallway at the biggest of the city hospitals. His arms dangled at his sides, and he didn't answer when Bill said his name. Bill put one hand on Jerry's shoulder and his other arm around me, and we three watched the ragged rise and fall of Muriel's breaths. I inhaled, wanting to do it for her, but there wasn't any air, only the smell of charred flesh. I sank into

Bill, trying to stay upright, closed my eyes against the sight of what had been Muriel's beautiful skin, against the endless line of gurneys.

In the months that followed, I visited Muriel faithfully, and I dutifully participated in the lie that Iris had survived, that she was recovering just a few miles away in another hospital. I brushed Muriel's hair because her arms were so badly burned she couldn't do it for herself.

"I held on to her hand," Muriel would say. "I held on to her as long as I could." That's all she could remember, except the hard yank from a stranger's hand, the hand that pulled Muriel by the hair under the tent to the outside, to the hot air that could be breathed.

I kept brushing Muriel's hair, kept offering the lie, until I began to half-believe it myself, that Iris was intact in a bed with clean sheets and soft blankets instead of having turned up in the Armory, one of the unrecognizable bodies on the long rows of cots that stretched through the great hall and scorched the air.

It's odd, but sometimes I would imagine that Iris was Little Miss 1565, the one body that was never claimed, the body with the lovely little face that slept on the front page of the morning paper. It made no sense: I went to Iris's funeral and stared at the small casket covered with flowers and ribbons. But I wanted Little Miss 1565 to have a name, even wanted to claim her myself. I had known for a long time how easily a child can be lost, how quickly a stranger's hand can arbitrarily bring life or death.

Now it's my turn. Now it's Muriel who spends silent evenings with me, her beautiful, dark hair pinned tightly into a bun as if it shouldn't be allowed to escape again. Long sleeves covering her scarred arms, she makes me a cup of hot water, brushes my hair before bed. The lie cracked open months ago. Muriel suspected Iris's death because she'd seen it in her sister's eyes, but she went along with the lie for everyone's sake.

Now it's Muriel's turn to give the lie back, to urge me to hold on and keep holding on to everything that's possible, to lie to myself, to put my trust in the hands of strangers who might deliver me. But I'm like the photo of Emmett Kelly in the newspaper: a hand shielding his eyes from the smoke, his sad-sack, drooping mouth, a pail in his hand, one small pail of water against all those flames.

※ ❦ ※

I hold on to what I can remember, the blueness of eyes, the whiteness of teeth, the roughness of whiskers. They're fleeting, filmy, like smoke curling around my head. I can hold them only briefly, and then they fade. Here in the darkening light, I wonder if I have the energy to get up or can find the abandon that will let me sleep. I don't want either, want only to hold on to Bill's head and keep it focused in front of me, insistent and solid.

My belly feels hard and unfamiliar. I can feel my own pulse, steady inside its roundness. I listen to myself breathe, the only sound in the room. There's nothing else, only my body, my breathing, the warmth of the bed, the shadowed air.

※ ❦ ※

I was inside out, as if my skin could no longer protect me, as if there were nothing between my flesh and the air. I wondered if all the adults could read my thoughts, see right through my young skull to what lay beneath. But no one seemed to notice me, just a girl sitting quietly at the table among chattering voices, dressed in my Sunday-best dress, dark red velvet trimmed with Mama's hand-crocheted lace. I watched my mother eating, watched the muscles of her jaw tighten and release. She spoke little, sat nodding politely at the conversations around her.

Papa laughed and joked, offered toasts, boasted. The more he talked, the more Mama's silent grin transformed into a thin, straight line, and her eyes turned sharp and hard. I watched them both as if they were acquaintances I was trying to remember, speaking a language I didn't know.

When the dancing started, Papa made a show of asking me to dance, and my cheeks burned as I walked with him into the crowd. We waltzed, flying smoothly across the floor. Barely tall enough to reach his chest, I couldn't see his face unless I bent back, dizzying myself in the whirling. Adrift, breathless, I was anchored only by Papa's arms.

✦

In the dream, I could feel my baby's presence next to me, tiny and thin, wiry. His toddler legs should have had trouble keeping up with mine, but it was the other way around. My feet were heavy. They could have been mired in mud or cast in concrete. I drove myself on, afraid to lose him as we ran, held tightly to his hand, small and warm and moist. He pulled me on with all his might, his little legs strong and sure.

"Don't let go," I yelled to him. "Hold on."

The sound was too much to bear, whistling and exploding bombs tearing trees from their roots, gouging craters in the road. Mud and debris were flying everywhere, and I could hardly see, pulled on only by my son's urging. I didn't know where we were running, only that we needed to keep running. All around us people were screaming, falling. There were bodies everywhere, their limbs crumpled beneath them, their faces eerily peaceful. I ran and ran, heedless of direction or purpose, clutching my son's small hand.

The baby gives a sudden kick, and now I'm in the dim room again, but it seems like just another dream, even less real than the world I wake from. I'd grown used to the screams of people and bombs, and this room seems too quiet to be real.

I wish I could feel his little hand, see the top of his small blonde head slightly out ahead of me, urging me on. I need him, a body outside my own, a voice, eyes, a hand pulling me. But all I have is myself and the pool inside me that contains him, unseen and unknown, a stranger.

I try to call Bill's face to me, his reckless grin, his sentimental eyes that spill over with love, as easily for an injured robin as for me. There's an endlessness I want now, want badly, some sign that I can trust beyond this moment and this room, a sign that something beyond me still exists. I need eyes, a face to look at, to anchor me, to keep me from being tossed overboard, to keep me from drowning.

    I pull an afghan around me and cross the room to the dressing table. I turn on the two lamps, and it's my face that appears in the mirror. There I am, a face made of flesh, shaped and rounded in the air. I stare into my own eyes, stare until there's nothing else. And a fierce love descends like a dream, a fierce and nameless love, for past and future, for earth and sky, for everything.

Anna

1981

A fierce love descended like a dream, a fierce and nameless love, for past and future, for earth and sky, for everything. It played itself throughout her body, vibrating as if she were a drum, thick skin stretched taut over a bone frame. The smallest touch of air or light moved percussively through her, all her cells pulsing in waves of sound. She seemed on the edge of a precipice, ready always to fall, ready always to stand, balanced in a fine and perfect tension.

Thomas remained silent, her witness. Anna knew he was there, his presence speaking to her across rock. She heard a birdcall, quick and lovely, from the maples across the clearing. And then a repeat call came from right behind her, just past her shoulder, and she sat up as if awakened in the middle of a dream. She felt dazed, searching for her bearings, trying to find her voice, words.

"I've been to a place." When they came, the words were vague, incomplete, but it was all she could say.

"And what happened there?" Thomas coaxed.

She fished for more words, waiting, and finally hooked what she could. "I found something. I feel as if my skin molted like a snake's, and I've emerged, my same self but more supple."

A red-winged blackbird landed nearby, made the same clear call that had startled her. And then another and another landed and sang. She watched their dark bodies, the flash of their red wing patches as more and more birds gathered.

"They sing like the first raw edge of spring, the day that comes in January when you know for the first time that winter will break up and disappear after all, and you can believe in green again." She could feel the sound in her body, deeper with each birdcall. "I want to live in that rawness. I've always known it was there, but I'd forgotten."

She thought she should cry, but there were no more tears, even when she reached for them. Instead, her mouth curved into a smile, like the band of red on the blackbird's wing. Thomas waited, silent again. Anna sat still, smiling, glancing from bush to bush, noting the play of light on the leaves.

"It's like getting sprinkled with fairy dust," Anna heard herself saying. "I sound like Tinker Bell."

"Do you like it?"

"Yes, I do. Yes, I like it. I wish I could feel this way all the time. I wish I could believe in fairy dust."

"What's to keep you from it?" Thomas's voice was gentle and easy.

"Well, there's my job, the bills, how I'm supposed to be. Well, there's nothing." Anna's heart began to pound.

"Yes, there's nothing. Let me tell you a story."

Anna turned to Thomas and looked at his face as if she'd never seen him before. His skin was smooth above his carefully trimmed beard. His hair was full and dark, and for the first time she thought about him as a man, a person with thoughts and a history, real. She realized that until this moment he hadn't been real to her, but rather a two-dimensional presence, a singular pressure. She noted how young he was, much younger than she, thirty perhaps, and handsome in a carved sort of way. She felt self-conscious and reached for her clothes, rose on wobbly legs and dressed as quickly as she could.

"I tried to die," he said after she'd sat back down, sounding as if he were asking for a menu or giving someone directions to a museum or bank. Anna looked at him again, his witness now, her eyes on his eyes, steady. She invited him with a look, feeling awkward and chilled but ready. She waited. Thomas stayed quiet, just looking at her straight on. Finally she sighed and he continued.

"I had nothing to live for as I saw it, no love, no spark, no hope, only a job, only snow I kept shoveling over and over, only to see it drift back again. I had everything I needed, a house, enough food, friends, a paycheck, hobbies, chores, memories—but no future—nothing I could see beyond dailiness and drabness. I had everything and nothing. So I took a bottle of pills and went to sleep. I lay on my bed with my hands over my chest like a corpse in the movies. I didn't pray. I didn't think. I wasn't afraid or desperate or sad. I just closed my eyes and waited to slide from nothing into nothing."

Anna waited again, his pause like a moment of stillness on a windy day, startling.

"But I didn't die. I woke. Some gap went by, some empty, missing time, and then I woke. I learned how to walk, learned how to run, how to eat, how to see. I started over from a clean, empty place. There was raw power in it, like the January day you described. I made everything that crossed my day. I made it mean something. You see, starting from nothing, it could mean anything I wanted it to. That's what I discovered, Anna, by not dying."

She continued to look at him after he stopped speaking and he looked at her, as if their eyes were connected by fine silk threads only they could see. He smiled, a red-winged blackbird smile, and she answered with her own.

Vita & Violet

1920

Behind them the candle rippled its glow against the wall. The light swelled and collapsed, its rises and falls staccato. They sat there for a long time, as if their eyes were connected by fine silk threads only they could see. Vita held Harold's letter in her lap, still sealed. And Violet, her flickering twin, held its mirror in her hand, an unopened letter from Denys.

"We knew the world would come someday, didn't we?" Violet's voice was thin and warm like tea. "But I didn't expect it so soon." Resting her fisted hands on the envelope, she pushed it into her skirt as if she could make it disappear. "The world is calling us, and how shall we answer?"

Vita's thoughts strayed to the window, to the darkness pressing on the glass. She felt strangely light, not quite inhabiting her body, as if she could slip away to a shadow world, slide under the casement and into the night. She felt a little like smoke rising, or heat, vaporous and ever expanding. Still her eyes held Violet's, shining in the vacant air, and her fingers held the envelope tightly against her trousers, the wool the only buffer between it and her skin. Words did not come to her tongue, only to her eyes, which spoke their silence.

Vita finally unhooked her eyes from Violet's, undressed and slipped into bed. She still hadn't spoken. Violet could see her closed eyes from across the room and they frightened her, their rounded lids perfect and smooth. *Alabaster*, she thought, the word polished and cool. She rose and rushed to Vita's side of the bed, knelt and laid her head on the edge of Vita's pillow.

"You must speak," Violet whispered, her voice scratching inside her throat. She waited and waited until her muscles grew stiff, but no sound came from Vita. Finally Violet undressed, blew out the candle, and slid into her side of the bed, lying as close to Vita as she dared. Violet could not shut her eyes, searched the darkness for something, anything.

They lay against each other, their backs pressed together in the center of the bed. The letters lay unopened on the writing table, one on top of the other, their edges aligned. The room was dark and cold, and the two women faced opposing walls they could not see. It didn't matter whether their eyes were open or closed.

Vita walked down the main street as she had so many times with Violet, but this time she was alone. Her boots clicked on the packed surface, her steps long and swift, her arms swinging. She drove herself on, as if stopping or slowing could be a deadly thing, as if a knife glinted toward her from the darkness or a runaway horse gained speed from behind. There was no one to see her, not at this time of night. Everyone was inside the windowed world asleep, dreaming their own secrets. She alone walked the street, her long legs slicing the dark.

The morning light jostled Violet awake as if she were on a lurching train that swayed dangerously toward derailment. She wanted to get off, felt motion-sick, felt a desperate longing for the horizon to steady her. She knew the bed was empty as soon as she woke, Vita's absence as tangible as her presence would have been.

Violet fled the bed's warmth, charged the window and tore open the draperies. The streets were there, she assured herself. The town spread itself out toward the sea. By rote, Violet dressed hurriedly, aware of each minute's passage, the tide going out continually, leaving only bare sand under her feet. She brushed her hair by feel and dashed out the door, pinning her hat as she ran.

The sunlight dazed her as she hesitated just outside the door. She started in one direction, only to spin around and nearly bump into an elderly couple. She murmured an apology and rushed the opposite way again.

"So sorry," she murmured over and over as she stormed ahead. People began to stare, to nod to each other with raised eyebrows as she flung herself past them. Violet's hands extended in front of her a bit, so she looked like a sleepwalker moving at high speed, a caricature of a human form caught on film and accompanied by a racing score on the piano.

Violet had given up and then she spied Vita sitting on a rock below, a rock completely surrounded by water. Vita sat still, gazing out to sea like a ship's captain in the fog. *Serene* was the word that came to Violet then, but she shook it off like a chill because it made no sense.

Tracing the shape of Vita's body with her eyes, Violet wanted only to hold her lover, to feel her familiar closeness, but the distance between them seemed to grow. The wind caught at her full skirt, and she lost her balance for a moment, leaning dangerously close to the cliff's edge before she righted herself. She studied the rocks below, imagined her battered body landing behind Vita without a sound, and she shuddered at the sight of her own end.

Vita kept her eyes on the horizon, a straight line where blue met blue. She felt as if she were part of the rock, cold and hard, water hitting against her incessantly, wearing her away. Little by little she eroded, and she wondered how long it would be until there was nothing left.

Violet climbed down the rock path that descended from the cliff to the beach. She moved like a spider, using arms and legs to keep from falling, wishing for the ability to spin a silken line to save herself. She had seen this path from the top many times and had wondered who could possibly use it. Now she knew: only desperate women whose lovers had sailed away and never returned. Women whose hands and legs were torn and dirtied like their dresses, whose eyes held to the horizon, searching, whose feet stumbled beneath them. Pebbles spun away under Violet's shoes and she landed hard on her wrist, flopping forward on her face like a rag doll. She lay shredded, dirt and stones against her cheek, her hair undone. She lay there unable to move, and then a sound escaped her, a moan that she let loose into a howl. She howled for herself, but the sound was lost, swallowed by the waves that chiseled the rocks below. Violet kept howling, water against rock drowning her voice.

Vita took the two letters from her breast pocket. She read one, then the other, and cradled them both in her lap. She looked again out to the horizon, the line that joined two flat worlds. Keeping her eyes on that thin line, she tore the letters into tiny shreds and threw them into the wind. She watched them flutter to the base of the rock, watched them snatched by a breaking wave, lost in white foam.

Madeline

1931

She'd watched them, snatched by a breaking wave, lost in white foam. Her heart took a small leap, and then they rose laughing, splashing, easy in the water's push and pull. Madeline watched her cousins as if they were on a stage, distant and contained, speaking lines and making gestures. They seemed to have fun at whatever they did, even small, stupid things like making faces behind each other's backs, and she envied them their lack of self-consciousness, their silliness alternating with sophistication. She was continually trying to measure up to some unseen presence that hovered over her. And always falling short.

Madeline wished for one unencumbered moment when she could splash in the waves without worrying about her fair skin burning, for one moment without something looking over her shoulder.

She'd set out that morning to walk the seven blocks to her cousins' house so she could follow them to the beach. Her mother had given permission as long as she didn't return late, meaning she had to get there before the potatoes were boiling and her father arrived home. Madeline followed her cousins along the sidewalk, past house after house, apartment building after apartment building. The two boys wanted little to do with her except torment, so she tried to stay out of their way. The girls condescended to having her along, a younger version of themselves before they had achieved breasts and mastered flirting. Madeline continued to frequent her cousins' house and their trips to the beach in spite of their disdain for her. Their house was much more interesting than her apartment, at least while her father was out looking for work and her mother was hell-bent on making every piece of furniture and every knickknack aligned and spotless. Some days Madeline's brother, Andrew, let her follow him around, but lately he'd taken to getting up before dawn to accompany the iceman on his rounds, so he could earn a chunk of free ice and once in awhile even a few pennies.

The seven blocks to her cousins' house were monotonous, one building after another with their tidy stoops. Madeline amused herself by making up stories about who lived inside, peopling them with eccentrics, shapely showgirls and kidnappers. Each day she added to her stories until she began to believe them. A chance encounter with one of her characters on the sidewalk would set her tales spinning wider and faster. Soon Madeline's head was filled with neighbors, and she began to find more and more of them in her dreams and on the sidewalk in her path.

Madeline felt like a creation herself most of the time, not a real flesh-and-blood person, but a paper character that had walked out of one of the many books she took out of the library. She seemed less and less real to herself, less and less substantial, transparent like ice.

Eastchester Bay seemed huge to Madeline, and she felt as puny as a pebble. She couldn't imagine what open ocean was like, waves that could crush, no sight of land. As she watched her cousins in the water, Madeline longed to be like them, rounded and solid, flesh and blood. She lay back against the sand, digging into it with her toes. She thought about joining them, about losing herself in the foam, but she knew she wouldn't, knew she belonged flat against the sand like a towel. Hot tears sprang to her eyes and ran through her hair and into her ears. She lay still under the burning sun, watching the colors swirl inside her eyelids, orange and red and purple.

"What are you doing, Miss Fancypants?" The voice was glimmering and playful. Madeline opened her eyes to Betty, the girl who'd moved into a house on her block during the winter. Betty had short dark hair and wore glasses, which Madeline found fascinating. Betty dropped to the sand beside Madeline, her hand shielding her eyes.

"I'm waiting for the King of Siam to come and take me away," Madeline answered.

"No, he's coming for me, there on his fine white horse, with his gold crown and his silver sword."

Madeline had meant it sarcastically and couldn't believe Betty was taking it further. Betty herself was nowhere near as fascinating as her glasses were. Madeline wanted to sink back into the sand, to become invisible, to drown in this parched desert. She wanted Betty to disappear, to shrink and fade and leave her alone.

"The King of Siam is dead," Madeline found herself saying. "He died this morning in an avalanche, and he left me his crown jewels, which I have to go home and polish." With that Madeline got to her feet, grabbed her towel and walked away. She climbed the stairs to the boardwalk and sat down on a bench, searching the foam for her cousins, but she couldn't spot them.

Madeline continued to the end of the boardwalk and crossed the street to start the seven blocks back to her cousins' and then the seven blocks home. She wished summer had never been invented, wished she could fall into an open manhole and never be seen again. Then she could live in a subterranean world, out of the sun, away from everybody.

She kept walking, each broad square of sidewalk the only thing she looked at, past all the houses and storefronts of her stories, past the pirates and the witches and the bank robbers. None of them interested her today. She wished she could be somewhere else, in a fairyland where everything sang with magic rhymes and everyone loved her. There would be holidays in her honor with parades and marching bands. The gathered crowd would point at her and roar, push and shove to touch the hem of her dress. She'd have three wishes every day, and they would be for a kind mother, a sober father, and a house she wanted to come home to. She'd laugh and have acres of friends, throngs of people shouting her praises, and she'd never have to be alone. She'd be sprinkled with stardust every night, and each morning the sun would make her sparkle. And she'd look into the mirror, and the face that looked back would be smiling.

Bill

1945

What's real and what's not? He wondered about it, not as a thought in his head but more as a feeling in his body. The forest was hilly and wet. It was something he'd imagined for six months, this walking freely among trees, and now here he was in the place he'd dreamed up day after day. He touched a beech trunk to steady himself, and the lined bark was there under his palm just as he'd imagined it. He was awed by this power to imagine and make real, the simplicity of the gates swinging open and his walking away.

"Come on, Bill," Tom urged, his voice pleading and strange. Bill left the tree behind and followed the voice, but he felt like a bridge between two places, suspended in the air and not quite anchored on either end. His legs moved, his feet walked on the ground, but he didn't know where to go. "Come on, Bill." He followed the voice and stumbled ahead, his weak body not giving out on him. Something propelled him, thirst, hunger, home, the raw edge of freedom to move somewhere, anywhere.

As Bill and Tom stumbled forward, the other men were lost to them, scattered in every direction. There were only the two of them now, ashen-faced, skinny and torn, remnants of themselves pushing through the trees. They had nothing, no food or water, no weapons, only the thin blankets from their straw bunks draped over what was left of their uniforms. They looked like begging monks who'd survived the plague but lost their minds, zigzagging through an old world in another century.

"Come on, Bill." If it hadn't been for the voice, he would have stopped to rest, to lie still and peacefully under branches and sky, to sleep undisturbed by thoughts or dreams or longing. But the husky voice insisted, and Bill lunged forward following its bidding. On and on they walked, bent and thin as sticks. They saw no one but each other, not even a sign of anyone. Finally the light brightened and the woods shrank, and they came to an edge where trees met grass: a wide field. Bill felt fear, hard and sharp, piercing his head and stomach. He instinctively stopped while there was still cover, distrusting open space. They stood side by side, laboring to remain upright, swaying slightly and leaning against each other, shoulder to shoulder.

The field looked peaceful, which made it doubly suspicious to Bill. The gray stalks of last year's grass were matted, but tough green shoots were finding their way through to the light. The carpet of green woven with gray looked so inviting, a bright place to lie down, to soak in the sun, to sleep. But fear took over, and Bill scanned the horizon, looking for signs he could hang his doubts on. There was nothing, nothing but flat land covered by old and new grass and the sky above it, blue and bright. His eyes hurt from the unbroken glare. He stood, swaying against Tom in the dirty blanket, a tattered man afraid of the next step.

In the morning the landscape looked just the same as they'd left it, trees at their backs, the field ahead. They'd lain huddled together all night, shivering not so much from the cold but from thirst and hunger, waking to find the same world. The two men sat up and surveyed the space in front of them, shielding their eyes with the blankets draped over their heads and down their backs. They formed a single dark shape that blended with the woods behind them, a mound rising from the forest floor. Finally they looked at each other. Bill's eyes were rheumy and yellowed, haunted by the man he'd been. Tom's eyes were clear and blue, as if they held the sky's truth, and Bill knew that they would have to cross the open field, or turn back the way they'd come, or stay still and die. There were only so many choices, none of them good, none of them reliable.

Bill looked behind them to the shadowed woods, remembering all the pines he'd planted by the reservoir before he'd gotten the munitions job. The planting crew had moved easily, their bending and digging and placing of sprouts transforming the landscape toward a future he'd taken for granted. He was surprised at his ability to think, to remember the feel of a seedling in his hand, and then the picture flickered out as quickly as it had come, and he was back in this place where only openness lay at his feet, openness and few choices. Yet he knew vividly, as clearly as the seedling had been in his hand just a moment before, that the time had come to go ahead, to risk everything for water, for a scrap of food, for the chance to be found, to be recovered.

"Let's go," Tom said. They entered the sunny field, and it turned out to be just what it seemed, quiet and new.

The endless field ended finally, broken by woods, and then the woods were broken by more fields. Scattered among them were the remains of lives, burned barns and houses, abandoned and silent. Bill and Tom found water along the way, a hand pump the answer to their unspoken prayers. Other fragments of someone else's life came as answers, too, a knife with a charred handle, a root cellar with its collection of seed potatoes. Their teeth felt loose when they chewed, so they cut the potatoes into small pieces and sucked on them until they turned mealy, the moisture cool on their tongues. They slept in fits and starts, unable to trust night or day.

They continued to walk east, fueled by moisture and need, watching the sun and stars for direction, always suspicious of edges, scanning the three-hundred-sixty degrees around them. They counted the nights, even though they didn't know the names of the days, only that it must still be May, the month when the gates had opened. They counted the nights to get some sense of time again, some semblance of human life, organized life, movement.

The human figure outlined against the horizon was as startling as the first open field had been. Both men saw it and glanced quickly at each other and back again. Neither could blink it away. There it was, sticking up on the horizon, along with the shape of a small intact house. They dropped to the ground as they'd been trained to do, lying side by side on their bellies, watching the figure and the building. Bill felt for the charred knife in his boot, just to make sure. They began to crawl, slowly and deliberately, their eyes stuck to the spot where the figure was, their bodies taut and strained. They crept to the top of a small rise and stopped.

Bill couldn't stop the thoughts in his head, the thoughts coming unbidden and unrestrained. There was a flash of the camp where he'd been held, and he wondered all of a sudden why he hadn't thought of raiding the kitchen before he'd walked out the gate. But then he recalled an image of what had been a soldier lying in the mud next to a pot of soup, and he remembered that food could kill a starving man. He wondered why these thoughts came now, when he didn't want them, when he had to keep his eyes on that figure and decide what to do.

"It's a woman." The words and the voice pulled him back from the camp. And he could see what Tom meant—yes, it was a woman. He could see the skirt distinctly now. He felt his body relax. Women had been a comfort all along, on the snowy forced march that went on day after day and on the endless boxcar ride, where the men had to take turns sleeping because there was barely room to stand. They'd huddle close together for warmth and allow a few men the space to lie down, to free their legs from the continuous pain of staying upright. The boxcars stopped once in awhile, just as the line of men marching through snow had occasionally halted, and a few generous women would sneak close with a pan of water or a handful of bread.

The fact that it was a woman silhouetted against the sky calmed Bill, and he smiled for the first time he could remember. His mouth felt awkward, as if the muscles were straining to work. They took a quick look at each other and then scrambled to their feet and began to walk toward her. Their blankets wrapped them like capes, knotted at their throats. They kept it slow, knowing that surprising her could be deadly, depending on who she was and where they were.

"Friend—*freund*," yelled Tom, his slender hands extended from his sides to show they were empty. As they came closer to her, she stood frozen, a small older woman alone in the yard. She looked and looked, as if they were apparitions and she had forgotten she'd conjured them up herself. Then as the sun caught the blue of her eyes, her face broke into a grin and she ran toward them, her arms outstretched as if they were her long-lost lovers or her prodigal sons. And a pouring of German words streamed from her mouth like a song.

Anna

1981

She had thought about it one way, but now she could see another view. She could see endless ways. They stupefied her by their sheer number. She had thought she wanted clear, simple answers, but she began to take pleasure in the complexity of things, to see endless beauty in endless ideas, as if she were seeing her reflection multiplied in facing mirrors, reflection after reflection growing smaller into infinity.

It had been some weeks since Anna had seen Thomas, since she'd slept by herself on the top of the ridge naked under the moon. Nothing had been the same since, not her days, not her dreams, not her memories. She never went back to her job, never even called her boss to tell him, ignored the repeated messages on the answering machine. Finally a pair of police officers knocked on her door, and after she assured them that she was unharmed and showed them the photo on her driver's license, they went away, and she continued to ignore the ringing phone and the recorded messages. Finally they stopped, and she liked the silence. She withdrew her savings from the bank, years' worth of careful scrimping, and she hid it in bundles all over her house, quickly forgetting where they were but stumbling on them in sweater pockets or under the sink just when her wallet was getting empty. She wasn't shocked at the change in herself, only took note of it calmly, as if noticing a sagging hem or a missing button.

Anna spent time sleeping when she was tired, eating when she was hungry, singing when a song came to her lips, walking when she felt like it, doing whatever came to her when it came to her. She didn't worry about anything, not the end of her money or what would become of her retirement plan or being alone.

She found that the past had reformed itself. It was strange but it didn't surprise her that she could remember being a baby, the time her parents rushed her to the doctor because she held her breath until her lips turned blue and she passed out. She'd been full of infant rage at having been born, having to depend on those two people for everything. She saw that both of her parents had loved her in their halting and inexperienced way, that they had wanted her. Her mother loved Anna so much that she would poke her awake just to see Anna's eyes, and Anna could remember her father's heartbeat when he cradled her. She saw that forgiveness was simple, a simple flipping over of what she'd always thought. Her mother's growing criticisms had been a constant stream of love songs, and her father's angry outbursts an uncontrollable yearning to keep Anna close.

Anna had grown up believing life was a long disappearance, broken by stolen moments of happiness. Her father had begun to fade after his first heart attack, little by little becoming less and less. His laughter grew tentative and his smile thin, his body haunted by his former self. Grandparents were holes in history, long-lost, two-dimensional people who lived in photographs. Even the grandmother she'd known had slipped away, her days slowly consumed by confusion. Now Anna could see that life was endless spinnings, one event linked to another in the whirling. But she could also see that all her memories vanished when she sat under the moon or lay beneath the sun, and she became just herself, pulsing and breathing, a hot patch of energy kindling the earth.

There was no end to her rememberings and no end to the joy she found buttering a piece of bread or pouring a glass of clean water and feeling it slide down her throat. Each breath she took seemed important to her, and the trees were taller and lovelier. She swore she could smell a change in the weather and taste the approach of dawn.

Anna wanted to see Thomas again to tell him her discoveries, but she didn't seek him out, even though she knew well the routes he took running. She waited, things reeling inside her at a faster and faster pace, then slowing to a long sigh she could savor. She thought about Thomas often, his thin body in his dark green running suit the first time she'd seen him on the road. She thought about the sound of his voice, how little they'd been together, but how important those moments had been. She wondered what he thought about, wanted to share his insides as fully as he'd shared hers. She felt that he knew everything there was to know about her, that nothing of her had been hidden from him.

Anna began to wonder about Thomas's parents, about the house he grew up in, about what he'd looked like as a little boy. She felt there was something more she needed to know from him if only she could think of the right question to ask. Yet there was no urgency to her thoughts about Thomas, no longing or need. There was instead a solidity, a knowing that sometime they would meet again, and he would tell her something that would make the spinning wider and quicker and her thoughts reorganized and new.

Anna sat on a rock at the edge of the river downhill from the cemetery, the sun warming the top of her head, her eyes closed, her chin against her chest. When her head grew cool as if a cloud had passed over the sun, she opened her eyes to find Thomas standing in front of her. He blocked the sun so she could see him clearly, his thin nose and bright blue eyes. She felt naked when he looked at her, not in a sexual way, but seen, thoroughly seen. She liked seeing herself under Thomas's eyes. She had a steadiness she'd never had before and a sense of peace about everything. The past was the past, the future was the future, and here she sat, simply herself.

"You don't need me," he said. "There isn't anything I've given you that you didn't already have yourself."

"But I'd never seen myself outside myself before," she answered, struggling for words. She was afraid he would leave her, and she wasn't ready yet.

"I'm just your witness," and the word seemed like the right one.

"Yes," she said. It was the only word that made sense to her, so she said it again, "Yes."

Madeline

1945

"Yes," Madeline whispered, feeling the baby's kick, the watery flutter inside her. She sat at the table peeling an onion for soup.

"It's good for your blood," her landlady, Marta, had said. "I got it for you fresh."

Madeline had an aversion to the sight or talk of blood, yet her dreams seemed to fill with it, a series of bloody faces: her father's, Bill's, her unborn son's. She drifted in a sea of blood all night and woke drowning, a thick, chafed feeling in her throat when she tried to swallow.

※

She'd managed to say the word that day so many years before: "Yes." It had come out small and meek, barely audible, her voice sounding much younger than her fourteen years. She'd tried to say it again on that long-ago day, but the energy was not there to move her tongue and open her mouth. Her brother and mother kept looking at her, but she couldn't move from the edge of the deep hole that held her father. The workmen were already shoveling in dirt, and it sounded with a dull thud up her spine and into her head.

Madeline was sure the world had ended, that it would never be right again. The sail that had been her father had fallen into the ocean, leaving only a stick for a mast poking at the sky. They were alone in the boat, she and her father, a tiny boat shaped like his coffin, and they were adrift aimlessly without a speck of land in sight. He sat rigid, holding the rudder, and even though the wind grew more and more furious, howling over them, they didn't move.

Madeline turned to look at her father and he began to cough, and then blood stained the corner of his mouth, and he coughed and coughed until his whole face was covered with blood and he fell back into the water and sank. Madeline was alone in the coffin boat in the roaring wind. Only the drops of blood on the boat floor told her he'd ever existed.

For a long time after her father's death, Madeline couldn't stand the sight of blood. When her brother, Andrew, had come home one day after school with a black eye and a bloody nose, she'd fainted. Madeline's mother couldn't stand weakness, so she shook Madeline conscious, pushed her into a chair and told her to sit still.

"Yes," Madeline said, nodding. She was still nodding when her mother came back into the kitchen with Andrew, his face scrubbed into a raw shine, the flesh all around his eye purple and blue and swollen.

❦

When the postcard came, Madeline couldn't really believe it. The postmistress came around the counter waving it and met her at the door. There were twelve words, each written on its own assigned line:

Darling. Alive. Prisoner Germany. Fine. Send peanut butter, cigarettes. A baby! Love.

The postmistress beamed, and all Madeline could say was, "Yes."

She walked all the way home holding the card in front of her like a sign, resting her hands on her rounded womb, the card between them. Each step was a yes. Yes. Yes. Yes. Yes. She walked her measured steps and then stopped, feeling a kick from her son, who lay in his own sea of water and blood.

Two days later a breathless teenage boy coasted on his bicycle down the hill to the house and charged up the back steps to pound on Madeline's door. He handed her a telegram, stood and shuffled his feet until she found him a coin. Madeline was afraid of telegrams but she made herself open it—and there were the words she'd waited for. The Army confirmed Bill's postcard. He really was alive, and she began to believe it, awed by the power of paper to make or break her. Madeline had been afraid of the radio, too, but the telegram gave her the courage to turn it on. There was a series of quiet, grim voices that blended together, but one advertisement caught her, the promise of a show about Bill, a gift offered over the air.

When the evening and hour finally arrived, Madeline sat with Marta and Fran, one of her friends from work, their china cups of hot water balanced in their hands. The voice of Cedric Foster spoke intimately from the wooden box, as if he were right there in the room sipping from his own cup, a good friend telling them the story of Bill's infantry division.

Cedric, as Madeline wanted to call the warm voice, quoted the division commander addressing the assembled men only months before, and his voice swelled with patriotic ardor: "'You are brand new. You have no past history to live up to. You have no past sins to live down.'"

Madeline could picture Bill's face, saw the smoke that rose from his cigarette curling around his head. He was enveloped in a murky cloud, but she could see his features, almost taste the smoke. Bill's division was called the Golden Lions, the place where they'd fought known as the Schnee Eiffel, a forest on the edge of Belgium. The tale was horrific: green troops taken by surprise just before dawn, the ferocity of German tanks and artillery bearing down on them. Out of two regiments, only three hundred men remained, the rest dead or prisoners within a few days. Madeline couldn't look at the other two women, but she knew they were looking at her. More than eight thousand men had disappeared, Bill engulfed in a tidal wave of the lost.

Cedric ended his talk by quoting the mother of one of the missing men: "'If only they had a chance to fight . . . to prove themselves.'" He went on for a few more sentences, using words like *magnificent* and *shining* and *glory*, but Madeline didn't hear them. She wanted to kill them both, the mother and the man on the radio, both complete strangers after all, and got up to silence the dial like a soldier snapping to attention.

That night when she went to bed, she dreamed of bloody, faceless bodies and explosions that tore her hearing away, so only soundless men crept through the woods, eyes and gun barrels glinting in the dark. She woke in fear that the postcard was too old to be true anymore, that the telegram spoke only of history. The postcard was dated more than two months earlier, and she knew from the size of her belly how much could happen in two months. Madeline woke heavy and slow, heavier and slower than a rock, weighted against the mattress by her nightmares. She had to force herself to get up, to dress for work, tying a string from the button to the buttonhole on the waistband of her skirt to make room for her roundness. Climbing the hill to the bus stop, one foot in front of the other, she willed the silent yeses that kept her moving.

Repetition kept Madeline going, one day merging into another, sameness wrapping her like a mummy's cloth. She felt resistance with every act, every breath, every swallow. She mailed a letter each day in care of the Red Cross to Stalag 4B, the place the telegram had given her. On the nightstand she kept a stack of sixty-odd letters tied with twine, all of which had come back to her stamped *Missing in Action*. The packet was thick like her waistline, an accumulation that had its own weight. Since she'd heard that there could be something beyond those stamped words, she'd made herself try again and again. She had no idea if her letters would reach Bill, but she made them cheerful and light, as if he were just a drive away in a neighboring town.

Madeline boxed cookies and cigarettes with one of Bill's sweaters and mailed it all off. The cookies had taken her whole ration of butter and sugar, but she didn't care. She wanted something to reach him, anything, a word, a sweet mouthful, a puff of smoke. She'd sent him peanut butter and cigarettes right away, the day after the telegram. Madeline imagined a word, one word in his handwriting, the word that formed in her mouth every morning. That was all she wanted: *Yes*.

It arrived one day almost three months later when Madeline argued with herself for giving up hope, when she felt the most hateful and doubted her strength to go on. She'd almost bypassed the post office and gone home—she was that bone-tired—but the setting sun caught her eye when she got off the bus, and she turned toward the walk that led up to the door. And there was the postmistress waving an envelope and calling her name.

"Yes!" Madeline answered, and she started to run, toward her and her open arms.

Part 2

It was the visions that were most important to her. She held scenes until they were fully developed, played in her mind like movies at the theater.

One image she played over and over: a huge ship docked at a wharf, swarms of people in jubilee, the very air buzzing with the war's end. Yes, the air would be full of meaning. And there she would be as soon as she caught sight of him, held in sunlight, her smooth, blushing skin, her blonde hair. And there Bill would be, too, at the top of the gangway, just ready to descend, suspended on the back of history. Their actual meeting, their touch, would be less important than that moment of first sight, that anticipation, always complete, needing nothing more than itself.

It was the same with the letter. Its image in the postmistress's hand and all it promised held Madeline in its grip. When the envelope passed from hand to hand, the moment was over.

"I'm so happy for you," the postmistress said, her eyes brimming.

"Thank you," Madeline murmured, and then she looked away. There were tears in her eyes and they were real, but Madeline was acutely aware that the moment had passed. She knew, too, that it was the image she would keep, forever and golden.

Madeline wasn't sure when it had begun, this living from picture to picture. As she walked up the long hill and made the turn to descend down her own steep street, the scene of Bill descending the ship's gangway played itself over and over, seeming more tangible than the letter in her pocket, unopened and thin. She wanted to carry the envelope there for a while, to savor the anticipation that would end the instant she tore it open and slid the paper out. She imagined herself reading it, her head in a halo, backlit by the sunset. She couldn't help it, picturing how each thing she did would be, the doing itself secondary, flimsy.

It had begun when she was a girl, she knew that much, or perhaps it had no beginning. Perhaps she'd been born that way, her large baby skull filled with ideas, her body growing meekly to try to catch up. She knew, with the letter a weightless secret in her coat pocket, that it must be the way she was made.

New images began to play themselves, new versions of old ones: her family around the kitchen table, plates of abundant, steaming food spread before them. Always there was light ringing her father's blonde head and her mother's dark one, flooding her brother's smiling face. They were all talking and laughing, the conversation bubbling and bright. She held this vision and slid into her girl body, so she could live inside. Madeline could hear the animated talk, the rippling laughter, and she smiled to herself. She held this scene tightly all the way to her door, and it fastened itself inside her, replacing the stone-cold memory that had been there before. She could live at that warm table, erase what she didn't want, her mother's blaming stares, her father's slurred attempts to speak, her brother's silence, her own rigid shame. They no longer existed, washed away by the light.

Madeline had had this power for a long time, the ability to erase and reform, to bathe the old and dark with a dawn she created herself. This she had done for as long as she could remember.

Bill

1945

The door slowly swung open. Bill froze where he stood, the woman speaking continuously through her tears. He felt for the knife in his boot. But framed in the door was a bent man, shielding his eyes against the sun. The man stepped carefully over the threshold, down the stone steps to the ground and stood there as if keeping his balance was the only chore he had left for the day. Finally he raised his hand in a stiff wave and began to shuffle toward Bill and Tom and the woman, who was now quiet. When she saw the man approaching, she ran toward him and offered her arm. In that instant Bill glimpsed how they might have looked strolling onto the dance floor many years before. The man was thin and wiry, small. His hunched-over shape made him seem even smaller than he was, made him seem too fragile to walk. Yet he continued and held his hand out to Bill, his mouth moving as if he were practicing a speech or reciting a prayer.

Bill stepped toward the man, extending his hand, and was surprised at the handshake he received. The man's birdlike hand grasped firmly and pumped the longest, heftiest handshake Bill had ever experienced. The two old people clucked around the two young men like mother hens showing off their chicks. It didn't seem to matter that the two soldiers looked as if they'd been dug from the grave, dirty, decaying, barely human.

Bill felt relief storm through his body after he and Tom searched through the barn and the little house and determined that they were truly alone. There were no hidden sons or spies, no weapons beyond the axe resting against the chopping block. The four had no common language between them, save smiles, nods and hand gestures. Tom pointed to his stomach and shrugged his shoulders at the woman. Bill rubbed his stomach and nodded, then bowed as if she were a princess and he a courtier. She nodded back and opened a cupboard door, then produced four medium-sized potatoes that looked light and dry like driftwood.

Bill had to sit down to steady himself, unused to such good

fortune. Tom kept cracking jokes, but Bill could reply only with a little wobbly laughter and then quiet. The world seemed too much to take in, even though right then it consisted only of a house, a barn, two old strangers, an open field and Tom, so much, plenty.

The old woman, who it seemed was named Lisbet, took a kettle out to the pump and filled it with clean water. Bill marveled at the water's clarity as it flowed jewel-like into the pan. The old man, whose name seemed to be Jakob, perched on a wooden stool and invited Bill and Tom to sit on a bench by the window while Lisbet cut the potatoes into chunks. Then she lit the cookstove, the firewood already neatly assembled inside. She covered the pan and placed four bowls on the table with four spoons alongside. The four sat together waiting. The house was quiet except for the sound of the fire and a ticking clock, and Bill felt warmth flood over him like tears.

In the morning there were three eggs, boiled and split four ways. Lisbet placed the plates before the men with a grin. The four ate silently, exchanging shy smiles. After breakfast Bill took Jakob outside and sat him under what appeared to be a fruit tree not yet in blossom. Bill took a stick and drew a map in the dirt.

"*Deutschland,*" he said, one of the few German words he knew that didn't sound like a reprimand or hate. He pointed to the middle and put a dot, randomly placed because he really had no idea where the prison camp had been. Then he drew the rudiments of a camp in the dirt beside the map and pointed to the direction from which he and Tom had come. Jakob took the stick and made a line that stretched from Bill's dot and crossed into the dirt outside the map.

"*Tschekoslowakei,*" Jakob said, the word resting like a feather on Bill's shoulder.

Over the next few days Bill, Tom, Lisbet and Jakob pieced together bits of their stories by trading words and drawings and making signs in the air. Jakob and Lisbet were refugees, bombed out of their home in Dresden. Lisbet acted out the bombings by beating a pan with a spoon and then crawling under the table and crouching with her arms folded over her head. Eventually she crawled back out and opened the cookstove door over and over, waving her arms wildly to spread the imaginary fire all over the house. The old couple had fled to the Czech countryside to join Jakob's cousin, but they'd found him ill with fever, and despite their diligent nursing, they hadn't been able to save him. They showed Bill and Tom the wooden cross Jakob had made to mark his cousin's grave, out beyond the well and the barn. Lisbet and Jakob were trying to live off what had been left in the root cellar and what they could manage to trade for in the village a few kilometers away. They feared Russian soldiers and seemed endlessly grateful for the protection they saw in Bill and Tom. Roughened and bent with the wear and tear of war and years, Lisbet managed to keep a spark in her eye and the will to rise every morning. They'd lost their only son in the war, a good son. They talked of him without sorrow, with only pride and warmth, as if he'd gone away and would be coming home any minute, just in time for dinner.

Bill glimpsed his own unborn son, a small hand wrapped around his finger and a blonde head of curls, when Lisbet showed him a photograph of her son when he was three. Bill could have wept when he looked at the boy, but his body had no moisture to spare. He looked around at the still countryside and thought of peace, a word that until that moment had seemed alien. Gradually he let himself think of home, of Madeline and budding orchards and perfumed Sunday drives in the greening hills. Those memories felt rusty like old wire, ready to snap.

After several days, Bill and Tom felt stronger, strong enough to take the two bicycles out of the barn and ride to the village. Their uniforms were clean and mended now, and they began to stretch their limbs in the freedom that belonged to them, now that they had time and a place where they could remember how to move, how to laugh, how to let calm settle around them at dusk. Bill had known little of the war but starvation, captured on his fourth day of active duty. Those four days had been full of terror, artillery smashing around him in dense fog, but that memory had faded to a forced march through miles and miles of snow, to bits of moldy bread and gruel flavored by scraps of rancid meat, to hard labor.

Every few days Bill and Tom rode the bicycles to the village, the only Americans in sight, and traded some small treasure of Lisbet's for powdered eggs or a cup of flour. A few villagers had discovered a cache left behind by German soldiers, and so, for once, there was food to be had. Bill felt as if he'd stumbled upon the cool, green bank of a river after being lost in the desert for as long as he could remember.

Madeline

1932

Madeline's walk to school was tedious, endless sidewalks and streets, houses and apartment buildings, storefront after storefront, the butcher, the tailor, the grocer, and on and on, block after block. On some days Andrew walked with her, talking a blue streak all the way. He was full of plans for trading marbles, for taking on the bully down the street. At fourteen, only a year older than she was, he warned her in his big-brother way to steer a wide berth around trouble, something he knew a great deal about. Madeline listened the whole way to his mind's wanderings, focusing on his moving face. On most days she walked alone, Andy off raising Cain with the other boys. She could have traveled with a mob of girls who gossiped their way to school, but she preferred the talk inside her head, the stories she could tell herself.

Madeline peopled her neighborhood with the tailor who loved his wife so much that when she died, he died, too, just a few minutes later; with the fire chief who set fires because he loved the color of flames against the night sky. There were the vegetable man who squeezed his baby like a ripe melon, exclaiming perfection, and the nun who dreamed of riding a horse across the plains, her black habit flying out behind her. There were endless stories Madeline found on the street as she made her way to school, each person she passed the keeper of some dark and glistening secret.

It's what Madeline wanted for herself, a secret she could keep from everyone. She wished for a hidden life that she could hold, smiling benevolently at everyone she knew, separate and set apart, holy. She longed for her life to be so pure or so malevolent that she could see everyone around her from across a broad boulevard or a massive bridge. Secrets couldn't be made up, though, she knew that, not like stories could. They had to be real and significant. So she waited for hers to reveal itself, to come like a shiver, uncontrollable and sneaky. Madeline drifted through school each day, lessons misting over her like fog, the other children cloudy apparitions. They were not what she waited for, even her cousins, older, beautiful and stylish. She'd always looked up to them, shadowed their near perfection, but lately they had thinned and become shadows themselves, insubstantial and insignificant. Their teasing no longer bothered her, their exclusion no longer hurt. She didn't need them anymore, not while she was waiting for her secret to be revealed.

Each day when she arrived home from school, her mother greeted her with a dozen questions: did she have homework, had she behaved, had she sinned knowingly, had she been punished? On and on they went, but Madeline let them slide over her smooth skin and offered only one-word answers in reply. Then her mother gave her the daily list of chores to do before Madeline could go back out into the neighborhood, to the other girls or her own restless head. She had given up questioning or resenting her mother's lists and instead moved through her tasks, biding her time, ready to slip outside and continue her real life. She had grown patient and quiet, a state her mother welcomed, a state she herself preferred.

Then a morning had broken bright and calm, the light cleaning away the street's impurities, the sidewalk cracks, the shabby storefronts. And Madeline had awakened, her eyes startled by the early spring light. She lay still and imagined herself lost in the desert. She let the light seem harsh, exploiting her parched skin and her terrible thirst. Finally her mother called her for breakfast and the awful glare dimmed.

Madeline dressed hurriedly, splashed cold water on her face, not taking the time for the hot water to rise from the basement through the pipes and come to her. The water smelled metallic and it was tinged brown. She didn't even wait long enough for that to go away, just rubbed it into her skin and then ran a towel over her face, leaving her hands damp and freezing. She dropped into her chair at the kitchen table and began spooning hot cereal into her mouth, spoonful after spoonful, as if she hadn't eaten in weeks. Her mother eyed her suspiciously, but Madeline kept shoveling the oatmeal in. She wanted to be gone from this chair, from this mother and this place, to find her rightful home, but the oatmeal kept filling her spoon. She swallowed, barely chewing.

Finally it was over, and Madeline edged off the chair toward the hall closet and her coat. Andy was just coming to the table when she closed the door behind her, but she didn't wait, didn't even pause, scrambled down the stairs to the street.

On the street things seemed different than usual. People were stopping to talk to each other, huddled over newspapers. Madeline looked around her, puzzled, alarmed. Somehow the world had changed while she'd been asleep, and all she could see of the new one was spread before her in tableaus, murmured in inaudible words. She kept walking, trying to understand it, absorb it, inviting it in. Finally she heard a newsboy's shrill announcement as she rounded the corner for the last stretch to school.

"Read it here!" he yelled. "Read all about the missing baby!" Madeline stopped in front of him.

"Can I see it?"

He shook his head in a superior way, extended his upturned palm toward her, shaking it up and down for the coin she didn't have. But on the top of the stack at his feet she saw the thick, dark words, Lindbergh Baby Kidnapped, and she stood still, her shoes heavy, holding her to the sidewalk. People rushed past her, flocking with their money to buy the printed words.

"Look out!" the newsboy shouted. "Out of the way!" He shoved her off the curb with his elbow. Madeline sat down, her feet suspended on the storm drain, her skirt buffering the cold, rough cement. She looked around at the air, at the shadows from the buildings jutting across the street. Yes, the world had changed and she was there to see the ragged aftermath.

Every morning Madeline got up early and waited for her father to finish the newspaper, so she could read the fine print that dropped below the headlines into her stomach. Each day there was something new to devour, lumping down her throat like oatmeal. There was no end to the details, lukewarm and thick. She stored them up, so she could pick through them as the day went on, poking at one after another inside her brain to try to make the truth.

At night in her bed she imagined the smooth, new skin held in some rough man's hands, the sleeping suit no protection against the cold. She imagined the cries, muffled by coarse fingers over the tiny mouth, the hunger that could not be satisfied, the fear that could not be comforted.

Each morning on the street she searched the adult faces to find the guilty one and all the accomplices, to distinguish them from the impostors. Movement startled her. She felt disembodied, unhooked from the earth and floating. In school she sat quietly, unnoticed, as she reconstructed clues: the ladder, the windowsill, the empty crib.

She knew her father would come after her if she'd been the stolen one. She pictured him awake all night with his pipe and his whiskey, making plans. He'd find her, too, emerging out of the darkness into the locked room where she was kept, smuggling her out under his cape to his waiting horse. The horse would paw the ground, its breath a cloud over its sleek black head, its nostrils flaring as it readied and then broke into the loud gallop that echoed from the buildings and reverberated into the night. The kidnappers would run on foot after them, shooting their pistols into hopeless air.

The fast ride would smooth her father's hair against his head, making his eyes more pronounced. He'd hold her securely with one arm, his other hand easily handling the reins. They'd ride and ride, the horse's hooves resounding through the narrow streets of the city and down the open road that led to the ocean. At the end of the road, where the cliff fell off to the crashing surf, was their castle, and her mother, the queen of the land, waited with her soft voice and jeweled fingers, smiling always.

A feast would be spread on the long table, and all the lords and ladies would toast Madeline's safe return. She'd be dressed in a simple white satin gown, a true princess, her shoulders proud, her hair piled on top of her head and pinned with rubies and pearls.

Madeline wondered day after day if the baby was cold or hungry. Did he sleep in a basket like Moses, floating somewhere in the East River? Did he cry himself into a fitful sleep? She dreamed of him night after night, the lost baby.

Surely Colonel Lindbergh would find him. If he could fly alone over the ocean, surely he could find his only son. There must be footprints to follow by flashlight, a trail. She looked at the Colonel's picture in the papers, tall and chiseled, strong. This was a man who had no doubts. He was merely waiting until the right moment to enter the hideout without a gun, with only the force of his voice to undo all the damage.

This was what fathers were supposed to do, after all, by the force of their singular wills, by the strength of their limbs and thoughts. Saving a baby would really be a small thing. Madeline smiled, keeping this idea to herself, safe, a secret she knew as well as her skin, as well as her name and the books of the Bible.

The stairwell angled on a steep decline. It formed layers, one set of narrow steps leading to a small landing, then a sharp turn down the next set into the dimness below, five sets in all, descending from Madeline's floor all the way to the front door. She ran down these steps every morning and climbed them every afternoon after school without giving it much thought until the Lindbergh baby disappeared. After that, every face she encountered was suspicious, and every corner and shadow was menacing, hiding something.

One afternoon Madeline came home in a late rush, and she was halfway up the first flight of stairs when she found herself hesitating, stopping, turning to look over her shoulder and over the railing, down to the basement door. That door was a place she usually avoided, haunted by the tension between her parents. Her mother had yanked her inside it to hide from Madeline's father when he came home blustering, singing off key and smelling of whiskey. Madeline and her mother had stood in the dark at the top of the basement steps while her father staggered up to the sixth floor where they lived. It took forever, and all the way he sang songs from the Old Country at the top of his lungs, half in English and half in Norwegian, hauling his heavy feet and legs up the stairs, his voice growing more boisterous as he climbed. Neighbors came to their doors and said, "Hush, Olav," in cajoling whispers or yelled, "Enough, Ole!" and slammed their doors when he laughed and sang all the more loudly.

Madeline and her mother huddled in the dark, and finally Madeline asked, her voice a little squeaky, "Why are we hiding, Mother?"

"I do not know," her mother answered, and she gripped Madeline's shoulder even more tightly. It happened over and over, the hiding and the sloppy singing. Each time, Madeline and her mother would eventually tiptoe up the steps to their apartment, and they'd find her father sound asleep on the sofa in his shoes, his overcoat and his hat. When Andy finally came home from the streets, the three of them would eat a silent dinner of boiled potatoes, while snoring from the living room echoed around them.

Madeline didn't know why she stopped on her way upstairs and turned back or why she opened the basement door, her heart thumping and her palms sweaty. She just found herself at the top of the basement stairs, a dark hope falling in front of her into musty air. She fumbled for the light, and finally her hand glanced off the string, which she grabbed and pulled, just as her heart grabbed and pulled in her chest. The light was dirty and dim, but she could see all the way to the landing and then the turn to the final flight below. Madeline stepped down and brought her feet together like a toddler first learning about stairs. The pungent smell of the dirt floor below bit at her nose, but Madeline kept going, step, together, step, together, heavy-footed and slow.

At the landing Madeline stopped and listened, sure she could hear footsteps behind her or below her, or maybe the noise was from filthy rats scurrying away from the light. Finally she stepped off the last wooden stair to the packed earth floor, the sound of her foot muffled. She stopped again, unsure what to do next, her hand still on the railing. She looked around, her eyes getting used to the dull light.

There was a sudden bang and Madeline shrieked, but then she realized it had come from the furnace, the fire in its belly sending heat up to Mrs. Knutsen on the first floor, to the Stenersens on the next, to the new people above them, and three more floors up to her own. Mr. Arnold, the furnace man, wasn't due back until evening, when he'd stoke the furnace for the night. Madeline wondered if the thing would explode, ripping her apart, crashing six stories of brick spectacularly to the ground, but still she went on.

She slunk past the furnace to the coal bin, three-quarters full, its dusty load blacker than the shadows around her. She'd never been this far into the cellar before, even farther than a few years ago when dares were exchanged between her and Andy and the Stenersen kids, and she'd run and touched the furnace door handle and then scrambled back up the stairs. Even though she and Andy had won the bet fair and square, the Stenersens wouldn't pay up, and so they hadn't spoken to each other since, except to trade taunts and nasty looks.

Now she was deep into the cold, clammy dimness, deeper than ever, and something caught her eye, something unclear in her mind, sticking out from the chunks of coal at the far end of the coal bin. It was a piece of fabric, pale. She touched it, a soft flannel, light yellow. She pulled, several pieces of coal knocking to the floor. This time she did hear a scurry for sure, and a rat, its tail thick and ugly, slithered away. She held in her scream and pulled until the fabric came loose, shredded and smeared with coal dust. Madeline put it in her coat pocket and backed away, then turned toward the furnace and raced for the stairs, her hand in her pocket all the way. She climbed noisily, her steps sharp against the wood and echoing around her.

At the top of the stairs, she pulled the light cord, then closed the door behind her, breathing hard. She took out the piece of cloth and rubbed it with her finger, imagining a small naked body buried in the coal, its eyes open and staring. She ran out the front door and to the sidewalk, bewildered about which way to go. Andy was at the end of the block with some boys, and she ran toward them waving the cloth.

"I found the Lindbergh baby!" she yelled.

"And I found a big bag of gold in the garbage can," Andy said with an obnoxious smirk, and he grabbed her elbow and steered her back toward their building while all the other boys laughed behind her.

"Really, I did," she said in a little voice, and then she started to cry.

They climbed all the stairs to their apartment in silence, and then Madeline slipped into her room. She hid the fabric under her mattress and cursed her brother and all his friends, invoking God's wrath on oafs and kidnappers.

That night Madeline dreamed of a flannel-lined cradle that held a sleeping baby. It rocked and rocked, without a human hand, without anyone near. Inside, the baby slept under thick covers. In the middle of the dream someone came and snatched the cradle, dropped it off the fire escape. Just before it hit concrete, the cradle sprouted wings and it rose, higher and higher over the city into the dark.

Anna

1982

"Alone or not, one still must face this truth," Thomas said in a voice that seemed distant yet right under her skin. Anna had been sitting motionless for more than an hour, next to Thomas under a white ash tree several hundred years old. Its roots were gnarly and thick, rising out of the ground like elbows and knees and then sinking to depths Anna could only guess at from the scale of the tree that reached way above them.

The ash grew beside an abandoned stone foundation, the remnants of a small colonial settlement that had faltered, after drought hit and then wouldn't abate year after bone-dry year. Anna had read about it in the town history published at the time of its bicentennial. She liked to read about older times when things seemed simpler and less threatening, an illusion, she realized, but a satisfying one. Anna liked sitting with Thomas atop history's remains. Earlier she had climbed down into the foundation and imagined lanterns set in its hollowed-out sills, a quiet family sleeping off a day's work and readying for another one. She had dug in the mound behind the foundation and turned up bits of broken crockery and tarnished metal. In the brush next to the foundation she'd found a snakeskin, intact even to the eyeholes, so complete it startled her until she poked it with a stick and discovered it was no longer inhabited.

Anna didn't reply to Thomas's statement, sat silently next to him. She knew she didn't have to respond or ask a question, just wait, and he would go on. She watched the light change, shadows creeping over her legs and arms, shivering her. She tried not to think, not to wonder why Thomas had chosen her, or who had chosen whom.

"Death is one truth," Thomas finally said. "Alone or not, each of us must face it." He looked at her, his eyes steady and sharp, focused somewhere inside her head. She had never met anyone like him before. *Intense* was the word that came to her, a word she would use if she tried to describe him to someone else. But intense like a black hole in space, not any earthly quality. Intense like a comet that appears only once every thousand years, taking your breath away and then burning into another hemisphere, no longer visible.

Anna didn't mind thinking about death. It made her feel closer to her father, who had tested those waters long ago. He went to sleep one night and never woke up, and that was the end of him, slipping into a dark river that she couldn't navigate. For a long time after he died, Anna felt she couldn't get enough air. Breathing deeply and slowly or rapidly and shallowly made no difference. Her lungs just didn't seem big enough to sustain her.

She had thought about death a great deal through her adolescence when her father recovered again and again from a series of heart attacks. His death seemed constantly on the horizon, and in the late afternoon sometimes she found herself looking out the front window until she spotted his car across the field on the road beyond, the dark blue Chevy he'd taught her to drive.

Anna wasn't afraid of death. Her father had paved the way, sliding gently through his silent sleep to the other side of the world. She didn't know what she believed about that other side, had discarded heaven and hell when she'd brought her Bible to the Goodwill donation center along with most of her childhood. But she didn't know what lay there, on the shadowed side away from the light. She wasn't afraid, just puzzled, and she accepted her puzzlement with a mild curiosity and calm. Even when Thomas had taken her again to the cemetery and she looked into another open grave, a grave with a name attached, she felt only wonder, not fear.

Anna mused for some time, her father's funeral remaining only as a blur. She could remember crying hard, tears dripping haphazardly down her chin to the floor until someone handed her tissues, a gesture that seemed irrelevant. She remembered the closed casket in the church and all the flocks of people who came to the house later and ate and drank coffee and filled up all the space. She couldn't remember anything about being at her father's grave, only being driven through the cemetery gate. Beyond that, nothing remained in her head from that day more than twenty years before.

"But death is nothing." Thomas's voice brought her back, her hands resting in her lap, one on top of the other like petals. "It's life that must be faced. Death is an afterthought, parenthetical, a mere fragment. It's life that needs to make the bold statement, be enunciated, be sung at the top of the lungs."

Anna turned toward Thomas and looked into his eyes. *Intense* was an understatement, she thought, his eyes holding her fixed and still, unable to look away. She had never seen eyes like his before, blue like lake ice in the coldest, clearest heart of winter. She found herself nodding, and for an instant she grasped his words, not as words with meanings but as sounds that entered her blood and flowed there.

"Life," she repeated after him. "Life," she said again, and the word took on a dimension she could begin to glimpse. She felt her heart race and her mouth go dry. She imagined being shot out of a cannon, heat at her heels, her body piercing through air. There would be no landing, that she knew. There was only the swift rise, the wide arc, her arms pressed tight to her sides, her head with its flaming halo aimed straight for the sun.

Anna and Thomas sat close together under the great ash in the quiet afternoon light. Side by side, they could have resembled lovers, suspended in time on an idyllic country day. But they were not lovers, not even friends. They were strangers come together out of two worlds, aligned. Anna became aware of her breathing, inhaling deeply and letting go a sigh. She could hear Thomas breathing, too. That was the only sound around them, breath. Thomas was the man who didn't die, the one who'd tried to, but life defied him. Defiance burned in Anna like fuel, hot and clean. She felt aimed, her ride out of the cannon not random, her path a straight line blazing its way through space.

Vita & Violet

1920

The full moon bears the profiles of my sons.
There is Nigel and there is Ben, back to back
like bookends, holding volumes of light.

For so long, I've kept them pressed into molds,
packed away, stored on dusty wooden shelves.
For so long, I have turned my back on them.

Here they are, gigantic. Their glow slides golden
and thick across the water, like spilled honey.
I long to lap them up, to taste their sweetness.

~~~

"Read to me, before I'm too weary to keep awake," Violet asked, her voice trembling as she pushed against Vita's silence.

"Nothing new to read, I'm afraid," Vita answered, returning to the same page of the book she'd been staring at for the past hour.

"Read something old then, please. The evening isn't right without your voice to grace it," Violet pleaded.

"Too tired, I'm afraid. Perhaps tomorrow night."

That morning a photograph had appeared on the dressing table, Vita's smiling boys. Violet didn't understand the hold of children, knew only that she feared them and the snaking tendrils they took for granted, rooted all through their mother's body. Vita could not shed them, could not free herself from the fine hairs that wrapped her veins and bones. Violet wished the boys no harm, but she could not love them either, not even as replicas of their mother, each Vita's molded twin.

The boys haunted the corners of the room, taking over the evening's quiet, sucking all the air and light, leaving behind in their wake—nothing. This was the darkness Violet had dreaded, the silent void that sealed Vita away in a vault. There was nothing

Violet could do to reach her, nothing she could say. They grew more and more silent, more and more stiff in the perfumed air that should have sent them into each other's arms.

Only thin basting thread, frail seam,
narrow strip where I meet myself.

Only frayed edges giving way,
torn beyond mending.

Only a void beyond the choppy sea,
beyond the ribbon of horizon.

Only collapsed sails to navigate the winds,
no safe return to shore.

Only my ship splintered against rocks,
my crew battered and drowned.

Only hollow, concave resistances,
two halves of the same planet.

Only an equator dividing them.
I cannot cross over.

Only air on which to stand,
my earth splits beneath me.

Dear Vita,

I know what it is to have everything. I have held you night after night, and we have met, luminous and willing, until we turned into fierce and burning suns.

I have come to know perfection, all I have ever wanted, and it fills me like the moon, like the rolling stars. I want nothing more or less than our stilled bodies and hushed voices, our vibrant light.

I imagine a sea inside me, roiling and foaming with endless speed. I have never known that love could be so pure, that my heart could contain so much.

It cannot be the end. My refusal is so strong, it has tied a knot inside me that cannot be loosened, cannot be undone.

How can we have come to this, a slow folding? I want a volcano, a tidal wave or forest fire, not slow silence, not quiet moonlit streets, not a warm spring morning that mocks me.

Not normality. Anything but normality.

Your Violet

Madeline

1945

Anything but normality. Anything but the thoughts that were in her head, turning and folding over one another in the hours before dawn. Sleep had come in spasms between long periods of wakeful rest, her body unable to be comfortable, unable to settle.

Madeline wished heartily for dawn, when things began to have fixed edges instead of melting into the blindness that spread unrelenting through the night. She'd been alone before, had grown up in a cocoon of aloneness that had rarely been penetrated. But this was different, death and starvation knocking on her doors and windows, whistling down the chimney. She imagined Bill as a skeleton with skin, his eyes bulging from deep sockets, his fingers unable to bend or hold. He rattled against the windows, scratched his bony fingers against the wooden doors. She wanted to let him in, but she was afraid of him.

This was not a dream but a waking image that would not leave her alone. She saw him circling the house on his stiff legs, heard him pleading with her to feed him. He named foods, the list growing endless in the night air, the names ricocheting off the walls of the bedroom and landing on the bedcovers. She was smothering in food, barely able to breathe. The baby churned and kicked inside her, and she was caught alone between the unborn and the undead.

Grayness slowly began to appear in the room and objects with it, curtains and furniture, the clock, clothes draped over the chair. Madeline felt so relieved that she looked around carefully, as if she'd lost something but there was still a chance of finding it. Then she forced herself out of bed to the bathroom and vomited. She could barely bring herself to take in food while Bill was starving, yet morning sickness still arrived faithfully each morning. She imagined the pencil arms and legs of the baby in her womb and felt horrified that she couldn't feed him, couldn't care for him, just as she hadn't been able to save her father when she was a girl. Bill had slipped into the vast terrain inside her head, and the more she tried to picture him, the more remote he became, except in his night hauntings. Instead, she tried to imagine the baby, fingers and toes and ears, but he, too, turned away, his cries inconsolable, his belly empty. He became for her the stolen baby, blonde curls resting in a shallow grave.

※※※

That day years before when Madeline was thirteen, she'd come home from school and the same headline she'd seen on the street faced out from her father's newspaper, left neatly folded on the coffee table. Big block letters told of the baby's kidnapping, and she'd felt her stomach flip over again and sink.

On the street people were still stopping each other and asking, "Did you hear?" even before they asked the everyday refrain, "Do you have any work yet?" Whispering in huddles on the sidewalk, mothers held on tightly to their children's shoulders, their eyes flicking up and down the street, their heads turning suspiciously with every passing car.

It was unimaginable that a baby could be missing, especially this baby, whose father had walked on wings, had flown an ocean. Whenever Madeline put her foot in the water at the beach, she knew it was the same water that had seen the belly of Lindbergh's silver airplane. Surely this was a man who could keep his own baby from a thief.

That day she'd worn her blue sweater, and she would always think of it as Lindbergh blue, the day the baby fell out of the sky and didn't land. It was everywhere, the great story, on people's lips, resounding from the radio, in thick letters stamped across the page. There was no escaping it, even by absolute disbelief—he was gone.

Madeline became fascinated with ladders, imagining one at her window each night, and thick, greasy hands dragging her from bed. What would her parents pay to get her back? They had nothing and so could not afford to claim her. She would float in limbo, never return.

Madeline watched for unsavory faces, for money hidden inside people's shoes, for babies that cried comfortless and loud.

Everyone and everything was suspect, waiting for her to solve the case, to rise up and save the baby, return him to his father's arms. There would be another parade, this time with her seated next to the Colonel, holding the baby in her lap, his curly head coming just under her chin, his chubby legs and arms heavy against her, his breathing quick and soft, his eyes wide and blue.

Anna

1982

His breathing was quick and soft, his eyes wide and blue. He looked at her steadily, his face expressionless, listening absolutely, absorbed in her words mixing with breath, her pauses, her pitch. Nothing she said caused him to waver, only to listen more deeply, as if he existed just for her.

For Anna, the depth of Thomas's attention was unnerving. No one had ever been hers before, not in this way, not by being a container that could hold her completely. She didn't leak anywhere but was wholly held by him, everything and anything that issued from her mind. Sometimes Anna wondered why Thomas had come into her life, why she'd felt pulled to stop her car. He was so odd, like some new alloy forged in a furnace of incredible heat. Yet she couldn't stay away from him.

Anna had thought her life was settled. Everything about it had been good enough: her job, her house, her daily routine, her handful of friends. She'd known what to expect, and it was all bright and smooth, each day unfolding with expediency and predictability. This was the middle age she'd hoped for, responsible and sound, her father's legacy.

So what had possessed her to stop her car and allow this young, inscrutable man to get in, to lead her on a path from everything she'd so carefully constructed? She'd asked herself the question many times, but here in the grip of his eyes, it didn't cross her mind to doubt him. He was simply there, eyes and ears, not wanting anything, hers.

Anna told Thomas everything, every memory, every petty human thing, every wondering and loss, and in his presence her life was transformed, became her real life, the one that had flourished inside her beyond the rhythm of her days. The result was an imploding, her life folding in on itself. She walked away from her job into an unscheduled existence free of worry. That was what really amazed her. She looked inside and there was no *what if*. She lived in moments.

In his listening, Thomas returned her life to her, each piece examined and then sent to join the others, a mosaic Anna was constructing from scratch. She relived every bit of it and saw each piece in a new way through the prism of Thomas's eyes. He seemed to have the ability to break light apart into its spectrum of colors and intensities, and he did this with everything she gave him, not by talking about it, but simply by being there.

When Anna asked Thomas why he'd chosen her, he smiled his crooked, pleased grin and claimed he hadn't chosen her at all, that they had merely converged on a point, that they would ultimately diverge and continue on. He said that was true of everything in life, that it was all convergence and parting, a symphony of notes played simultaneously and independently. When she wanted to know more about him, his history, his lineage, he avoided her, glancing off her like light. She had stopped asking after he said that what mattered was that he had chosen death but death had rejected him, catapulted him back into days and nights, breathing and moving and following the insides of his mind. His life had started then, he'd said, from nothing, and what he'd made since was meaning. Anna hadn't understood him then but vowed to accept what he said, not to question or doubt him, for she'd never met anyone like him. Thomas didn't have to say or do anything. His presence was striking, powerful and compelling, pushing her to edges inside herself she hadn't known existed. She kept coming up against herself and finding more, and more, and more.

Anna looked at Thomas's eyes, and what she saw was herself, revealed in all her nakedness and glory. She felt unsettled and unsound, as if she were cracking and coming apart, but she found herself welcoming it, standing on the edge of an abyss and hoping for a fall. Thomas asked nothing of her, nothing but this looking, and everything she gave him he accepted humbly, holding it for her in his vast heart and hands. She realized that she trusted him completely, though she knew nothing about him. She didn't have to know, only to accept his presence, his rapt attention.

"I loved my father more than anything or anyone," said Anna, and Thomas nodded. "I was so young when he got sick, and my heart broke. When he died, I thought I'd never love again, and I chose ugly, loveless surroundings, nothing I could claim or that would claim me." Thomas nodded again, and she felt herself relaxing into her story. She stopped, her statements hanging between them complete, nothing more to add.

"Your life was over because you'd had everything, perfection and wholeness, and then it was gone, erased. You wondered if it had ever existed, your life, because there you were, left behind with only love, love and a gaping hole that had been your father."

Anna nodded. She kept nodding at the truth of it and felt a small bird fluttering in her heart, its tiny heart beating, its tiny wings stretching and arching. As it spread its wings, a smile spread over her face, and she felt so much love, bottomless and lasting, flashing over her like sunlight. She could see drops of water sparkling in the pines, remnants of a passing storm. There was such perfection in a drop of rain hanging from a green bough by chance, ready to fall, clinging moment by moment. Anna saw everything at once, the drop of rain and the wide ocean it drew from and then replenished. It was all there, right in front of her in Thomas's eyes.

Anna watched the moving clouds, the sky that held them. She knew that she belonged in the world. Thomas picked up her hand and held it, and she felt their equal warmth, skin against skin.

"You came to save me," she said.

"No, you saved yourself." Thomas smiled again and Anna smiled back, the shadows of the overhanging pines spotting their faces. She was not one to be able to receive gifts easily or gracefully, but this one she would take. She would take it, awkwardly and completely, and hold it like the sky until it became smooth, expansive and blue.

Vita & Violet

1920

Violet would take it, awkwardly and completely, and hold it like the sky until it became smooth, expansive and blue. This was her only course of action, because Vita could not do the holding herself. No, Vita was juggling great orbs in a high wind, so it would be up to Violet to hold the space where Vita could return. Violet knew she would have to become larger than herself, larger than her own hot need. But her single-minded passion led her, and so she knew she could find the way.

Each morning when she rose, Violet recited a litany, over and over, "I hold you like the sun, like the sky, like the moon." She repeated it softly, as if she were at peace and contented, until she believed it. Then she would go about her day, a brisk walk by the sea, a warm meal, and an afternoon of painting in the open air, the pigment moving under the swirl of her brush like a miracle. She focused entirely on the paint, on its slick, oily texture, and on the colour, vivid and pure. She rendered a rocky coastline, the great sea and the greater sky, so much blue she could taste it, and to her it was bittersweet.

Vita sometimes accompanied her, but Violet could see that Vita was becoming a shadow or a band of light, transparent and thin. Vita was slipping away into the world of orbs—one for Ben, one for Nigel, one for Harold—that she had to keep airborne, flying deftly from hand to hand. It was all Vita could do, so Violet had to be the one to support the sky that held them. In her heart there was enough space, for she had known perfection: perfect beauty and perfect peace.

At the urging of their mothers-in-law, the two men had agreed to share the hired airplane, then the hired car. They'd made a plan along the way, but when they'd arrived inside the *pension*, they hadn't been able to meet each other's eyes. Finally, in a silent pact, each man squared his shoulders, and they climbed the staircase.

"Please, you first." They said the words in unison when they reached the top and stood before the carved door. Their plan had not specified this moment, so they resorted to what they knew: politeness. Then Denys stepped forward and knocked several times. The sound was loud and hollow. They waited.

"Perhaps they're not inside," Harold offered.

"I think they are," replied Denys. "Open it!" He shouted the two words in the same voice he'd used for giving orders to his men during the war, a voice that did not question obedience.

"Please, Denys, let's not make a scene." His jaw clenched, Harold tried a restrained triplet of knocks. Still, they were met only with silence.

As they discussed how long to wait, what to do next, each man was aware that they were merely trying to use up time, their politeness with each other exaggerated. Harold's long practice as a diplomat took over, his stance and language tempered by a grave sense of patience, as if he might be negotiating a treaty, there in front of the closed door. Deeply engrossed, neither man noticed the sudden current of fresh air that rose toward them. But they halted when they heard the laughter of their wives. And their wives, arm in arm, stopped short at the bottom of the stairs, each taking in the men at the top.

"No!" Violet shrieked. "I will not."

"Not here, Violet, please," Vita said. She freed her arm, turned and grasped both of Violet's hands. "We knew this day would come. You must calm yourself, dear. Let's go inside." Vita held herself erect, her trousers, boots and jacket making her appear even taller as she began to climb the stairs, holding Violet's hand.

"I will not," Violet repeated, her lowered voice trembling as she followed Vita past the men and into the sitting room.

Part 2

"My dear," Harold said, his eyes brimming, his hands resting lightly on Vita's shoulders.

"Harold. Dear. Harold." Vita's voice was flat, formal, as if they were at a state occasion, her eyes avoiding his.

"I will not be claimed," Violet said when Denys took her arm, his fingers rough against her flesh, so different from Vita's muscled touch. She tried to pull away, but his grip tightened, his anger barely contained, hot and focused on a single point like sunlight on a mirror that can start grass burning until the whole meadow goes up in flames. Violet realized it was fruitless to resist, let Denys lead her from the room, her eyes briefly meeting Vita's vacant stare. She left Vita behind in the room with Harold, could hear their muted voices between her own and Denys's sharp footsteps.

"I hold you like the sun, like the sky, like the moon." Violet spoke the familiar words defiantly and felt the release traveling through her body as she matched her steps to Denys's down the long hallway and steep stairs to the street. She wouldn't flinch from her firm resolve. Vita was lost to this moment, but Violet refused to believe it was forever; she held with steadfast stubbornness to the future she wanted. She would hold the wide expanse of blue in her mind until Vita could return to her and they would find their place again.

> *Dearest Vita,*
>
> *I write this to you so you will remember that I exist, that I live under the same sky you do, breathe the same air. I ask nothing from you except remembrance, to hold me sometimes in your enormous mind, to cradle me there beside you in the night.*
>
> *I hope that you have found your children well, that they are everything you dreamt of, that you cradle them also in the close and comforting dark. I did not want you to lose them, never would I want you to lose anything, but really to have everything. I have found it, in the perfection that was our life, and I shall keep it here, where you will always know that it is safe. Out to sea there is a storm, the grey slanted rain rushing from the clouds in sheets, but here in the harbor, all is still and sunny.*
>
> *I hold you, and I will always hold you, like the sun, like the sky, like the moon.*
>
> *Your Violet*

The letter was bound to come, though Vita had erased from her mind its probability. When it did come, finally, addressed in Violet's hasty hand, she'd traced the envelope's letters with her fingernail, the ink so crisply defined against the fine, pale paper that the words might have been raised from the surface like embroidery.

Violet had been silent for months, giving Vita the opening back into her country life, the gardens flourishing, the large rooms echoing with the rounded family—husband, wife, sons—complete and unbreakable. Yet until the letter arrived, Vita hadn't understood that she'd been sitting in her familiar chair, writing in her familiar room, stepping through her expected days like an automaton.

Vita held the letter in her hands and read it silently again and again, her sons' voices bounding up the stairs from the library below, where their nanny read aloud to them. She could hear the boys' laughter and Nanny's spirited voice urging them on.

Across Violet's words spilled a new truth. In its light, Vita's two halves fell away from each other, leaving a core that was warm and pulsing. She saw that she was neither self, that love possessed a third possibility. She listened to the letter speaking and to her sons' sweet and quick voices, and for the first time she sat between her two halves.

Anna

1983

She sat between the two halves of her life as she'd known them. The past and the future had fallen open, leaving a core that was warm and pulsing. She could look forward and back at the same time and see with clarity what was behind her and what she reached toward.

Before she'd met Thomas, Anna's past had enveloped and blinded her. As she'd revealed her life to him piece by piece, she'd come to understand all that had happened, to see that the past was separate from her. She'd needed to remake it, not in her image, but true to itself. All that the past had given her was still hers, unaffected by need or desire, there in its own right. She could examine it at will, laid out before her, clear and translucent like water, and she could see beneath the glossy surface all the way to the bottom.

Anna didn't leave her past behind but instead took it with her, keeping it polished and new. And in Thomas's light, the future became a bright hope, glistening in the rising sun, not a cause for worry or grief but only wonder and awe.

Thomas didn't have a past, at least as far as Anna could tell. It had been erased in the deep sleep that had brought him back to life. She tried to imagine it, waking to a clean slate, everything behind her gone. Her own past had been so strong, its grip powerful, and now that she had remade herself in its open face, it held magic for her beyond any she'd known. It was difficult for her to imagine what it might be like to be Thomas, to move so fully into the blaze of life that all else was seared away, the past sloughed off like sunburned skin.

Thomas seemed to lack all need and desire, moving into each moment completely. Anna had asked him if he ever grew uneasy with the pulsing speed of it, but he had shaken his head and smiled. When she first knew him, Anna was afraid that his smile was mocking her, but she had grown used to it and saw that he gave the same smile to everything he encountered. Everything was a source for his wry joy, not the sentimental, sappy kind, but a sinewy amusement, stripped bare of flesh. Everything gave Thomas equal joy, and for that Anna envied him. Her sense of joy was different, slow and selective.

Anna found it difficult to talk about herself to anyone but Thomas, who seemed to be the only person who truly saw her because he actually looked. She visited with her friends from time to time but found herself checking her watch, anxious for solitude or for Thomas. She knew he wouldn't be there forever—he'd already warned her of that—but while she had him, she wanted what time there was with him, so she could be the self she was becoming.

When she was with her friends, she caught them exchanging glances. She evaded their questions and took only superficial interest in their talk. It wasn't that she didn't care about them, for she loved them dearly, but she could no longer quite settle into herself with them. And so she tended to stay on the outside, where she could perch briefly and then move on.

Anna never knew when she would see Thomas. She'd go about her business and then he'd appear in the produce aisle, at the fish market, or running on the shoulder of the road. She was always glad to see him, glad for one more time of being with herself with him. And he always seemed happy to see her, yet surprised, as if he'd opened his door and there she was, an uninvited guest he'd make room for at the table.

Anna and Thomas did simple things together, walking in the woods, sitting by a brook, sleeping under a full moon. Sometimes they'd start off together and then Thomas would disappear, and Anna would go on without him, the path rich with colors, the water noisy and strong. In the beginning Thomas's disappearances had alarmed her, and she would call after him and walk in aimless circles. But she'd grown as used to them as she had to his smile, until she barely noticed his absence, like stepping over a root onto solid ground. His appearances had unnerved her, too. She'd be choosing pears at the farmers' market, and his hand would reach toward her, offering a beautiful piece of ripe fruit. But she no longer felt jolted when he came, as smooth as breath and as regular.

Anna wouldn't have used the word *love* in relation to Thomas. Their relationship was well beyond that. Thomas was like air, ever present and necessary, beyond choice. She had given up wondering where Thomas went when he wasn't with her. His presence had become solid and real, whether he was physically there or not. It was simple. She was grateful for him.

Anna had begun to understand simplicity, to feel joy at its winged touch. She didn't need complication anymore, or confusion, or uncertainty. She could grasp the completeness of a moment. That's all there were for Anna after she'd met Thomas: moments, one after another. She slid through time like clouds crossing the sky, and there was no stopping her.

In her old life, Anna would have made a plan: the next job, the grocery list, the yard chores. But she no longer thought in lists, no longer saw things in columns labeled *Pro* and *Con*. Anna mused about the future with Thomas sometimes, sitting next to his droll smile and clean eyes. She'd drop her ideas like rocks that made concentric circles in the surface of the water and then disappeared. She knew they were just musings, that the future was arriving each moment. It wasn't way out ahead of her, always out of reach. Thomas was like water, but not the rushing kind. He was a great pool, calm and dark. She couldn't see into his depths but accepted their mystery.

Anything Anna tried to explain fell apart in the analysis, and so, over and over, she arrived at *mystery* to account for why Thomas had come to her, why she'd been ready to meet him, why her father had loved her so and died. Everything became a mystery to her, a mystery of the deepest kind, like Thomas's still waters.

Anna rose early to sunshine and blue after a week of unrelenting rain. She ate a banana on the way out the door, dressed in her sweats and walking shoes. She would go adventuring on foot, see where her feet led her. The air was cool but the sunlight was warm, and she delighted in the simultaneous sensations on her skin. She looked up and smelled the wet, earthy air and the fragrance of lilacs. Turning out of her street and onto the main road, she headed east, with the morning sun full on her face. Her steps were quick and her arms swung at her sides as she paced her own rhythm in the warming air. She listened to her steps on the asphalt and her matched breathing. Anna felt centered on the ground, her steps light but firm, and she moved easily and freely, smiling to herself. The sun was blinding, but Thomas had taught her how to look just past it, so she could take it in without even shading her eyes.

In the distance on her side of the road, she could make out a familiar figure running in the same direction she walked. Thomas, as usual, was dressed in his green running suit, his arms beating the same steady rhythm as his feet. She admired his form, his comfort in his body, watched him until he disappeared around a bend in the road. It made her happy to know that he was there, that she followed in his footsteps. For a moment she had the inclination to run, to see if she could overtake him. But she was satisfied to walk and know she followed him. She heard robins singing in nearby woods and reveled in the generosity of spring. She noticed the shape of each maple against the sky, the pale leaves unfurling slowly overhead.

Anna was so absorbed in her surroundings that when she rounded the bend where she'd lost sight of Thomas, she didn't quite take in what she saw ahead of her. Then she realized it was Thomas she saw, leaning forward into someone's car window, his hands resting on his hips, elbows out behind him. She kept walking toward him and the silver sedan, its shadowed windshield masking who was at the wheel. Thomas was standing on the double yellow line in the center of the road, the car on the other side pointing toward her. Abruptly Thomas rounded the car and got in. It began moving, seeming to coast at first but then picked up speed. As it flashed by her, Anna waved, but the side windows were tinted, and she couldn't tell if Thomas responded. Anna kept walking, eventually heading up the side road that skirted the river.

After a mile or so, Anna came to the cemetery road and found herself turning in. She didn't know what drew her, but she kept going as if it had been her plan all along. The dirt road continued to rise beyond her up the hill, graves meandering among oaks and maples and old stone walls. Anna leaned against a big oak, its branches pruned haphazardly by ice and winter storms, the brown remnants of last year's leaves lost amid the new crop of yellow-green. The shade felt good to her, cooling the top of her head. Then she could hear the churning sound of a car coming up the dirt lane and turned to see the same silver sedan that had stopped and picked up Thomas. The car raised dust, climbing steadily, its engine droning, arriving finally at the top of the hill. Anna walked out from under her oak tree to get a better look. She started to walk up the hill, but something stopped her and she held back, rooted at the bottom of the cemetery.

Anna watched as two figures got out of the car: familiar Thomas, whose lines she would know anywhere, and a stranger, a tall woman in slacks and boots. They walked to the edge of a newly-made grave, stopping at the foot to look in. Anna felt queasy, as if she were watching a violent act she could do nothing about. Her stomach seemed to flip and turn, and her heart quickened, pounding through her body. The couple stood side by side for some minutes, and Anna couldn't pull herself away. She stood riveted, her eyes unable to stop staring, and a shiver passed through her, her palms damp and cold. She wanted desperately to climb the hill to them, but just as desperately, she couldn't bring herself to move.

Long after the two figures returned to the car and drove away, Anna stood on her spot. She heard the car pull onto the tarred road and then stop across the bridge. She heard two car doors slam, and in her mind's eye Anna saw Thomas and the woman climb out onto the flat rock shelf that jutted into the stream. They would sit there, she knew, listening to the water, would take off their shoes and dangle their bare feet in its coldness, the kind of cutting coldness that makes bones ache. She swore she could hear the two of them talking, even make out some of their words, though that was absurd, because the bridge was half a mile below. Anna thought about walking there, but again she couldn't move, so she stayed where she was until her legs grew stiff, her knees locked. Finally she stretched, turned, and began her way home. Her limbs felt heavy and awkward, her morning lilt having evaporated.

Anna couldn't understand her feelings. Surely Thomas knew

other people. Surely their relationship was far beyond petty jealousy or possessiveness. But Anna felt betrayed, as if Thomas had taken the most intimate details of her life and splashed them on a billboard or in the evening news. She knew she was being irrational. She knew Thomas wasn't hers. But her sense that she had been chosen, perhaps not by Thomas but by mystery itself, had become a foundation for her life, her days and nights, her every moment. Anna longed for Thomas, for the words he would use to help her think this through, for the silences that would follow, but at the same time she knew she would never ask him. She felt doubt and fear, so unfamiliar to her lately that she didn't know what to do, now that they engulfed her.

Anna let herself in the front door of her empty house, boiled water for a pot of tea, and sat heavily at the kitchen table. She watched the liquid flow from the spout into her cup, the steam rising and then disappearing. The truth came to her, stark and staring. She would never see Thomas again. The gift was over. Tears rose to her eyes and overflowed, dripped into the hot tea in her cup. She realized that what she had wanted most since her father's death was closure: a last touch, one more look into his eyes, a word. And she knew she would never have it, something even Thomas couldn't give her, Thomas who had left her behind to sort out all the details by herself. Everything was raw and unfinished, frayed, and she wondered if she could seam it all together again.

Yet at the same time Anna couldn't deny the sense of momentum she felt, relentless and unpredictable, driving her forward into something she couldn't see.

Bill

1945

He felt a new momentum, relentless and unpredictable, driving him forward into something he couldn't see. It came when he realized that he was no longer starving, that the bits of potato and egg, turnip and coarse meat, were holding his body together, keeping it from being eaten away. He could actually feel energy, a rising in his blood and muscle, rather than the dragging stupor he'd lived in for so long. With this new feeling came a forward movement, and he began to think again, to remember, even to hope. He and Tom took turns every few days to bicycle into the village with Lisbet's offerings and return with what they could scrounge, one day even a chicken. Jakob's eyes filled with tears when he saw it, and he plucked it himself, presenting the naked bird to Lisbet as if it were a jewel. Lisbet hummed to herself when she lowered it into the big black kettle and then later added the two potatoes she had left.

At the start of the meal, the old couple bowed their heads briefly, prayer mixing with tears, and then the four had the feast of their lives, laughing and winking, their lack of common words making no difference. Bill could feel the warmth in his belly and the end of his shivering, imagining his blood growing thicker and redder with each bite. In the prison camp he'd imagined food every day: pot roasts and lamb, sweet boiled onions and cherry pie with fresh cream. Each day had been Thanksgiving or Christmas, the menus stacking in his mind, each item juicy and delicious, perfectly cooked. But this meal was different, real, eaten as a free man with a future.

Sometimes Lisbet and Jakob's exchanges in their own tongue would stir memories Bill had buried: a shiny black boot in the groin, nothing but snow to eat for hundreds of miles. He'd never been warm since, not until now, when he had his back toward the stove and something in his stomach. Memories surfaced like fish, and rings stirred the water long after they dove. A German soldier with a pistol moved from man to man, taking anything of value, watches and rings. Bill could see him coming down the line, moving closer and closer. All he had was his wedding ring, and his sentimental anger rose, bubbles breaking the smooth surface. He slid the ring from his finger and slipped it into his mouth, held it in the hollow under his tongue. He rubbed his ring finger to smooth the crease left behind, and when the soldier got to him, Bill held out his palms, then turned his hands over and back again, over and back. He was sitting in the snow, his legs and buttocks burning, ice pressing through his pants into his skin. His mistake was not to protect his groin as he uncurled from his huddled position to extend his hands. When they turned up empty, the soldier grunted and kicked Bill again and again in the soft flesh of his belly. Bill tightened his muscles as hard as he could, but the wind left him in a rush, and he couldn't hold himself taut. The last kick hit him hard, and Bill felt something rupture. He kept his face rigid, though, and the soldier moved on. Bill curled his tongue to trace the gold circle beneath it, and he smiled to himself in defiance. His righteous anger and the gold metal tasted strangely sweet.

After their feast of chicken stew, the four refugees lingered at the table. Jakob made a short speech, which neither Bill nor Tom could understand, but they could tell they were being toasted and thanked, toasted with good, clean water. That night Bill could afford to dream: Madeline's arms around him, her voice soft in the hairs at the base of his neck. Then he was visited by another dream: snow, the endless march, ice spreading inside his body and over the land. Most of the men marched in their stocking feet, limping more and more with each mile. But Bill had kept his boots, and he continued to be able to feel his toes against the roundness of the leather, long after the others had started to hobble.

When the two German soldiers had come down the line, forcing each captive to give up his boots, Bill took the knife he had hidden just behind one ankle and hacked at the leather until the boots looked worthless. With any thought, someone could look and know that the important parts of his boots were still intact, but these soldiers weren't thinking, so once Bill let them find his knife, they passed his boots by. He dreamed this scene again and again, the dogged German soldiers moving down the line, the sharp orders, then the snow engulfing the small, slow figures that crawled across the vast landscape.

But in the dream Bill could feel his feet and the wedding band under his tongue, and so it wasn't a nightmare. When he woke, he fingered the ring, back in its rightful place. He saw the beginnings of dawn, and he knew that in a small, finite number of hours it would be light on the other side of the ocean.

❧

Bill and Tom lived their suspended life for some weeks, each day feeling a little stronger, gradually feeling enough strength to help Jakob fix the barn door, split some firewood they'd gathered from the distant woods, and turn the soil in the area that would again become a garden. There were no seeds, but Jakob and Lisbet had saved some seed potatoes, going hungry some evenings while Bill and Tom ate, in order to safeguard their planting. The old couple had nowhere else to go, no home to return to, no son, nothing waiting for them. They would have to make do where they were, and their gratitude to Bill and Tom was boundless and jovial, a return to living after so much barren grief.

Bill began to wonder who the enemy had been, not these two sincere and grateful people, even though they'd given their son to the war. He could have been the one who'd kicked Bill in the groin, but it had stopped mattering. He could feel his wounds closing and knitting, his dreams becoming welcome in the night. Madeline didn't cry anymore but reached toward him as if he could cross over.

❧

Bill stood in the doorway trying to understand what Jakob was telling him when Tom rode up the long lane toward them, whistling and waving his arms. The bicycle swerved and he almost went over, but he grabbed the handlebars in time and managed to stay upright. Jakob took one look at Tom and seemed to know right away what Bill couldn't seem to grasp. Jakob rushed to the barn, wobbling as he went, and wheeled out the other bicycle, which he presented to Bill. Lisbet came out of the house and Jakob spoke to her. She gestured to Bill quickly, shooing him away with her hands. Bill looked into her eyes, puzzled, and she threw her arms around him, then let him go, pushing him toward the bicycle Jakob was still holding. Jakob laid the bike down, patted Bill on the back, then threw his arms around him, too, and his words came out halting and broken. Bill mounted the bike and rode around Jakob and Lisbet, his circle widening as he went. Standing side by side, small and stooped, they waved to him. And then Bill pedaled toward Tom, who was still whistling and yelling and veering on the dirt lane. Over his shoulder, Bill could see the old couple waving, wishing him home.

Vita & Violet

1921

Beneath the woven sky, the wind at her back, Violet watched the bent grass. The wind was strong enough that she thought she could almost fly, her skirts a wide bell lifting her off the ground. She stood in the glade overlooking the sea and watched the endless waves, heard the sound that roared without rest. She stood at the edge of the cliff, the trees behind her now, in front of her only air. She felt weightless, as if she could step off and hover there, buoyed by the sea air, never rising or sinking. A few metres away stood Denys, sleek in his long coat, solid as an oak, not shifting or bending in the blow.

Violet had made peace with Denys during the long months since she had returned. She did it not by apologizing or trying to stifle his sharp anger, but merely by being there, at dinner each evening and at breakfast each morning. He came to her in the night, and she was there, too, opening to his touch. Slowly his anger cooled to simmering, and they rarely talked anymore about the time when she was missing, about his shame. After the first painful months, they settled into a pattern as if they had been together for decades and were growing more rooted as they aged.

This holiday at the seaside came after the long winter, a promise they had made to each other when the first violet bloomed. When she saw the sea again, Violet felt the waves rise in her chest, and she framed inside her head all the letters she would send to Vita. Denys didn't resist her writing to Vita, so deep was their truce, and he even posted them himself from time to time.

> *Oh, my dearest Vita,*
>
> *I have come again to the edge where land, water and sky meet, and here you are. I nearly can fly, hovering just beyond the cliff, descending slowly to skirt the tops of the waves. You are here in the great waters that wear the rocks away, slowly turning them to sand, slowly erasing the land.*
>
> *You are with me, my dearest love, and I trust that you can see the cresting waves beneath me and the wind that holds me aloft, as I hold you.*
>
> *Your Violet*

Violet no longer asked Vita to come to her. Instead, she held open the possibility of Vita arriving in twilight, settling in as darkness bent over the land. Violet simply held the hour and space for it to happen.

Vita wrote long letters in reply to Violet's, about her growing sons and gardens, about Harold's next posting abroad. Between the details, Vita's language dazzled Violet, and as long as that continued, Violet kept hope. When she finished reading a letter from Vita, Denys burned it, according to the arrangement they had made. Violet watched the fine paper flame, darken and fall apart. The first time, she'd rubbed some of the ash into her skin, and all evening she could smell its sharpness.

Vita sat inside her writing room day after day. She, too, had created a routine: her diary in the morning, letters in the afternoon, occasionally a poem. The room was ancient and dusty, history layered beneath her. She had chosen this room because it was solitary and set apart, and she locked herself inside like the poor miller's beautiful daughter, spinning her golden words without the help of any little man. She had the gift of language that really did transform straw into gold, and each day she did her spinning.

Violet's letters arrived with a steady flow, and Vita wove them into the suspended hour between morning and afternoon, wove them with the threads of day and her pen. When she wrote her replies, Vita kept to daily things, the new roses, her lovely, wild boys. She wrote to Harold, too, off again to Paris, meeting with heads of state and protecting the interests of the Crown.

Vita's letters were full of news and anecdotes, yet below this surface ran a poetry so sublime that it reached to both Harold and Violet and tied them together with a magic knot that couldn't be undone, not by Rumpelstiltskin or any evil queen or even by Vita herself. She had united Violet and Harold, and her words provided the thread, the same thread she was using to stitch herself back together with a strong, invisible seam.

Vita was beginning to understand roundness: the staying in one spot, the traveling, the easy return to the same spot again, over and over, circular and whole. She was becoming a globe, harboring everything on her continuous surface, never ending, always beginning.

Madeline

1945

She was becoming a globe, harboring everything on her continuous surface, never ending, always beginning. As her womb grew rounder, Madeline also grew round, and she began to feel that she contained more than her unborn son. She became accustomed to holding a sea inside her, accustomed to her swelling breasts with their larger, purple nipples. She had a new smell that reminded her of warm milk shooting from a cow's udder into a metal pail.

Many times Madeline had milked her uncles' cows during the endless months after her father died. Her mother found work as a domestic when she could, cooking for people who could afford meat, dusting their fine furniture, scrubbing their polished floors and washing their fancy clothes. She moved Madeline and Andy back and forth between city and country, depending on when she could manage to keep them. The best times had been when they got to stay at their uncles' farm, but their unmarried uncles wouldn't keep them long, didn't think they could properly provide for them with no women in the house. Within a few years Madeline and Andy had to board all the time with strangers, their mother forced to give up their apartment and take a live-in position as housekeeper.

The cows' musk and the fragrance of warm, fresh milk came close to her own smell now, and Madeline began to feel as if she could feed the whole world herself. The baby was developing inside her, a boy she would call David, the small one who fights a great enemy. He grew inside her like hope, and she welcomed him, reclaiming him from her nightmares, letting him be solid and real.

It had not come easily, this acceptance, this belief in a future. Just a few months earlier, fear had gripped her throat, making it impossible to swallow. Food had been her adversary, a continuous test she had faced morning, noon and night. It had been a powerful force that she couldn't seem to tame, haunting both her sleep and her waking hours. She had tried forcing it down her throat, a cracker or a spoonful of soup, but she always seemed to choke, even vomit. She'd felt guilty, knowing that her landlady, Marta, and some of her friends gave her a portion of their meat rations to keep her strong. Madeline began to hide her attempts to eat, so no one would find out about her battles with food. Guilt was the only thing easy to swallow, especially when she thought about the baby inside her, who seemed such a weak and frail thing, unrecognizable as human. She could barely get food to go down, or keep it there when she did, and the more she tried, the more victorious it became.

Then one Saturday Madeline had heard Marta climbing up the back stairs. Marta's three legs, her two human ones and her cane, made slow, thudding progress. Madeline went to the door, knowing it must be something important to bring Marta there, her rheumatism lately sticking her like knives. She could hear Marta's heavy breathing, hear her stop to get the next breath. When Madeline opened the door, there Marta stood with a bowl of fresh strawberries, sugar sprinkled lightly over the top.

"You've got to start eating or you'll lose that baby," Marta said between breaths, extending the bowl with its red, juicy offering. Madeline felt tears she didn't know she had spring to her eyes, and she helped Marta up the last few steps and into the kitchen. She had no idea where Marta could have gotten the berries, perfect in their ripeness. They were Madeline's favorite food, and somehow Marta had conjured them out of a hat. Madeline placed the bowl on the kitchen table and began to cry hard, her hands over her face. She knew Marta was right—she had been trying to kill it, the life she couldn't imagine living. Marta stood over Madeline, stroking her hair and neck, murmuring what sounded like a lullaby. Finally Marta went over to the drawer and came back with a big spoon.

"Eat," she said. "It's good for you." Madeline ate every berry as Marta nodded and smiled and hummed, and Madeline kept the whole bowlful down.

※❧

When they'd arrested the baby's killer, Madeline was in school doing geometry. Numbers came easily to her, so she sped through the problems drawn on the blackboard in her teacher's neat hand. School was Madeline's haven from her mother's scorn and her father's lingering death, the suspended time when she didn't count hours and minutes. She loved it all, the reading, the formulas, even the tests, all the time she was alone with herself and her mind, quick and bottomless. Her only real challenge was penmanship, forced to switch from her left hand to her right, so her letters always came out crooked and uneven.

In the evening she'd try to help Andrew, who was a year older but less inclined to accept anything handed him by stern elders, especially those who used a ruler so freely. Andy grew more and more stubborn and defiant, but in the evenings he'd let Madeline come into his room and lay out the books on his bed. She'd coax him to spell a few words or describe a famous battle, mastering his work long before he did. She'd soothe and tease him into it, and she could even get him to write a few sentences for his English theme or memorize a required passage to recite out loud. Madeline had infinite patience with Andy. She worshipped his adolescent cockiness and his possessive protectiveness of her on the street.

The day the police descended on 222nd Street, she'd used a different route home from school and missed all the commotion, taking a shortcut through an alley a few blocks west of her usual way. Her mother had asked her to stop by her cousins' house to see if she could borrow some sugar for Andy's birthday cake, a spectacular prospect in those days of mouths to feed and little work. Madeline had taken to eating less and less at the table, saving the choicest potatoes and bits of meat for Andy and her mother. She was growing thinner, like a stick. Madeline's clothes hung on her, and she didn't seem to grow any taller, her hems remaining adequate for far too long. Rather than letting the seams out, Madeline's mother had to take them in, clicking her tongue with dismay at every stitch.

The possibility of a birthday cake for Andy thrilled Madeline, and she knew she would let herself have a piece even if it made her sick. Andy didn't know that their mother had been hoarding flour for weeks, precious as gold. But sugar was nearly impossible to come by, and so Madeline was sent to see what she could beg from her plump and cheerful aunt and her more comfortable cousins who still had a father.

By the time she got home, her pocket bulging with the borrowed treasure Madeline knew would never be returned, Andy lay on the davenport next to the radio, king of the birthday evening. He was covered by an afghan, crocheted and embroidered by their mother's careful hands. There was a rough spot in one corner where Madeline's practice stitches merged into her mother's perfect ones. Andy looked thin and peaked, so like their father in the months before his death that Madeline's heart seized. She stood in the doorway without moving and looked in her brother's hand for the telltale bloody handkerchief their father had taken such pains to hide. She half expected her father's usual greeting.

"Hello, little swan," he would have whispered, and then he'd motion for her to sit down next to him on the cushion's edge. She would have felt his bony legs at her back as she perched gingerly, afraid to jostle him and make him cough. But this was Andy, and she shook herself into the present and crossed the room to touch him, just to be sure.

"Listen to this," Andy said, his voice his own, and their father's ghost evaporated.

The story unfolding on the radio was outrageous beyond belief, and Madeline recalled the tiny body in its shallow grave, dead leaves masking the hasty digging. And she imagined the Colonel's face as he'd told his wife, his jaw muscles tense, his words clipped but soft. His wife would have sobbed, Madeline knew that much, her only child muddy and limp. These images had haunted Madeline's dreams, but now there would be a new one, even worse. There were actual hands that had done this, hands attached to arms, to a body containing a mind that thought and planned and plotted this terrible thing. Real hands, with fingers and thumbs and palms, capable of smothering the life from a baby and then digging a hole to throw it away in, as if it were so much garbage.

And these hands, attached to this mind, lived around the corner from her in the house numbered 1279, with the garage the police had begun to tear apart.

Madeline had walked past this house on her way to school and back, again and again, never once knowing it to be the place where the killer of the golden baby ate his meals and drank his morning coffee. Where in the dark of night he'd hidden the stained ransom money and then went to sleep as if the world were still in one piece.

His hands were huge, this much Madeline knew, huge and dirty, powerful, inescapable. They were hands that could take a tiny sleeping breath and snuff it out, turning the whole world upside down.

Anna

1983

Anna thought of Thomas's hands, gesturing nimbly in the air, punctuating his sentences and speaking more than his words. Slender, beautiful really, with long fingers, his hands were elegant in the way they would lie like birds in his lap, folded like wings, and then rise, buoyed by air, to illustrate a thought. They were hands capable of ballet or opera, graceful and disciplined, hands that could turn the whole world upside down.

Thomas wasted nothing, not time or ideas or words. Each thing he said was thoughtful, pressed out of his mouth in smooth, even tones, as even as a slow-moving river idling along its banks, yet responsible for a whole region's commerce. Anna had lived most of her life in a polite, civilized realm where everything was *thank you* and *how are you* and *excuse me*, where everyone kept their circumscribed distance and Anna was rarely herself. Thomas's voice came like wind into the quiet reaches of her mind, the place where she really lived, and it pushed open the door without knocking.

The thing about Thomas's hands was that they reminded Anna of her husband's, the hands of a sculptor and painter, hands long dead. This was the one story she had not yet told Thomas for some reason she didn't understand, perhaps because Thomas had her husband's hands, ghosts attached to his arms and fluttering around him. But now that Thomas was gone, moved on to someone else's story, Anna could begin to tell it to herself.

It was a twenty-year-old story, old enough that whole days and even weeks went by when Anna didn't think of him, new enough that a certain angle of light or a song on the radio would send her back there, immediate and raw. She sat by the picture window looking out over a sea of trees, full of erupting growth, green and vibrant. Her old life returned on a flutter of wind that lifted the leaves and revealed their silver undersides, a whisper of fog slipping into a sunny day. Anna could picture her husband still, his soft brown beard, his thin face and pale blue eyes. And his hands. She could call up his sadness, especially at the end, when nothing she said mattered and she had no idea how to reach him, trying herself to stay afloat in their sinking world. This was a story she wanted to turn upside down, to find the silver underside that held the secret.

It was a story about how easily Anna could love, unwisely and quickly, thrusting her whole self into it, and once she loved, she loved forever. Her heart was big enough to hold it all, but sometimes cracks opened up, gulfs that she couldn't narrow or bridge or repair. Thomas's leaving her was like that, and she dreamed about him almost every night, his beautiful hands and eyes. Thomas had returned from the dead to find her, and with his leaving, he'd opened a chasm in Anna from which all her stories could escape. They danced before her in the air, and she could snatch them one by one to look at, not just at their surfaces, but at their undersides. Sitting on the other side of glass from all those green leaves, Anna plucked her husband's story from the air and retold it to herself, detail upon detail opening like bird wings.

The day she went through all his clothes was a gray, misty day. Even the air inside the house seemed gray, not the sad kind, but comforting like flannel. She played the same record over and over, the only sound she could imagine hearing, a solo flute, notes sliding up and down inside her skin, keeping her full. She was so full of feeling that everything she did had import, each move of her body or head, each breath, suspended above the regular world in a place where everything mattered. Anna had left work early to do this thing, to sort through her husband's most personal possessions and move them out of her life, opening space for herself, for what she didn't know, knowing only that this had to be done and this was the day for it.

She held his wallet in her hands, the wallet the nurse had handed her at the hospital, all that was left of him then, rounded and worn. She'd sat with it in the vinyl hospital chair, turning it over and over, wondering how his life could fit into it. It seemed so small and finite, yet it was heavy and solid, a weight. When the nurse said the authorities needed someone to identify his body, Anna sat holding the wallet. Her friend from work, Allyson, had driven her there and was sitting quietly in the chair next to Anna. The two friends looked at each other as the nurse stood waiting.

"I'll do it if you want me to," Allyson said. And Anna nodded. She knew what she wanted. A clear stream moved her forward by instinct. While Allyson was gone, Anna sat alone with the wallet in the waiting room among the orange vinyl chairs, hers cold against her back. Finally Allyson returned.

"It's him," she said softly. Anna sat with the wallet a while longer and then rose, and she and Allyson left the hospital together. In Anna's memory it was raining. It rained most days in her memory, the sun coming out only sporadically.

Anna sat on the misty flute-music day with the wallet in her hands, and finally she opened it. There was a twenty-dollar bill, his driver's license, an insurance card, a library card, and on and on, things that had allowed him to go about his days. There was a picture of Anna, her high school graduation picture, dog-eared and cracked. They had started going together that year, when Anna was seventeen, shy and reserved, pained in her discomfort and self-consciousness. Her smile in the picture looked strained.

She remembered the story her husband's friend, Jake, told about the guy in his unit in Vietnam who would sit for hours smelling his wallet. When Jake finally asked him why, the guy said the smell reminded him of his father. Anna tried it, but her husband's wallet smelled only like leather. She threw it away, burned all the cards and the picture of herself in the woodstove. She felt tender and angry and alone, each thing she did momentous. She'd never been alone until then, moving from her father's house into the home she'd made with her husband, the wedding presents neatly in drawers and cupboards, replicas of their parents' lives. Now Anna was by herself in a dim, rainy world where everything felt deliberate and new, weighted by history.

She began with the socks and underwear because they were utilitarian and easier, laying them in a big green trash bag, feeling

Part 2

queasy as she converted her husband's life into garbage. Moving methodically through his clothes, she was surprised by her ability to be washed in so much tenderness, yet thinking at the same time. She sorted out what would go to the dump and what would go to the donation center behind the building where she worked, not quite able to imagine someone else wearing them, yet not wanting to waste anything. It wasn't as hard as she thought it would be. She didn't get hysterical or even cry. She was brimming, though, nearly spilling over, close to tears.

When she came upon his green flannel shirt, it was a complete surprise, hung back in the closet after he'd worn it, still seeming to hold the curve of his shoulders, the bend of his elbows. She sat looking at it on the hanger for a long time, the last time she would see him, imagining his hands at the ends of his sleeves, his long, thin, beautiful hands. Finally she took it from the hanger and sat back down on the bed, hugging the shirt to her chest. His scent lingered in the cloth and she buried her face in it. She lay with him on the bed long after the flute stopped, while the needle clicked and the turntable kept spinning. Anna lay there smelling the shirt, mist surrounding the house, the needle ticking on the last band of the record.

Madeline

1945

Madeline laundered all of Bill's clothes, ironed them, hung them back neatly in the closet, the hangers evenly spaced. She checked them now and then for wrinkles, touched them up if they needed it. She polished his shoes, straightened out his sock drawer. Everything was ready, poised for that singular moment when he'd walk in the door. She had taken to wearing his sweater on cool nights, a brown cardigan that was too long for her, but she rolled the sleeves and wrapped the length and width around her as she curled up on the couch with a book she never seemed to get through. Now and then she could hear Marta bustling downstairs, opening and closing cabinets or closets, clanging pots, humming. Madeline liked the sounds Marta made, welcome in the looming, empty house. Sometimes Madeline went down and had a hot drink with her, most often hot water because there was rarely tea or coffee to be had anymore. Marta fussed over Madeline, offering her hot biscuits, brushing her hair, and Madeline had come to need her, a word or a bit of butter giving her the will to go on.

Madeline found courage in small things, a washed window, a swept floor, anything that promised a day beyond this one. She'd never liked waiting, fidgeting in movie theater lines or on the bus to work, but she was beginning to learn how to get from minute to minute, how to pass the clock's slow tick.

❧❧❧

She'd lain there, smelling the shirt, mist surrounding the apartment building. She'd looked small on the bed, younger than her fourteen years. The world had shrunk to this room and this shirt, everything else fading into shadow. The shirt was the one her father had worn the last time he'd been strong enough to go out, before he took to the davenport and never got up. There wasn't much of him left in it now, not since her mother had laundered it, starched and spotless. The smell of starch reminded Madeline of Sons of Norway festivities when she'd danced with her father, waltzing around the candlelit hall. Her mother was a reluctant dancer, stiff and unsure. Madeline was certain that she was her father's favorite partner, eager to whirl with him while her mother sat balancing a cup and saucer gingerly in her lap. He was graceful, smooth and light like silk, and he loved to dance. His whole face lit up in a smile that matched the candles' glow.

The shirt was what Madeline had left, a whiff of her clean and elegant father on the dance floor. She lay crumpled on top of it in a dark place where she had no thoughts or feelings, just nothing. Madeline's father had died while she was at school, and she'd missed his last breath, the last words he might have given her. When she'd left in the morning, he was still asleep on the sofa, so she blew a kiss from the doorway and went down the stairs to school. When she came home, he was gone, the living room tidy, the floor scrubbed and polished, its wood grain gleaming in the windowed light. Her mother had erased him, the sofa pillows fluffed, the blankets put away, even the medicinal smells that were better than nothing—gone.

Right away Madeline recognized the different quiet that echoed through the apartment—the ordered silence and empty light. She sat on the sofa trying to sense him, listening for a hint in the air, looking for a wavering of shadow. Her mother was busy in the kitchen and didn't say anything, her movements over the pots thick and graceless. Madeline ran to her parents' bedroom and tore the shirt from the closet, then flung herself on her bed and went limp. Finally Andrew came home and coaxed her to get up. They sat side by side on the davenport, Madeline still clutching the shirt until her mother grabbed it away.

"Look how you've wrinkled it, and it's the one he'll be buried in," she'd said sharply, and then Madeline could hear her in the kitchen sprinkling the shirt with water, rolling it up in a towel and putting it in the icebox. Madeline heard the ironing board folding down from the wall with a creak, the iron clunking on the stove to heat. All the while Madeline said nothing, but Andy took her hand. When the hot iron finally touched the shirt, it was Madeline that burned, with a flame almost as real as the one that had caught her hair several years before. She'd leaned too close to the candles on the Christmas tree at Julefest, and her father had saved her then, but he couldn't save her now.

Madeline and Andy stood next to each other at the cemetery, their mother on the other side of the grave. No one spoke except the minister, who droned on about rewards and mercy. Madeline thought she would die right there, standing by the mounded dirt, her father in a sealed box. She heard Andy sigh and tried to follow him, but her lungs seemed to have shrunk. She wanted to lie on the cool dirt, to rub her face in it, to dirty her clothes. She didn't know how to stand there any longer, waiting through the minister's words, her mother staring angrily at the ground. Madeline wanted to run screaming across the green cemetery to the street and then beyond to the river, to board a boat that would move and never stop, but she stood there next to her brother.

When it was over they went home, where a flood of relatives passed through the apartment. Madeline and Andrew sat on the sofa until their mother shooed them away to make room for aunts and uncles. Each time someone sat down, Madeline cringed, the hollows her father had left behind transformed into some other shape than his. She wished she could make everyone disappear, so she could lie down in the space that had held her father, with his wool blankets and his pillow, the crisp pillowcase pure white from bluing.

She would lie there until the space grew smaller, if it ever could, or until she grew big enough to fill it herself. She didn't care how long it took. It would be better than this waiting, for the good china cups to be back in the cupboard, for all the voices to echo down the stairs, for the quiet to return, the quiet that enveloped everything and would allow her a chance to find him again.

Vita & Violet

1921

Vita allowed herself little chance to find him again, to feel his strength. She pushed him far inside her ribs, her bones rigid in their protection. She relegated him to her deep interior, where he might come out in a dream but never disturb her well-ordered life. Violet's letters to Vita kept him breathing, but he was safe there between the lines. Vita's letters to Violet never mentioned him, and she abandoned the novel where he'd had his own life as Eve's Julian. Vita's trousers hung in the wardrobe, increasingly moving toward the edges, past her skirts and dresses, occupying the position of the rarely worn.

Vita had to hide him away, to settle fully into her life once her boys' images abandoned the moon and came to rest again on their own warm faces. She slid into her female body with dexterity, donned her fitted skirts and tailored blouses, feeling again her lines and curves from the inside. Vita was home in a solid way, rejoicing in her sons' long limbs, their soft necks and sweet hair. She couldn't get enough of them, and they seemed to forget her absence, ready to find a new day in her embrace. She suspected that Harold had prepared them for her return, for the smooth wind that brought her safely into their harbor, her sails unfurled only enough for a landing that barely stirred the water.

Vita wore her old life until it began to feel like skin. Harold's comfortable wit animated her as she brought her own intellectual powers into a ready match with his. When Violet's letters arrived, she could open them without the threat of losing her equilibrium, answer them without fear of harm. She kept Violet's letters in a box lined with purple velvet. When she added one to the collection, she admired the growing depth of the stack, then closed the box firmly, never rereading, never dwelling on what the envelopes contained.

She would live with Violet this way, live without her.

※⚫︎※

Violet knew that Vita underestimated her patience, her ability to wait, to hold focus and space. She held open the place where Vita's male body could be kept alive, in well-placed phrases on fine writing paper. Violet's capacity for love only grew with time and separation, channeled into her pen and brush, into her open gaze that took in the wonder of petals and clouds and oddly shaped rocks. Violet was surprised by the fact that her desperate longing could be utterly transformed into something so endless and faithful.

She had made her peace with Denys, and they lived in a tense quiet that was tolerable, that sometimes fueled his passion for her, his passion for what he could not control or even know. He was content to be in her presence, a simmering anger giving way to something new: respect.

Violet was no longer the girlish and flighty object of his conquering, but his match, in her stubborn intensity, in what she held back, hers, safe from tampering and loss. Violet had discovered the best in herself and welcomed it. This new and subtle freedom was not something she and Denys had words for, but it permeated their days and allowed them to live, not on top of each other, but side by side.

Violet's canvases grew more unique, her use of colour more original. She saw the world with different eyes, its imperfection wonderfully perfect, its ordinariness striking. Shadows became orange and green, trees magenta and purple, because this was what she really saw when she looked beyond the obvious. It was her power of sight that allowed her to wait, to translate into pigment on canvas what she had learned about perfection and what she had known of herself with Vita. She could wait forever as long as she had colour.

Vita

1922

"I believe we have made our acquaintance before, sir, have we not?" The man stood before Vita as if at attention, his posture elongating his tall, thin frame, his smile graced by a carefully trimmed mustache and beard. He was dressed in the latest Paris fashion, a high-waisted jacket and cuffed trousers. Vita couldn't help but think him a dandy, in spite of the fact that she had donned a bit of Paris herself, in her wide silk tie and belted jacket. Lost to the borders of her wardrobe for so many months, her trousers had begun to feel familiar again during her secret, solitary train ride to London.

"Not to my recollection, sir," Vita answered, keeping her voice husky and low. The man seemed to take her words as an invitation, settling himself into the adjoining leather chair. Vita turned the page of her newspaper, swirled the liquid in her glass and took a sip, claiming a pause to calm her irritation. She'd concocted a ruse to gain entrance to this place exclusive to men, St. James's Club: a letter of introduction on members' stationery, bearing a careful copy of Harold's signature. Successfully inside, she'd planned to disappear behind a newspaper until she recovered her bearings. Glancing at the man, she was envious of his boldness, decided in that instant to assert her own.

"Perhaps you would join me for a cognac, tell me something about yourself. Perhaps I will remember," Vita offered, folding her newspaper and giving a subtle nod to the waiter, who floated like a ghost at the edge of the room. Without a word, the waiter placed another snifter of bronze liquid on the table between them, offered a cigar to the stranger. "Remind me of your name, if you would be so kind, sir. I meet so many people."

"Thomas Burlingame, sir. You are Julian Somers, are you not?" The stranger looked Vita in the eyes as he spoke, and all she could do was to stare mutely, her heart speeding like a runaway horse. Who was he and what did he want?

Explanations raced with her pulse: her mother had sent the

man to force her to return from London. Or Harold had employed him to deliver a message from Paris, a possibility that made her only more alarmed. But they didn't know her whereabouts. And her maid, Agnes, hadn't been told Vita's destination when she'd packed trousers and shirts, when she'd carried the suitcase downstairs, stone-faced and silent. Only Violet knew about Julian, about the novel Vita had set aside. Perhaps she had sent the man, her idea of an amusement. Yet even Violet had no knowledge of where Vita was.

No one knew that Vita had made a mistake in not burning the manuscript. No one knew that she'd rediscovered its unfinished pages in a stack of papers, and she'd compounded her error by reading them. Only Vita knew that Julian had summoned her, and she'd begun to work on the novel again. She'd thought she could control him, keep him contained on the page, her third mistake. Her old torment had reared its unbearable head, and she'd boarded the train to London as the person she could no longer abandon.

"Why, Mr. Burlingame, of course. I do remember you. Lovely to see you again." Vita delivered the lie with a smile, hoping to mask her panic, still searching for an explanation. Violet had to be behind the charade. The thought calmed her. She spoke again, as if she could will the situation to make sense. "How have you been occupied since the war?"

"I have been occupied. A trip to America, which I do not recommend, I'm afraid." The man chuckled, ran his finger absentmindedly along his lapel. His laugh was soft and alluring, and Vita relaxed enough to take a breath, as he added, "And what about you, Mr. Somers?"

"Isn't it pleasant to be able to travel freely again? I have been occupied as well, a bit of a vagabond myself. What brings you to London, Mr. Burlingame?" Vita was growing interested in the man. Was he an actor? Perhaps Violet had met him at the theatre, and they'd planned this little drama together. Perhaps he'd been frequenting the train station, looking for an opportunity to follow Vita and play the trick.

"I was waylaid. I'd planned to go to Greece, but there is too much unrest, as you know, so I'm taking a short holiday here to decide my next move. Never any harm in enjoying London, is there?"

Part 2

"Oh, no harm in that," Vita replied. She motioned to the waiter and accepted a cigar when he presented the silver humidor. As her smoke joined with the stranger's and rose toward the sculpted ceiling, the room took on the appearance of an elaborate stage setting. "I do so like Greece, don't you?" she asked, although she had never been there, and the Aphros of her novel was completely imagined.

"Yes, but I saw enough fighting during the war, so I'll go nowhere near the place until it settles down." He placed emphasis on each word, as if he were chanting or saying a prayer, and Vita wondered if he had practiced his speeches. Perhaps Violet had written them herself, rehearsed with him—she could picture Violet's delight in the play. The man shifted in his seat, checked the time on his pocket watch.

"Are you in a hurry, Mr. Burlingame?" Vita asked. She watched as he lifted the cigar to his mouth again, as the end glowed from his draw, relishing the thought that his script had run out and he was stalling to find more words.

"Oh, no, I never hurry. Best to take one's time with everything, so that time can lead us where it will. And you, Mr. Somers, are you in a hurry? Where are you going?"

"Nowhere. I am perfectly content here."

"Are you?"

"You are becoming a bit impertinent in regard to my private feelings, Mr. Burlingame. Take care where you step, sir." Vita hoped to make the man squirm, to win the game before he gave it up, a triumph she would report in exquisite detail in a letter to Violet.

"There can be no impertinence on my part, Julian. I have known the intimacy of the trench, of death—their stench and their sweetness. You may call me Thomas."

"Sir?" Vita did not know what to make of the man, his abrupt swerve in topic and tone. Perhaps Violet had chosen him for the terrible blue of his eyes. Since he had raised his wager, Vita would raise hers. "I will not call you anything, if you proceed in this incautious manner."

"Look, Julian, I'm in no hurry, but I don't have a lot of time. Let's talk about what matters, about how one cannot create a self by wearing different clothes or changing one's name or running away. Stake your claim, Julian. Mine your life for its rare metals. Forge a new substance. Alchemy is simple, like breath or birth. You have given birth, Vita, so you know exactly what I mean."

"Did Violet put you up to this? Who are you?" Vita's voice rose in pitch, and throughout the room, faces turned in her direction. She cleared her throat, drew on her cigar, and the men returned to their books and conversations. "This game of yours is no longer amusing, and I ask that you take your leave if you cannot control yourself, sir." Her hand shook, and she lowered the cigar to the ashtray.

"No one has sent me here. I arrived, that's all. I arrived, and here I am. I shall leave you soon, but not yet. This is our chance to meet, and so we have met. Believe what you wish, but none of it is true."

"You speak in riddles, Mr. Burlingame. I cannot understand you. I wish to be left alone and in peace."

"Please, call me Thomas. I am a friend to you, not an enemy. The war is over, and there are no enemies. There is only peace."

"Then tell me who you are."

"I have told you. I speak the truth."

"I have nothing to say to you."

"And I have much to say to you, if you will hear me, Vita. There is no game."

Vita had no reply, mustering her strength to remain in the chair, to avoid making a scene. The man leaned toward her, his eyes glowing in the lamplight, his hands with their long, thin fingers resting lightly in his lap. She met his eyes. It was strange, the way he no longer seemed like a stranger, but instead someone she'd known all her life, and she fought to keep her composure, to keep from disintegrating into tears.

"Thomas," Vita whispered, "what do you have to tell me?"

Alone in her garden on a summer morning that smelled of lavender and roses, Vita spied a messenger approaching the house. Harold and the boys were off for a ramble in the woods, and the servants had gone to chapel on the neighboring estate, so Vita went to meet the stranger. He handed her a neatly wrapped package, about half a metre square, flat and light. It was addressed to her in Violet's uneven hand, a small flourish at the end of Vita's name.

"Thank you," Vita said to the man's back as he walked away. She took the parcel to a sunlit bench. Balancing it in her lap, she carefully untied the string. The wrapping fell away, exposing the back of a framed canvas that bore an inscription:

> *To Mitya, my Julian,*
> > *whom I love in all his wild fury,*
>
> *From Lushka, your Eve,*
> > *who accepts all things, even perfection.*

Vita stared at the words, read them through several times, the quiet of the garden and the blue, sunny air gathering in folds around her.

And like a soft garment, a realization settled over her body—there had been something familiar about the messenger.

"Thomas?" Vita called, leaping from the bench with Violet's painting still in her hands. But he was gone.

When she turned the painting over, Vita was greeted with herself, a mirror of him that she held inside her bones, freed in magnificent colour, his cheekbones highlighted with dusky orange, his hair backlit, his face more handsome than any Vita had ever seen. He was golden, and his eyes held an entire miniature landscape of ocean and rocks, tumultuous and uncontrolled, let loose, no harbor in sight.

Vita felt her bones crack open, the marrow freed inside her, its cells migrating into her blood, pounding through her body. In that moment she truly knew that she was neither one nor the other, but both.

Anna

1983

It had seemed like a small thing at first, a feeling that crept through her body and gradually came into her mind, arriving like dawn, like light that seemed to come from inside things to make them visible. Anna had caught a glimpse: she was neither the past nor the future, but both.

At first she hadn't wanted to look, at least not to look back, but instead to begin again as Thomas had, to leave the shattered past where it belonged, and the fragmented future, too, so she could come to rest in each moment. Thomas truly could do that, live from one moment to the next, constructing a web that reached in all directions. Anna had wanted this ability and had thought Thomas would give it to her by explaining, by osmosis, by some means that would transfer it whole.

Anna had thought that Thomas would stay in her life until what was between them was finished, until she understood. He was the only person she'd ever met who didn't have a constructed self, one that he gave the world while keeping his true self intact. Thomas was Thomas in all moments, and that was what Anna had longed for, to unmake her public self and find her real nature. She could glimpse it with Thomas, but she couldn't seem to hold on to it. And now that she was sure he'd disappeared entirely, Anna began to lose hope, to feel frozen and stuck. She mourned Thomas, lost from her, the future missing, the present a dull waiting.

So Anna turned to what she had left: the past, the place where she didn't have to change. The memory of Thomas's hands had brought her there and left her to rest. She looked at her own fingers, turned her hands from back to palm, made them into fists, then opened them flat again. She was flesh, bone, somehow a mind that connected, that could make her body move. She formed tight fists, held them until her forearms ached. She wanted to burst through as Thomas had, to break apart the barriers that remained.

⁓❦⁓

The knock on the door was even and quiet, and at first Anna didn't recognize it for what it was. Then she heard it again. She didn't want company, not now, not without a way to speak about herself that was true. She tiptoed to the living room window and eased forward slowly, not wanting to be seen. The gentle knocking came again, and she could see the person's shape, leaning forward toward her door.

In that moment Anna realized that it wasn't just Thomas's hands that reminded her of her husband. It was the shape of his body, too, the length of his neck, the curve of his shoulder. There he was on her front step, still knocking, haunting her. A shiver went through her, and then she opened the door.

Thomas stood looking at her, his eyes her mirror. She could see her own face reflected there, a double image in blue. He didn't say anything, just stood. Anna felt funny, lightheaded, as if her feet hovered over the floor instead of standing on it. She felt made of light or air or water, intangible and moving.

"I walked until I saw this house," Thomas said finally, "and it was yours." Anna's feet seemed to touch the floor again at the sound of Thomas's voice, and she realized that he hadn't known where she lived, hadn't ever been to her house before. It was enough that he'd found her, and she didn't question it. Instead she gestured, inviting him in. Thomas stood inside the door, looking around.

"It's a beautiful place," he said, "spare and full at the same time." Anna still hadn't spoken, reached out to touch his shoulder, brushing it quickly as if with a feather.

"Come in," she said finally, her voice faraway and odd.

"I did," was all he said.

The house was quiet, the only sounds a passing car and a distant barking dog. *The world still exists out there*, Anna thought.

"Come in," she repeated, and Thomas smiled. Anna gestured again, and they walked through the house and onto the back porch. Thomas settled into a wicker chair, looking over the stretch of grass that eased down to the shore of the lake, the water calmly reflecting the sun.

"I live on a lake, too," Thomas said softly. "My view is much like this one."

"Sit down," Anna said. Thomas looked up from his chair and smiled. Then she sat in the chair next to him, a small table between them. She looked out to the water, too, noting its smoothness. They sat together for a long time, the water their focus, the sun pouring on them.

Without looking at Thomas, Anna said, "My husband killed himself. I never told you that. He put a hose on the tailpipe of his car in the middle of the woods and died. You have his hands."

Thomas shifted a little in his seat and looked down at his hands, then over at Anna. He reached toward her over the space between them and took her hand in his. Anna could feel the warmth, the solidity in his relaxed and easy grasp. She held on. A ripple of wind passed over the lake and then the water flattened again. A frog spoke from the shade at the water's edge.

"Look toward the sun," Thomas said. Anna glimpsed the fiery mass and the porch went dark around her. She could feel Thomas's hand, firm and warm. She held on.

Inside their yellow car Anna's husband breathed evenly and deeply. She could see his closed eyes, his head back against the headrest, his feet braced on the floor. She saw tears gather under the lids, then spill down his face. He had one hand resting on the steering wheel, one in his lap.

Anna reached toward him, put her hand over his, closing her fingers gently. She lifted his hand from his lap, held it in the space between them, felt his fingers slowly tighten, returning her grip. He hand was dry and soft, his fingers strong. She sat holding his hand while the engine ran, vibrating the car. Outside the car window the sky opened above the thick, green trees.

"It's okay," she whispered to him, "you can go." She listened to his breathing, regular and deep, one breath after another.

"It's okay," she said again. Gradually space grew between his breaths, longer and longer. Finally there was a slow exhale, the sound flowing and even, flowing and fading to silence. Anna felt his fingers loosen, a small movement as quiet as breath. She squeezed his hand and let it go.

Bill

1945

She'd squeezed his hand and let it go. As Bill pedaled away, his hands tight on the vibrating handlebars, he looked back over his shoulder at the two figures who should have been his enemies, and he no longer could make sense of anything the world had rested on for so long: who was right, who was wrong, even where home was. The uniformed guards who had beaten and starved him and all the men of the barracks seemed far away and flat compared to Lisbet's eyes and Jakob's half-smile.

Bill hated goodbyes, had avoided Lisbet's face and concentrated on her hand, clasping his and then slipping away. In the weeks he'd spent with them his hunger had stopped eating him away and his cold anger had turned to memory. He was still gaunt and weak, but he no longer felt starved for anything, not food or drink or warmth or company. He'd returned to the living, his ready burst of laughter surprising him, then quickly going unnoticed, a natural part of the slow evenings in Jakob and Lisbet's borrowed house. They'd lost everything, their son, their home, their country, yet what they had left they gave away without expectation to Bill and Tom, the prodigal sons who happened to return.

Lisbet's hand was rough, aged beyond her years by work and deprivation. She'd held Bill's hand as if it were the last human thing on earth, tightly, bone to bone, as if the flesh were just in the way. And then, light as a cloud, her hand released, and she'd nudged Bill toward the bicycle, then waved her hands as if shooing chickens, urging him away. Bill had mounted the bicycle awkwardly, his reluctant limbs not quite obeying him, still watching her fluttering hands. Then Bill's eyes caught Jakob's; he saw the sadness there and the acceptance Bill had bathed in through recent weeks, as he'd slowly found his way back.

Bill pedaled away, hardly believing in the world that he and Tom were riding toward. He was stuck in mid-air, pedaling furiously toward something he could hardly remember, away from the only things that seemed real: a rocky farm, kindness.

Her hand had seemed so big to him, so enveloping. He'd played with her fingers, tapping each one, straining his small hand to span the breadth of hers. He'd sat by her bed during the whole endless afternoon waiting for the doctor, feeling her hand tighten and loosen with each passing pain. His father had taken the wagon and team into town to fetch the doctor, many rough, slow miles away. Bill felt important and little, watching over his mother, keeping her from harm. He sang every song he knew, told her every joke he could remember, rewarded by her smile.

Finally she whispered, "Not now, Billy," and he'd sat in silence, holding her big hand. When she asked for a drink of water, he held the glass to her lips, and he moistened cool cloths to lay on her forehead, just like she'd done for him when he'd had the measles. The few things she asked for he did, always returning to hold her hand.

When the doctor finally came, Bill was lost in the bustle, nudged out into the yard. He climbed up on a wooden crate outside the bedroom window and watched while the doctor placed the mask over his mother's mouth and nose, trickled liquid over it with a dropper and then took it away, her face no longer tight and squinty, just asleep. He saw the doctor cut his mother's side, her blood bright and red everywhere. He saw his happy-go-lucky father turn grim and serious, following each of the doctor's barked commands for clean rags and boiling water, for applying pressure and unrolling bandages. He watched the doctor sew his mother up as if she were a shirt that needed mending.

After it was all over, he watched his father cry and his mother sleep, watched the doctor leave. Bill stood on the crate until his legs ached and he shivered in the dimming light, until his father came to the kitchen door and called him. Bill refused supper, and instead sat by his mother's bed until his father made him go to his own room and lie down for the night. For a long time Bill couldn't sleep, but he finally gave in, lulled by the rhythm of his father's pacing.

The next morning Bill ran to his parents' room, but it was all different, empty except for a replica of his mother lying in the bed. Her face was gray and expressionless, and her hand was cold. Bill stood in horror next to the bed, wondering what kind of monster the doctor was to do this and why his father had helped him. When the women from the neighboring farms swooped in and shooed him from the room, Bill returned to his crate outside the window and watched while they bathed the statue of his mother and dressed it in her best clothes.

○○○

After Tom pedaled up, shook Jakob's and Lisbet's hands and passed them a precious loaf of bread, he leaped back onto the bicycle and started away, shouting, "Come on, Bill! The village is swarming with Americans."

Bill's hand dwarfed Lisbet's, but he could feel the strength of her bones and the warmth of her flesh. When she let go, he knew there was no turning back, only going forward, only getting onto the bicycle and riding down the dirt lane.

Bill watched Tom flying away and mounted the other bike, his limbs operating on their own without him. He kept looking over his shoulder as he pedaled away unsteadily, weaving down the lane.

"Come on, Bill!" Tom kept shouting, and Bill pedaled. He kept looking back at the two figures standing side by side, their hands waving.

Part 3

*Rise up nimbly
and go on your strange journey
to the ocean of meanings.*

*The stream knows
it can't stay on the mountain.
Leave and don't look away
from the sun as you go,
in whose light
you're sometimes crescent,
sometimes full.*

Rumi
translation by Coleman Barks

Vita

1923

24 May

I kept looking back over my shoulder at the two figures standing side by side, their hands waving. They were small and growing smaller, but their presence seemed to fill the horizon as they perched at the edge of the lawn watching my roadster recede. I was engulfed—by love for their long limbs, their boyish reaches toward manhood—but I had to look away, to aim the car properly down the narrow lane ahead. When I glanced behind me, the boys were gone. I felt a tug pulling me back to them and then a release, and I could look forward again, down the lane to the open road beyond, to Violet.

This time I felt no frenzied tearing apart, but only a sense of being all in one place, inside the open car that carried me. I no longer have two lives, one behind and one ahead, but only movement, as if I am a swan gliding through calm water between verdant islands.

I return to the boys and to Harold—with Violet's blessing—and with Harold's blessing—I return to Violet. It has become a simple circle: not either, but both.

I have expanded enough to be able to hold everything and everyone at once, even my joined self. The place where my two halves were knit together is invisible, no stitches, no scar, only smoothness. I am fluid, not held back by dam or dike, but flowing with my full liquid power, the force of the ocean that swept across the painting's eyes.

This time, with Violet, there is no pain. There is only the joyful return that erases time, a brush that with a stroke paints us together again.

28 May

The ocean is our home.

Violet and I watch its changing colours, the way it absorbs and reflects light. We see dawns and sunsets, midnights and moons. With pen and brush we record our changeable world of rock and water. It is no longer a place we have to, or wish to, keep to ourselves.

I write long letters to Harold and my boys, telling them the story of light, how it changes in an instant, how it changes everything in sight. And they write back to me, each having his own unbridled say. Their letters are seamless, weaving together Harold's caricatures of his fellow statesmen along with the boys' stories of their dogs and horses, their daring at cricket.

Their home—the home I share with them—is of the land, solid and safe.

Violet sent them a painting of me standing atop a rock, arms outstretched, like a tall mast on a great ship leaving port with sails unfurled.

4 June

My life with Violet is no longer stolen. Our days are expanses of contentment we can count on. The world has changed. Colours are more vibrant and sounds more intense. Each day we set out to capture it on paper and canvas, and each night we savor it fully and long.

My habit is to rise early and walk to the sea, my steps light and sure. This morning I slowed on the landing halfway down the front stairs as I caught myself in the mirror. I stopped and looked from the toes of my boots, up my long trousered legs, to my jacket and hat. Then I looked into my own face, my own eyes, the curves of my cheeks and chin. I stepped back to take in my whole figure, tall and strong.

"This is who I am," I said out loud, and I smiled, a smile I kept as I strode down the rest of the steps and out to the street, down to the path that borders land and water.

10 June

There is nothing I long for. I realized it this morning with a start and kissed Violet awake.

"I never thought I could have everything," I told her.

"It's not me or Harold or the boys you ever really longed for," Violet answered.

"Yes."

I could feel the word vibrate through the air, expanding and expanding, floating out the window over buildings and trees, over all the waking city to the sea, beyond rock and water to the sun breaking over the horizon, burning the air, setting fire to the very air.

The sun heated my face, and I didn't look away, only closed my eyes, let it flame through my blood—everything I've ever wanted.

Anna

1983

She didn't look away from the sun, only closed her eyes, let it flame through her blood, giving her everything she'd ever wanted. She could feel the sun inside her, rushing like a waterfall or an avalanche, out of control and gloriously powerful. Her blood carried its brightness, a furious pounding that wore away the jagged, rough edges, polishing her to a smooth gloss. Everything else fell away and she became complete, possessing a fullness she'd always known was hers, lost beneath layers that had settled over her, a curved fullness that could hold without resisting and remain without flaw or decay. She'd wanted this, always wanted this, more than love or ambition or safety, a wordless and infinite longing, defying definition, defying understanding, knowable only in its lack. And she'd come to know it in the blinding, burning light, a sense of herself beyond all things, a capacity to hold everything at once because there was nothing to hold on to now.

Anna blinked and the room came into a kind of focus, a glowing of objects among the shadows: the porch windows, the wicker chairs, the wide floorboards, the potted plants, and Thomas, sitting next to her and smiling. Thomas nodded as if miming in slow motion, and Anna looked directly into his eyes. There was nothing to say. They sat in the perfect silence, in the bright sunlight. Anna looked at Thomas's hands loosely folded in his lap, at the gracefulness of his fingers. She, too, smiled and nodded.

"Yes," she finally said.

She heard Thomas rise, felt his hand brush her cheek. He moved quietly through the house to the front door, and Anna heard it open and close, a low squeak followed by a click. She sat still, feeling her back against the chair cushion, and then spoke, her voice firm and strong.

"Thank you," she said, and her tears were the happiest she could remember.

Anna found herself walking. She was aware of the road beneath her feet, solid and stretching before her. Flowers dipped in the breeze; the scent of peonies rose around her. She'd never seen anything so beautiful, the layered heads weighing down the slim stems. She stopped and held a blossom in her hands, bent down and buried her face in it, breathed in the luscious fragrance. Sunlight glinted from its polished leaves, and its shadow bridged grass and pavement. Anna walked toward the sun, following its shiny trail, letting it pull her as if it were a magnet and she were made of metal. She felt finely forged, like surgical steel, her tensile strength heightened by fire. The sun drew her and she followed, the light lengthening as afternoon turned to evening. The sun's round glory heated the world.

As night fell, things became less defined, and the air more toned. Anna watched the color leave, green draining to gray, red darkening to black. Slowly, things were lost to her eyes, and she could only hear the night, the breeze in the leaves, the occasional closing of a door, an airplane high above her. She saw lights go on in the houses she passed, creating enclosed and defined spaces. People moved inside lighted walls while Anna slid past in the dark air, still smiling, still nodding. She waited for the moon to clear the trees, her skin taking on the coolness of the night, and as the moon rose, she stopped and watched it, not quite spherical, a few nights before full. She turned in the moon's direction, let it pull her back toward home, the silvered road before her, her shadow trailing out behind.

When Anna woke, she wasn't surprised to find the morning. She lay where she'd landed, fully dressed on the couch. She had closed her eyes to darkness, opened them to light, gladdened by the simplicity of night shifting into day. Stretching her arms out as far as she could reach, Anna looked at her hands, their slender grace.

Steam curling from her coffee cup, Anna sat on the porch and looked down the back yard to the lake, to the ruffled water flashing in the sun, a scene she had risen to morning after morning, but this day the colors seemed more vibrant, the lake fuller and more beautiful, the light more pure. She sat for hours and took it all in, every last detail, for this would be her last look, of that she was sure.

Anna sat down to write a note. She didn't know who would find it, a worried friend perhaps, or her neighbor, someone who missed her, who noticed that she no longer came and went. It wasn't a note she'd planned, and it came out all at once, like morning.

There should be a term for the opposite of suicide. What would it be?
Committing life. I'm committing life, among sunlight and green trees, among wind and dirt and flowers nodding from long stems.
Take this house and live in it happily. I'll miss it only as the butterfly misses the cocoon, flying on painted wings toward the sun that gives it color. I'm shedding this place and taking only my painted body into the warm air, my wings carrying me lightly away.

It wasn't hard to decide what to take: a small clay sculpture her husband had made, a few gifts from friends, her favorite clothes, her favorite books. She packed it all into two big suitcases and loaded them into the trunk of her car, then went back inside and put the house in order. She straightened up, watered the plants, dusted, made everything look inviting, well kept.

Anna signed the note and left it on the kitchen table, closed the door behind her. She backed out of the driveway and onto the street, turned right toward the main road. At the intersection she turned left, heading west, driving toward the sun.

Madeline

1945

When Madeline received the third telegram, it was an ordinary night. She sat with her friend, Irma, small talk occasionally breaking their silence. Madeline was growing even rounder, the baby inside filling her out, pressing on her with all his restless insistence. He squirmed and kicked, never letting her forget that he was there, living and waiting to spill. Waiting was finally taking a shape.

She'd tried to imagine the prison camp, but she had nothing to picture, only general grayness and bleakness, a hungry cold. The closest she could come was the mine at the Old Newgate Prison, narrow, low, frequented by skeletons from the Revolutionary War. Her few ventures down the shaft, blinded by thick darkness after the glare of the shiny new dance floor above, had left her shivering and afraid. She tried to imagine Bill locked behind doors and barred windows, but his face kept flickering, thin and bony. She could imagine his hunger, for now she could never get enough to eat, enough sleep to ease her tiredness. But the baby's kick would bring her back from Germany, and she thought she could see his little face, round and soft, framed by blonde curls.

At the intersection on that long-ago day she'd turned left, heading west, toward the sun. She couldn't seem to help herself. It was her usual route everywhere now: to school, to the grocer's where her mother sent her with a memorized list, a minimum of cash, and an apology, asking Mr. Werner if he wouldn't extend credit just this one more time. Mr. Werner tended not to be harsh with Madeline, though there was a price she paid when his eyes moved slowly up and down her body and his voice fondled her in forbidden places. If she could get Andy to go with her, Mr. Werner would let her alone, but then she could buy only what she had money for and she had to face her mother's blank face.

Madeline's mother had grown even more silent and stern. Her mouth seemed stitched shut. She'd forgotten how to smile, and laughter was a luxury she couldn't afford. Madeline skirted around her mother as much as she could, to keep from making trouble or asking too much. In the months since her father's death, the apartment could have been the inside of a coffin. It was immaculate, everything in its place, dust and window streaks banished, and its clean emptiness forced whispers from Madeline and Andrew. The quiet was stifling, as if there was not enough air in the rooms even with the windows open.

Andy spent more and more time on the streets, and Madeline became her mother's appointed emissary, bridging the gap between her mother and the rest of the world. Madeline wondered if she would wear a trough in the sidewalk, with all the comings and goings dictated by her mother's needs and whims. She looked at meat in the butcher shop window, then asked the price in her bravest voice, running home to gauge her mother's reaction and then back again to barter or beg. Most often it didn't work at all, and meat just wasn't to be had, potatoes their mainstay. Her thoughts took on the rhythm of her feet, and she looked for roundabout routes to travel that would give them more room. At home, the muffling silence seemed to breed a vacancy without thought or feeling, where Madeline existed in her body but not in her mind and heart. Sometimes she stared at her father's photograph in the living room, just to make sure she was awake and hadn't dreamed him.

Madeline kept returning to that place around the corner more and more regularly, working it into the beginnings and ends of her meandering routes. She'd walk up one side of the street and down the other on that block, sometimes again and again, so she could look at the house and disassembled garage. The house looked ordinary—that's what was so startling. Madeline could imagine living there, her family at home in those rooms, that maple outside the bedroom window a daily, comforting sight. But then she'd shudder to escape the haunting that seemed to slow her steps and direct her thoughts.

The man who had lounged on the sofa in that living room,

who had backed his Dodge out of that garage and into the street, kept lingering there and following her around, reaching toward her. He'd calmly eaten his breakfast in that kitchen and bounced his son on his knee and thanked his wife for a good meal. He'd kissed his son goodnight, stroking the child's soft hair, without a thought of the tiny cracked head and the little chest that no longer rose and fell in sleepy breathing. Madeline couldn't imagine how he'd managed to live his false life, living and breathing himself, going to the movies, waking slowly out of dreams. The baby was dead, and he'd killed him with his bare hands.

Sometimes after her mother had gone to bed, Madeline climbed out of the living room window to the fire escape and held the metal bars in her hands, imagining the man in jail, his small eyes scanning the corridors and planning his breakout. The first time she'd climbed out, she'd found her father's last whiskey bottle, tucked back in the corner against the bricks. She'd held it to her chest, the glass cold and slippery and hard. There were a few inches of liquid left in the bottom, and she tilted the bottle back and forth, heard the whiskey slosh from side to side. She uncorked the bottle and sniffed, the biting, familiar smell rising, and she quickly tipped the bottle into her own mouth, the hot, harsh taste a shock. Jamming the cork back into the neck, she held the bottle out between the bars, opened her hand and let it fall, making a spectacular crash in the alley. Then Madeline held the bars in her two fists and cried, silently, so her mother wouldn't hear her. She thought about her father's body weighted with dirt, his bones cracking. She thought of the baby's body covered by mud and leaves, his beautiful skin smeared. And she thought of the cold man living in the barred cell, the wrath of the whole world pointed at his head.

The telegram arrived without warning, a knock on the door coming as if from some other place, sharp and loud and rapid. Irma went to answer it, then called Madeline, her voice quick and shrill. Madeline pushed herself up from the couch, her legs a little

Part 3

wobbly, and held out her hand to the young boy with the official look on his face. The paper felt flimsy, as if it had been softened by continual use. It felt insubstantial, unable to support the letters that announced like a brass band that Bill had been *returned to military control, date unreported*. That was all it said, the words stark. But they meant something. They meant Bill would be coming back after all, coming home.

Madeline thought about that word, *home*, and she realized that it was here, where she was. She realized, as her legs weakened and she stumbled to a chair, that home was what she'd held for so long, a place where something could grow, a baby, a possibility, a space that could be filled, finally, a hunger that could be fed.

Madeline sat with the telegram in her lap and thought about that word, *home*, a small word. It was where Bill was coming. On a certain day the door would open, and there he would stand. It was here. Home was here.

Anna

1983

Home was here. Anna hummed the phrase into a simple melody as she drove. *Now there is no home* was the second verse, the tune growing more complex and boisterous until she began to sing it out loud. She was aware of everything, her hands on the wheel, her foot on the gas pedal, her taut calf muscles. Her voice sounded deep, uncovered and bare. There wasn't much left to her, muscles and bones, a moving car, a clear head.

Eventually she found herself on the side road that led to the nursing home. It was familiar enough that the car seemed to steer itself, and Anna watched the grassy fields go by, prime for haying.

"Make hay while the sun shines," she sang loudly, a phrase she hadn't heard since childhood.

As she pulled the car into the circular driveway and around to a parking space, there was no hint of the knotted stomach that had always been a part of nursing home visits for her.

※

"She's not coming back. And it's too painful for me to visit her," her mother had said in response to Anna's questions. "You don't know what it was like. I had to declare my own mother incompetent in a courtroom full of strangers."

"Then I'll go." Anna threw the words at her mother with all her teenage might. "She's my grandmother. The only one I have, in case you didn't notice."

"Don't you use that tone with me, young lady. And how will you get there, might I ask."

"I'll get there. You can't stop me."

"Well, if you're going, at least run a comb through your hair." Her mother's voice was shrill, a sound not unlike fingernails on a chalkboard.

"Nana says I'm beautiful, no matter what you say," Anna snarled as she grabbed her purse. "She's in her right mind about that." She slammed the door behind her, stalked up the street to the bus stop. It took three transfers to get there, her stomach tensed into rock the whole way. She forced herself to sit still while her grandmother ranted about her lost savings and her lost home, while her grandmother rocked back and forth in her straight-backed chair, railing against Anna's mother, the lawyers and the Beast, which Anna pictured as a dragon that belched not fire, but slime.

"I know, Nana," she said when her grandmother took a breath. "I'm on your side."

That first visit became many more, spread through the rest of Anna's teens and well into her adulthood. It never occurred to Anna not to go. Gradually her grandmother lost track of most of her life, her capacity for anger giving way to a quiet forgetfulness, and she transformed back into the sweet grandmother of Anna's childhood. When she died, Anna and her mother and her mother's minister held a scanty graveside service, the only people in attendance, and Anna paid for half the headstone, splitting the cost with her mother.

It had seemed fitting, the thick stone resting over her grandmother's head. The size and bulk of it fit Anna's sense of the weight of her family's collective misery. She had never been certain what she was guilty of, but she'd carried it all on her shoulders like a yoke, as if she were an ox working the field, hauling the mower that turned grass into neatly cut hay. She'd carried her father's faulty heart, her failure to save her grandmother, the sin of being the plain daughter her mother didn't want. She'd carried, too, her husband's death in all its accusatory harshness, all of it chiseled into her side of the stone that stood at her grandmother's head, the stone owned jointly by Anna and her mother.

It was to her mother that Anna went now. It was her mother who now lived her days in a nursing home, a frail shadow of her former self, flickering on the screen like a silent movie. Anna walked the shiny linoleum hallway to her mother's room and was struck by how tiny her mother had become, her body turning into bones, her face sunken around the high cheekbones she'd always been so proud of. Anna's mother had been a great beauty, and everyone had wanted her all of Anna's life—her friends, her parents' friends, her relatives, strangers—all of them were taken by her mother's beauty, her blonde hair and blue eyes, her fine chin, her perfect skin.

Anna sat down near her mother, who was dozing in the huge red vinyl chair next to the window, her hair yellow-white, her skin blotched with age. She looked so small and harmless. Anna thought about her mother's power to maim, about the one line that had issued from her mother's mouth when Anna had gone to tell her about her husband's suicide.

"Well, I never wanted you to marry him," Anna's mother had said. She'd gone on to tell Anna how hard widowhood was for her, how much she missed Anna's father, and that was that. Anna looked closely now at her sleeping mother. How big her eyes appeared, in their closed sockets over hollow cheeks.

Anna's eye fell on the newspaper beneath the potted plant in front of her mother's window. She saw a headline that captured her. *Innocent?* it read, and she slid the yellowed paper out from under the plant. It was a review of a new book, one among several on a similar theme, the critic said. The book's author claimed he'd uncovered evidence that Bruno Hauptmann, executed for the murder of the Lindbergh baby, had been wrongly accused.

The critic noted the irony of all the blame cast toward the German man, Hauptmann, juxtaposed against Lindbergh's fixation with Germany during World War II. He went on to describe Lindbergh's anti-Semitism when he'd argued bitterly against America entering the war, his eerie obsession with eugenics that mimicked the Nazis' own. Yet somehow, the reviewer wrote, Lindbergh had proved to be a Phoenix, the fallen hero rising out of the fires of the war's aftermath, embraced by a forgetful public willing to forgive. Hauptmann's fate had been a different kind of burning—his head shaved and his pant leg slit open to receive the electrodes. The thick leather straps to hold his body in place, the mask draped over his face, the jolts that pinned him to the chair, the smoke that rose from his head.

Part 3

Anna took her time reading the long article, her mother breathing softly next to her. About halfway through was a picture of Hauptmann's wife, an old woman by then, a woman named Anna, pleading at a press conference for a meeting with the governor to clear her husband's name. There was also a picture of the baby, pale curls ringing his chubby little face. *The trial of the century*, the article called it.

Anna thought about what was left of a person after he dies, a body that deteriorates, a whisper, earth. She tried to imagine the wrath of a whole nation turned against one man. What if Hauptmann had been innocent? What if a whole nation's collective guilt had been pressed against him, so that from the outside he looked one way, but on the inside, the lonely, singular inside, he knew the truth?

Anna's mother didn't know her anymore. When her eyes fluttered awake, she looked at Anna's face as if it belonged to anyone, a stranger. She took Anna's hand and counted her fingers out loud.

"My, you're a pretty one," Anna's mother said, and her face broke into a grin. Anna laughed, struck by the irony. Her mother had been after her all her adult life to wear lipstick, to curl her straight hair, to wear shorter skirts, to be anything but who she was. Her mother had prefaced any statement about or to Anna with how pretty she could be, if only she'd do something with herself.

"My, you're a pretty one," Anna's mother said again.

"Thank you," Anna said back, and she meant it. She let her mother hold her hand, let her stroke the hair back from Anna's face. They sat together for a long time, Anna remembering her mother's clear laugh against the backdrop of her aged, gruff one. She remembered pulling her mother down on the couch beside her on rainy afternoons.

"Tell me a story, Mommy," Anna would say, and her mother would oblige with tales of Danny, a heroic talking horse, and the little boy named Randolph that he always saved from disaster.

"I'll tell you a story," Anna said to her mother now.

"Oh, yes!" and Anna's mother clapped her hands.

Anna told her mother a story about a woman who had found something lying on top of a ridge in moonlight and looking toward the sun with a man who had her husband's hands. She told her mother about a woman who had shed her guilt and her skin because they'd grown too small, a woman who took all her savings out of the bank and left everything behind.

"Oh, yes!" said Anna's mother, and her eyes shone with tears and what Anna could only call love.

Bill

1945

"Oh, yes!" Lisbet had said, the English word sounding natural in her voice. Her eyes had shone with tears and what Bill could only call love. He pedaled like a machine, as if his feet and legs moved by their own will, as if he were attached to Lisbet and Jakob by cables, and he had to pedal with all his might to break free. *The milk of human kindness*, he thought. He had drunk of it freely. It was a hard thing to keep pedaling, to snap the cables holding him to the place where he'd turned from a limping stick figure into a human being again, found a home. His knee ached as he bent and unbent it, and his feet still felt a little like blocks, with frostbite damage from the long march through snow. But he pedaled, Tom calling him forward.

Bill kept looking over his shoulder until he couldn't see Lisbet and Jakob any longer, until the farm was erased, and then he put the brakes on without thinking, feeling the last tug of the cables, cables so thick they could suspend a bridge.

"Come on, Bill!" Tom yelled, and so Bill went. And as he rode, Madeline's face came to his mind, and he saw her blink back Lisbet's tears and then burst into a grin. His pace quickened, and then he caught up to Tom.

The village was in chaos, vehicles everywhere, jeeps, tanks, trucks. They all moved quickly, an endless line of machines and men, flowing like a river at flood stage. The two men rode to the steps of the minister's house, and Bill dismounted and hammered on the door. The minister's wife finally understood after much signaling and shouting of Lisbet's and Jakob's names over and over, and she called to her two sons. Bill and Tom had nothing to give the two boys except handshakes, and then Bill watched as the boys rode away, back toward the farm, against the noisy flow of traffic. He and Tom hailed a truck, which slowed down just long enough for them to scramble in. Tom had to help Bill up because his bad knee had given out. The truck was crammed with men, and the two found seats on the floor where they'd landed when it lurched forward.

It was hard to know where he was. Even with the smell of exhaust and sweat, the hard bumping along the rutted road and his thirst, Bill managed to fall asleep, pressed against the men surrounding him. Wedged together, they leaned as one mass, shifting around corners and coming to rest upright on straightaways.

When he woke, Bill could taste milk, the dream had been so real. He saw it pour cold and smooth from Lisbet's pitcher into the sparkling glass. It filled his mouth and when he swallowed, he could feel it all the way down to his stomach, then radiate out to his limbs, and he tingled with the warmth and strength it brought him. Lisbet smiled and filled his glass again. The smile transformed her face and she was Madeline, her arms outstretched to him. As he went toward her, she unbuttoned her blouse, took him in her arms and suckled him. He woke still feeling her nipple in his mouth, her cool hand stroking his forehead. He was surprised to find his arms and legs so long, for he'd been a baby again, Madeline's and Lisbet's faces merging into his mother's face. He stretched his arm up as high as he could reach and looked at his hand, his fingers, his wedding band. For the first time since he could remember, Bill wasn't hungry.

Bill lost Tom among the mass of men being sorted into endless lines. He listened for Tom's voice in the eternal repeating of numbers and fingering of dog tags, looked for his tall, thin figure across the delousing tent and in the mess tent, but he never found him.

All Bill had was the dull tick of time, restored to him now, yet suspended. He was waiting for the second hand to speed up, to pull the minute hand with it, and with their combined force to push the hours. Bill didn't talk much to the men around him. The future still seemed as far away as the horizon, and there was nothing to say about the past. But he liked hearing other men, hung on to their phrases, their laughter, the variation of accent and tone. It was like a well-tuned band with its tight rhythms and solos, its rises and falls. He didn't feel a need to speak, just to take in, gulping the sounds like food.

His son screamed in the night, "Scared, Daddy, scared." Bill gathered him up in his arms, amazed at how perfect and small he was, all flailing limbs and crying. Bill held on to him tightly, afraid to move, afraid of dropping him or losing his grip. The boy continued to scream, and Bill held him, waking with his arms feeling like knots and his heart thumping.

Bill had gotten used to limping, to the strength of one leg and the buckling of the other. He'd gotten used to the stab under his knee and his loose black teeth. He worried his teeth with his tongue, pushing them slowly and feeling them give. He'd gotten used to getting winded and having to stop, imagining a canary inside the thin bars of his ribs, caged, failing, unable to hold air. The yellow bird folded its wings, and its tiny chest vibrated, its beak open, its tongue like a shriveled petal. It made little wheezing noises inside him, and its head nodded to one side with the effort. Bill had gotten used to it all, his aching body, his aching hunger, the dead stop when it came to thinking of home.

Now he could unravel it bit by bit, the tight knot that held home. When he wrote the word in the letter to Madeline, he felt the knot give just a little and he tore at it with his fingers. Then he dared to remember her, her hair, her eyes, dared to imagine the bulge of her womb that was his son. He took a deep breath when he handed in the letter, the small bird in his chest raising its head, a note passing from its beak, dry at first but then clear, followed by another note, and another.

Madeline

1945

The bird inside her heart had been wounded long ago, a gash torn in its side, and it had folded its wings, tucked its head underneath and gathered itself. Over time it had become weak and thin, its bones growing brittle. She hadn't known how to help it, so she'd just let it be, let it stay choked up inside her heart sharing her blood.

Madeline thought it had begun, this folding up, when her father had taken ill. His illness had crept in slowly, and at first it was hard to distinguish it from his sleepy life with the bottle. Madeline couldn't remember how it had started, the creeping realization that her father would never be the same. She knew only that something had collapsed inside her, wings that could no longer fly but only protect. More and more she'd kept to herself.

She'd tried to curb her mother's harsh judgments, to protect her father, by doing the same chores over and over until their apartment was spotless. The sicker her father became, the sharper those judgments had been, as if her mother could hold on to him only by berating and belittling. Everything was his fault: the lack of money, lack of work, lack of health, lack of any life beyond the current day. It had seemed as if all the suffering of the nation was his responsibility, the fall from plenty to lack. He was the cause of the bread lines, the men standing in the streets with nowhere to go each day, the empty grocer's shelves, the empty kitchen cupboards.

As Andy grew even more sullen and moody, Madeline had dedicated herself to entertaining him. Only she could get him to smile, to stay a moment longer in the hushed apartment before he slammed the front door and tore down the street, returning hours after dark without any explanation. Madeline had gone to bed each night exhausted, but even so she'd had trouble finding sleep. Madeline remembered imagining herself the Colonel's daughter, lost at birth and landed in the wrong family. She'd wondered what it was like to fly alone across the ocean, surrounded by blue in every direction, flying straight through day and night. The Colonel would have taken her along, she'd been sure of that, to witness, to keep him awake. And she would have ridden next to him in the great parade that filled the streets with people and streams of paper and unbelievable sound reverberating through the tunnels the buildings made, carved out of the bright sky.

But when the baby was snatched away, when the whole world held its breath, she hadn't been able to imagine what the Colonel's face looked like then, crumbling, falling, crashing into the sea. She wouldn't have wanted to look at his face, to see it change into something unrecognizable and faraway. And when the baby was found, not fat and alive but dead and unwhole, she hadn't been able to look at her father's face, turned toward her as he lay on the sofa, his breaths growing more and more shallow, like a stream clogged with sand.

That must have been when Madeline started looking past her father, when the bird in her heart had become cold, folded tightly and barely breathing. And months after her father's death when the arrest was made, the man Hauptmann living just around the corner, Madeline had known that evil could reach anywhere, could change a family and a world, its hands choking and strangling everything in its reach. That must have been when the little bird died altogether, a hard knot of bones and feathers and coagulated blood.

⁂

The bird's unfolding came sweetly, so sweetly it felt to Madeline like pain. There had been flutters when she'd met Bill, but they were cautious and small. Madeline had accepted them, though, thinking they were love, all that love was. She'd lived on flutters for months that turned into years, but always tentatively, imagining how easily Bill could crumble. When he'd disappeared into the war and then vanished entirely, she'd known how the Colonel's face had felt from the inside.

But the baby fluttering inside her womb seemed to wake the bird, and nothing Madeline did could still it. The bird grew stronger as the baby grew, and once or twice she felt it stretch its wings, slowly and stiffly, as if reminding itself of flight.

When the letter came, the letter in Bill's handwriting, bearing the word she could never quite believe in, the bird opened its beak and remembered how to sing. It startled her, the sweetness like pain. Tears burned her eyes and ran down her cheeks, and the Colonel's crushed face reconstructed itself into her own.

The bird sounded a few raspy notes, then broke into song and rose, wings outspread, into the blue air. She watched it rise and remember how to soar, watched it cross the Colonel's ocean to the place where Bill stood looking back. Madeline could see Bill's face turned toward her, could see the bird land on his shoulder. She could see it nuzzle its small, beautiful head into Bill's neck, see the vein pulsing there, carrying blood through Bill's body, warm and real.

It was true, all of it. Bill was coming home. The word sang over and over from the bird's mouth, the sound reaching over the sea, the wings an arch that joined everything.

Madeline was coming home, too.

Vita

1932

She was coming home.
The long lane stretched out ahead,
lined by stately elms that stored
the days of the land. People had come

and gone, lived and moved and died
among the trunks that reached toward sky
and moon and summer lightning.

And the trees had held their ground, acres
of water pulled through their veins, sent
to new leaves year after year after year.

For the first time, she returned to the place
of her birth, the place the men of her line
passed from one to another:
grandfather, father, uncle, cousin.

She knew it as well as she knew her skin,
the only place on earth where tendrils shot
from her body, anchored her. Here, the paths
knew her feet. Here, she knew she'd be led.

Sun darted through the leaves, a vibration
of light on her upturned face. Each step
returned the lean muscle of her youth.

The ground beneath her was old, older
than the elms. She felt primordial, as if
she'd stepped back in time, before ice ages

and ancient floods, the lone human
in a vast, overpowering landscape. But
she wasn't small—she filled this place.

It no longer mattered whose name
was on the deed. This land was no larger
than she was, and so it was hers.

29 June

My long passion for astronomy and my unwavering passion for the land of my birth collided on this date, exactly on this date, five years ago. I was innocent then of the consequences of heaven meeting earth. I shall call to that time now, that faraway time, force myself to remember what was unleashed.

In that remembrance I shall give this new poem its due place. I shall know the poem for what it is.

The beginning was a celestial event, an event so cataclysmic that the face of the earth was altered. And soon after, my reflection in the mirror would become the face of a stranger, though I did not know it then.

The predictions were everywhere, in salon conversations, in newspapers, even in hushed whisperings among the servants: On 29 June, 1927, a total eclipse of the sun would be visible in Britain for the first time in over two hundred years.

I went to Knole to watch it with Father, spent the night in my old bed chamber, rose early that morning, for the sun would eclipse not long after it dawned. The sky was heartily cloudy, muffling the stars and my excitement, for I feared this great occurrence would come and go invisible. Yet dawn arrived, and with it the sun broke through with a radiance that seemed biblical. I watched, wrapped in a sweeping cape as if for winter, Father by my side.

In truth, it lasted only a few minutes, but time was not relevant as the fiery globe was replaced—inch after slow inch—by shadow, until it became a black disc defined by a thin circle of light. The earth grew chill. Birds ceased their singing. Colours were mute. I lost Father in the dark, though I could hear his soft breaths.

And then I watched the sun resurrect itself. Father's smile lit his face, and I thought that brightness had returned to the world for good.

    Yet only seven months later, my dear, gentle Father was dead, and the earth was once again shrouded in darkness. My beloved Knole passed to my uncle, and the earth became chill. Someday Knole will pass to my cousin.

    The simple, painful facts do nothing to explain what I felt then, the kind of pangs amputees feel coming from their phantom limbs. I dreamt night after night of walking at Knole with Father, of our matched steps over the green lawns, of the tumbling gardens, the peculiar blue of the sky overhead. I couldn't get him—or the place—out of my system, tiny thread-like roots dangling from my body but unable to find soil. They reached helplessly for water, but they received none. A brutal gardener had hacked me from the ground, and I'd been thrown aside to wither. I was catatonic, my body so weighted by sadness that I could barely leave my bed, my chair, could barely lift a fork, the stubborn tendrils knotting themselves around me and keeping me still. I was senseless, did not know myself in the mirror. Perhaps it was all a dream. Perhaps it was all too terrible to be real.

    I had to give it up: Knole, where I was born, where my first son was born, where my stillborn son lies in his tiny grave, where Father was born and is buried. Knole: the place that could not pass to me, my father's only child, because of a law that makes it so, a law made by men for men.

    No matter that Harold and I bought our Long Barn. No matter that I bore my third son, healthy, in London. No matter that I have found space and time to be with Violet. No matter that Harold and I have now acquired the most lovely home, Sissinghurst, which we are making new.

    I had to give up Knole to have any of it.

    And the way, finally, to give up Knole was to visit there, to walk again upon its earth, to know that it no longer owns me.

    Everywhere I have lived, I have planted flowers. I like the warm dirt in my hands, like the idea of putting in seeds that *sprout and root and grow. My desire for flowers is insatiable, and I endlessly admire the cycle of the seasons, the seedlings breaking through the earth, the wild flowering, the withering and death. I've watched it every year, no matter where I've lived, in the houses Harold and I have bought, in the series of rooms Violet and I have taken. Always there is space enough for a patch of ground that can bear blossoms. I like to take off my shoes and stockings and feel the bare ground beneath my feet.*

If I were told I had only one hour to live, I would spend it digging in the dirt, feeling the soil with my hands and feet.

I walked the familiar grounds of Knole, and a smile bloomed on my face, the kind of smile that an art critic, no doubt, would call inscrutable when dissecting a painting. But on my living face it was a simple smile, a smile of peaceful joy.

I need nothing to be different than it is. It is not just acceptance. It is far deeper and more profound, yet simple as dirt. I need no person, place or thing except myself. Everything else is beautiful luxury: my sons, Harold, Violet, my pen and paper, my possessions, my memories. I no longer crave them, no longer try to force them to define me. They have all come to me unbidden, and I have finally opened my heart to them.

As Thomas predicted, I have stepped into my name. It's mine, like my skin.

Anna

1983

Anna's hands on the wheel felt sure, as she watched the landscape unfold before her, laying itself out for her to examine. She welcomed all of it, every tree and fleeting bird, every cloud and threatening storm, realizing slowly as she saw the land wander and flatten and rise that she no longer craved anything, no longer wanted to be defined. The land inside her was all she needed, and she followed a map that led deeper and deeper, until she couldn't tell the difference between the craggy turns and waterfalls on the roadside and her own mind and heart. She became what she saw, and her eyesight was clear and unencumbered.

Anna used her own kind of navigation, driving always away from dawn and toward sunset, sure that west was where she was going. She found that driving and looking out her car windows was enough to occupy her, to frame the thoughts that arose randomly and rode across the horizon. She followed them—thoughts, memories, flickering images—and marveled that the outside landscape mirrored the one inside her. She was wide open and capable of filling the land around her.

Anna stopped the car when she saw something that pulled her, a bird bending a branch on takeoff, a field shorn of its cover of grass, leaving amber stubble and inviting a red fox to search for exposed mice. She studied what she saw, storing it in the vast reserves she'd created by leaving so much behind.

She spent a whole day sitting under a big old oak tree, her back pressed against its trunk, its core drawing moisture from the earth the way her heart drew the blood through her body. Studying the tree's limbs and her own arms and legs, she watched a trail of ants take a shortcut over her calf and partway up the muscled tree trunk. She leaned her head back against the bark and wondered if she could read the tree's mind, sure that it possessed one as mysterious as her own. She fell asleep finally and dreamed that she became a tree, storing water and sun for days and nights and human history. Waking slowly, Anna was surprised to see her skin where bark should have been.

Anna studied water, how it pooled, how it ran, how it flowed with a power that could cut through rock, how it flooded with a strength that could rearrange towns and cities. She spent the day beside a stream, watching the water curve over rounded rocks and the suction of eddies, studying the undercut bank and the deep, slow places. She took off her clothes and stepped in, feeling the cool water lick her legs, and then lowered herself into the shallows and lay on her back. The water pulsed over her, and she could feel its quiet pressure wearing away her years. She looked up through the sheltering cottonwoods to the sky, felt the sun sparkle over her body as it lit the water. Anna breathed the wet air, felt the water cascade off her breasts and then engulf them again as she exhaled. Her head supported by a flat rock, she slept and then woke to a fast water snake darting past like a graceful current. Wading into a deeper pool, she swam like a snake, letting the water form her movements, her strokes becoming more and more subtle.

Many nights Anna rejected the comfort of a motel bed and slept alone out in the open, the stars mapping the sky overhead, forming pictures and giving her signs. She rearranged the constellations and made up her own, naming The Great Tree, The Small Brook, The Water Snake and The Gathering Cloud. After a while she could see into the night sky as if she wore 3D glasses, some stars receding and others moving to the foreground. As if hurtling through space, she could look closely at the stars rushing past in great streams. Anna was learning to fly, teaching herself to leave the earth and borrow the heavens. She sailed toward the moon, its glowing, ragged landscape sharpening and becoming familiar, and then in the morning she soared toward the flaming sun as it cleared the horizon and burned the night away. She rose with the sun, arcing over the noon sky and falling toward the flat afternoon, rode the sun until its last fire burned out in the west, the moon at her back rising again.

Anna spent time with a dandelion, watched it open in morning light like a small sun, welcome bees and butterflies, fold up at dusk and disappear into a munching hare's mouth, the stem following like a piece of spaghetti. She spent days with rocks, with sand, with toads, with mud, with vines, listened to baby birds begging to be fed and desperate adult birds who lost their young to hawk or eagle. She watched a Canada goose teach her young to fly, their awkward wings seeming too small to lift their bodies.

Anna watched everything. There was nothing too small or too large to escape her attention. She saw the land level into broad plains, saw it cut by wide rivers, saw it thrust into rocky peaks. She could feel it all, feel herself widening and lengthening, losing her limits. There was nothing to define her anymore. She found herself unmade, unknown and unfamiliar. Yet she always knew where she was. Her map was sturdy and true. She followed it carefully, paying attention to where she led herself, where she was drawn. She obeyed every impulse to stop, every impulse to keep going. She was self-contained, her own pilot.

One morning waking early in a meadow brought her a doe and two fawns. Anna propped her head on her palm, her elbow bent underneath, and watched them graze. They seemed unaware of her, or at least unafraid. She watched the two fawns, still spotted, try to nurse, nudging their mother at first, then pushing their way in even harder, shoving the doe from opposing directions. The mother was strong, but the two young ones were stronger in their combined effort. The doe was blown from side to side as if by a great wind, until she finally had enough and leapt away. Anna chuckled to herself, awed by the mother's easy power, and she stayed out of her car that day and hiked, feeling the muscled strength of her lower body. Focusing on the trail and her legs, Anna found she could make leaps and land exactly where she wished. All day she played with how her strength and flexibility felt from the inside.

That night Anna dreamed about a great blue heron gliding over a bay, squawking cries that seemed alien to its elegant grace. In her dream Anna watched the heron fish, watched it stand endlessly on one leg, its wings hugged tightly to its body. It darted its long beak into the water and came up with a small fish, gulping it down its slender throat. The movements were so quick Anna thought she'd imagined them, the heron now settled back into stillness. But then it came again, the quick thrust into the water, the fast swallow, and then perfect calm again. The next morning Anna practiced stillness, sitting without moving, as if wrapped in her own folded wings.

Anna missed nothing, not the scattered pieces of cone left behind by a squirrel or the streaked clouds like ribs in the sky. She watched a spider attach its strong elastic line from leaf to leaf, anchors for the bull's-eye of its web. Then she saw a complex of webs glinting in sunlight, each spider waiting and ready. A relentless line of ants charged forward over open ground, many staggering under the weight they carried, bits of berries or leaves larger than they were.

One night Anna saw lightning split the horizon far ahead, and then she listened for the thunder that came several minutes later. She pulled her car over and walked into the woods until she came to a cluster of firs with a clearing in the middle. Sitting in the center of the opening, her clothes folded neatly next to her, Anna waited with her eyes closed, her head tilted upward. There were flashes, followed with some minutes in between by rolling thunder, the storm still some distance away. In one of the booms she could almost hear her father's voice, warning her. It was the voice that had told her to check her oil and tires before she left the driveway, to be careful driving on wet roads. She smiled to think of him there with her now, gesturing wildly and yelling at her to get to her car and away from tall trees.

But Anna sat on, listening to the space between lightning and thunder grow shorter, feeling the wind begin to rise. She could see light though her closed eyelids, a quick glow and then blackness. Sitting like a heron, still and breathing softly, she didn't flinch with either the flash or the following rumble. The wind rose and rose, and then the rain neared. Anna could hear it come, rapid drops that built into a crashing rush until there was no separation. Lightning and thunder and rain joined into a crescendo that vibrated through Anna. She could feel it in her whole body, an electric vibration that charged through her. She could feel it peak, the instant of absolute height, the sounds and rain battering her, lightning all around. The whole world lit up and cracked, engulfed by rain, until the air became light and water.

And then in an instant, Anna sensed it was over, the crescendo past. The storm moved on in all its ferocity while she sat in her small circle of calm. She continued to listen and to watch through her closed eyes the storm's steady movement away from her. The flashes of light grew subtly weaker and the roar of the thunder gradually diminished. Anna continued to sit to the very end, until the air returned to quiet. Then she opened her eyes to stars.

Bill

1945

Bill had never seen so much space. He'd lived so long within walls that he felt a kind of vertigo if he tried to let go of the rail. The ocean spread before him, endless and dark. The rail he gripped and the ship beneath him vibrated with the engines' roar. Bill felt suspended, adrift, even though he trusted the ship's steady progress and clear course.

In the wide expanse of sea and sky he felt tiny and large at the same time. He marveled at the sense of humility and power he felt, as if he were bigger than the night around him and yet smaller than the point of light at the sky's farthest edge. With both hands tight on the rail and his feet apart for balance, Bill stood and cried for the first time since he could remember. He cried without shame, without awareness of anyone around him. Then he opened his eyes to stars.

The ship was crammed with men. In every possible space was a cot containing what was left of a man and his possessions. There were waves of talk and laughter, card games and betting and fights, trading of cigarettes for candy or contraband liquor, all going on in a constant rhythm through the days and nights.

Bill settled into a routine of eating and sleeping and resting. He didn't talk much, except to name the first things he would do on land, the first glimpse of Madeline's face, the first hot meal of his choosing. His conversations would peak and then fall away to quiet. He liked looking around, observing the endless activity among the countless men around him. There wasn't a lot he needed to say anymore. Lingering between the past and the future, he was comfortable with silence.

Bill dragged his cot up to the ship's rear deck and wedged it into the space at the end of a row of cots and sleeping men. He lay down on his back, covered himself with his rough blanket and looked at the stars riding above him. He felt like a space traveler, the stuff of fantasy shows on the radio, suspended in the dark, the heavens above him vibrant with starry light.

Bill dozed and dreamed that Tom offered him something in his slender hands, something Bill couldn't remember when he woke again to the night sky. It seemed that he dreamed it, too, a beauty beyond what he had ever known. He lay for as long as he could with his eyes open, welcoming for once waking to the dark, giving in to sleep only accidentally.

It seemed to Bill that he'd lived forever anticipating, waiting, rebuilding hope, only to lose it again. He didn't know how to do anything else now, how to experience a moment without slipping ahead. He knew the feel of cold and warm, the trained response, hunger and thirst and the small gesture of a small meal to keep them both at bay. And he knew love as a shock that could come in the middle of danger, rescue as a shared grief, a shared roof, a shared meal conjured from debris and litter, eyes that spoke beyond the language of mouths.

Bill lay under the night sky and felt the wide places inside him that hadn't been killed. He felt himself expand, growing to fill the space canopied above him, a sky that never ended and never began. It came as an utter surprise to him, cradled among a mass of men aboard a hulk of metal that he was not only living—he was alive.

Morning came to the ship slowly. Bill sensed the first shift in darkness, the entrance of light. He watched the sky change from a dense black to a thinner one, the stars fade from sharp clarity to softened blurs. Gradually the sky grayed and the stars vanished, displaced by the sun that altered everything long before it appeared. Bill lay still while the men around him rustled and turned. He watched the night recede and the day replace it, watched the air begin to glow.

Finally he edged out of his cot and stood by the rail to see the first blaze of sun rim the horizon. The sky began a slow transformation from gray to blush to blue, a blue Bill swore he'd never seen before. He stood at the ship's edge and followed the edge of day as it emerged into full light. He watched the blue he'd never seen before become even bluer, and he knew he could never want for anything again, not in a hungry way.

As he watched the sun burn the sky blue, Bill knew what deliverance was.

Vita

1936

3 January

    I know what deliverance is. I know its taste and smell, its colour and texture, like afternoon in a garden, riotous colours blending with silence, the air raising scents that linger, fade and then renew. I know how to claim it now, the sweetness of deliverance. The irony is stunning—while parts of Europe are embracing fascism, I have managed to break free of my own. I am at liberty to walk the earth and take my home with me as surely as if I were a nomad who conquers the desert by vanishing.
    I can walk anywhere with anyone, Harold or Violet or my boys, and know who I am and where I am going. I trust my own two legs to take me. And I trust my home to be with me—the home I cannot inherit, the home I make with Harold, the home I make with Violet—all these I keep, whole.
    And I have wings. I sit at my writing desk and fly, lifting into thin air, pen in hand. Over the garden walls and into the ether, where I can breathe deeply and exhale with my full force. I rise at will and look down over the earth, my layered home, and see its rises and falls, its floods and dry plains, its lush trees. Sometimes with Violet I find myself suspended in the night sky, rocking like the crescent moon. Or with my boys, home from school on holiday, I sit by the fire surrounded by my three men and follow the smoke in its hot current up the chimney. I survey the stone roof beneath me as I rise above remnants of setting sun. The upper sides of clouds and the underside of the moon are resting places.
    At last I belong here—beneath this sky, on this earth.

22 February

It is deliverance that I can offer the Lindberghs, without reservation—I was certain right away when Harold proposed it. It is easy to offer Long Barn to someone who has known flight but has no home, who cannot walk the streets unrecognized, who cannot spend a night without fear of invasion or murder. It is a small thing to give a resting place where it is so sorely needed.

When they arrived yesterday, I took them under my great wing—that is exactly how the woman described it, and so I know that my wings are even larger than I'd understood. The man is tall, even taller than I had imagined. And she is so small and brokenhearted. Their toddler is robust and healthy, but they both hold him like porcelain, waiting for him to break. It will take great effort to keep them in one piece, I can see that clearly.

They live in an immense shadow, and the most I can do is to lessen its cold shade, its darkness. I will do all that I can to bring them warmth and light. But the greatest gift I can give them is quiet.

Yesterday when they arrived, I greeted them without questions, spoke only when they spoke. I will do my best to cradle them in silence, leave them in peace.

30 March

Little by little they tell me their story, bits and pieces quilted together to cover their grief. His singular flight over the ocean, his life utterly changed when he'd landed—if only he'd stayed in the air. They are haunted, not only by the ghost of their stolen baby, but by every face that has ever looked at them, every voice that has ever insisted on questions, every word that has ever appeared in print. The thing that is their story has taken on its own telling, separate from them.

It is the place that I have known so well, the place where the story separates from the teller and goes on to tell itself. I cannot explain how I've brought them back together—my own story and my own telling—only that it is possible. I have learned this lesson from Violet and from Harold, from their great love.

And these two people with their breakable child are willing to live on the basis of possibility—and love—for that is what they have left.

16 May

I bring them flowers from the garden, choosing the scents for their effects on the body, soothing or graceful or bright. I place them outside the cottage door every few days, a gathering of fragrance.

I bring them a few of Violet's seascapes, choosing them for their colours, for how the greens and blues become iridescent to the eye, how sky becomes water, how rock becomes sky.

I leave them love poems on the doorstep, my most intimate words.

I am careful to ask nothing of them, only to leave them quiet morning gifts. I am careful to wish nothing for them, for I know the power of things that arrive unbidden, the power of holding enough space for anything to happen.

My great wings hold me aloft, let me settle softly back on the ground. They shelter against my body everything that means something. I keep my story there, the old story and the new story woven together by the telling I give myself. I hold Violet there, and Harold, and my sons.

I have room enough, too, for the wounded man, his sad wife, their fragile baby, the raw memory of their murdered son, and the relentlessness of public curiosity. I make a home under my great wings where they can stay as long as they need it, where gifts show up on the doorstep.

And there is still space in the haven of my wings, space

enough for possibility, polished and precious, light as air and heavy as blood, hard-won and always new.

30 May

This morning I was greeted on the cottage doorstep by a wisp of paper, kept safe from the wind by a small stone. I knelt to receive it, a poem of thanksgiving in the woman's careful script. On my knees I received it:

Love is
the only prayer,
the prayer's
only answer.

Madeline

1945

Madeline woke in the mornings now facing the light squarely, without a cloak of grief around her shoulders. There was space enough for possibility, polished and precious, light as air and heavy as blood, hard-won and new. She rubbed her round belly with her open hands, amazed at all she could hold within her. She knew the baby was a boy as certainly as she'd ever known anything. She could even imagine his face, tiny and round, ringed with curls. Each time he kicked, she responded with a rub and talked to him, calling him by name.

"Little David," she'd murmur in a lullaby voice, "we've won. We've won our own little war, you and me." And he'd answer with an elbow or a foot. She loved watching him as he swam inside her, making his own current across the globe of her womb.

※※※

The day he came began normally enough, but then took a totally unexpected turn, for David arrived early, a full month ahead of his time. Madeline was wiping the kitchen counter and trying to picture the ship Bill would soon be boarding to bring him back from the dead and over the sea, when her water broke and she stood still, awed by the ocean that spilled from her. The pains that followed were sharp, and Madeline went to the top of the stairs to call to Marta, who summoned the neighbor across the street, the only person left who had a car with gasoline in it. Madeline sped to the hospital, her hand clutching the dashboard and armrest as she rode the waves of pain.

David was very long and pitifully thin and yellow. He was whisked away to an incubator, where he lived for two weeks before Madeline could hold him. The yellow faded slowly, a bit each day, until finally he turned pink. The first time Madeline picked him up he cried, his tiny face puckered and red. She talked to him softly, her voice husky, and he opened his eyes and looked straight at her. She laughed and hugged him to her breast tightly, knowing that in spite of his bony thinness, he was strong and could hold up to love. She took him home and put him next to her bed in the cradle Marta had given her. Lying awake nearly the whole night, she listened to him breathing, feeding him every few hours when his breaths grew shallow and he began to whimper. Madeline was amazed that someone so tiny could take up so much space. He seemed to fill the whole room, the whole apartment, and she couldn't imagine how she'd ever lived without him.

The bells began like a whisper begins, so at first Madeline wasn't sure what she was hearing. But then the sound grew and converged from different directions. One by one, all the churches and the town hall and the library joined together in the ringing of bells. It was a noise that was solemn and joyful, a clamoring that peaked and peaked. What started as a whisper became a roar, and Madeline put down her laundry basket and ran over to the cradle she'd set on the grass.

David was stirring, his eyes straining to open, and Madeline knelt down beside him. She touched his tiny arm and put her finger inside his loose fist.

"David, wake up," Madeline whispered, and then she picked him up and stood. He struggled awake, his eyes fluttering.

"Listen," she told him. "The war is over. Across both oceans it's over." She lifted the small baby toward the sky.

"Listen. It's peace." And then she began a slow dance, lowering him close to her chest, his head nested in her hand. She sang a made-up song, soft and off-key. They danced until the bells stopped, and then they kept dancing, and Madeline kept singing. She and David danced in wide circles around the yard, growing wider, growing wide enough to take the whole world in.

Anna

1983

Anna stretched her arms out straight and began to spin, faster and faster, her eyes returning to the horizon, blue upon blue, as it whizzed by. She danced in a wide circle, growing wider, growing wide enough to take the whole world in. She'd arrived at the world's edge, where the land dropped away to the Pacific and the horizon was new.

As Anna spun, the landscape around her disappeared into the blue blur, and she entered the landscape inside her, close and dark. Gradually her spinning slowed to reveal the scene around her again, and Anna came to rest there.

At low tide she walked out to a small, mounded island, where she could be suspended between land and water. There was so much life: deer bedded down behind driftwood logs on the beach, an eagle hunting overhead, pelicans skimming the water in a long line. Sea lions growled on a rock several hundred yards out, and then as she focused there, a gray whale surfaced behind the rock and then dove. Sea otters floated in big mats of kelp, undulating with the waves. Bright puffins dotted the rocks below. Anna sat still on the top of her island, watching it all. This was the place she had come to see.

She looked around her, the wide ocean, the long beach, the tall cedars behind with the mountains rising out of them, the domed sky above. This landscape was big enough for her to grow into. Anna could feel time and space spreading out everywhere. All those who had come before her assembled at her back, and Anna could feel their presences, their collective strength. She knew she carried them in her blood and bones and that they had joined to bring her here.

The world was open. She scanned the sky, absolutely clear, a blue she swore she'd never seen before, clean. Anna sat the whole day on the top of her island. She could feel the sun's movement, the peak and wane of its heat. She was a living thing amid a vast array of living things gathered in this place.

The sun descended rapidly toward the line that separated sky from sea. Anna felt its glint in her eyes. She watched the sky around it as the sun touched the horizon and began to disappear in all its flaming beauty. Bit by bit the sun dove to the other side of the world. The light lengthened toward her, blazing the water. Finally the last edge of the sun disappeared and just then a flash of pure green lit the sky where it had been. Anna closed her eyes and kept that green, the way a seedling keeps the color of its birth.

The Man Who Loved Sky

1927

When he approached the airplane in the early morning dark, its shape was obscured. The wings were not as apparent as the nose that urged itself into the rainy air. Lack of sleep, lack of proper food, lack of quiet all pushed against his body as he walked. For the first time, he doubted himself.

He had always known the smell and taste of danger. For God's sake, he'd been a wing-walker. He'd landed in farmers' fields pocked by gopher holes. He loved speed and lift, the feel of wind against his face. It all made the blood move more quickly in his veins, tingled his skin. Anticipation had always been equal to the real thing because he knew what the real thing was, each takeoff and landing, each time he felt the instant the air took hold of the plane.

But this was different. It wasn't that this was the flight of his life. Of course, he knew that made it different. No, it was something more, something he felt in his body, unclear to his head. He wasn't a religious man, far from it, so praying was not a natural act for him, but this time he almost wanted to, to give himself up to whatever could be greater than himself.

It should have been easy to talk himself out of it, not out of the flight—no, he was too far into it for that. It should have been easy to talk himself out of whatever was creeping over his limbs, making him heavy and dull, as if he were walking under water. It should have been easy to brush it off—after all, he wasn't one to give feelings much sway. He shook his hands into the cold air as if he could shake it out of himself. But it didn't help. The airplane looked little and faraway—how could it possibly lift his weight, his mortal weight, into the sky?

Still he walked, the throngs of people scattered like black bubbles under their umbrellas. Later he would write to the first man to walk on the moon that he wondered if the astronaut had felt as he had, that when he landed he would have liked some time to look around.

But he didn't know this yet as the plane loomed so small before him. He knew only a vague feeling that had no name. Later, after he became the first, not to try it but to land, he would be called Lucky, but he didn't know that now, and luck was certainly not what he was feeling. His legs kept him moving toward the tiny plane, but something besides his legs carried him, pushed him into the mist. He kept going—all he knew to do.

Once in the plane, he checked everything and then rechecked. He didn't have to think about it since he'd done it so many times before. His hands and eyes knew what to do by themselves. The movements were comforting, the familiar repetition, what was known in the face of so much that was not.

As the ease of familiarity settled over him, he realized how little he knew, how little he understood. It was not arrogance that rose in him in that familiar seat. He was smaller than the small and flimsy ship that surrounded him, and he knew it.

When the time came, when the propeller was cranked and it began to spin, when the engine made its expected roar, he simply went forward. The wheels were unchocked, and collectively men pushed until the plane had enough momentum to move on its own. The stick felt feeble in his hand, but still he went.

The plane seemed reluctant to leave the ground, slowed by mud and gravity, the horizon muddied by mist. Yet he rose, pulled away from earth. Even then the airplane balked, hitting down again. Finally, just in time, it rose with him inside, cleared the last manmade obstacles—tractor, ditch, power lines—and flew.

Once he was truly airborne, the force of flight took over, and his hands were steady despite his aching tiredness. He loved the sky, loved its endlessness. In all conditions, rain or snow, opaqueness of night or clarity of day, he loved it. It still amazed him to ride the sky, nothing holding him up but wings.

This time was different, he knew. He would be flying in the place where ocean met sky, blue everywhere. The only ground below him would be water. Later he would have a wife and she would learn to navigate, but he didn't know that now. He'd have to find his own bearings.

Later he would write that somewhere in that completeness of blue, he got the feeling that he was not alone. He wondered who was with him in that expanse of space, riding over waves of air and water, who joined him in that wicker seat when he didn't know down from up, when sleep kept edging over him, when hours dragged and dragged, buoyed only by thin air.

Later he would write that dim, transparent forms moved in and out of the space behind him, spoke with voices he could hear. He didn't know who they were, but he listened to what they had to tell him.

Those who shared his seat would never know it, would know only that they had touched him somehow, only that they went forward when their limbs were tied to earth, their wings remote.

As the airplane continued to rise, he felt the engine's strength, the stick's reliability in his hand. These were what he had to keep him aloft, these and as much fuel as he could carry. He'd left even paper behind so he wouldn't have extra weight.

As he banked one more time and began to level off, the first glance of morning sun broke through the thinning clouds and hit one of the wings, caught him in the eye. He righted the plane, made of sticks and cloth and wire—righted it and flew.

Acknowledgments

For background about Vita and Violet's story and a sense of Vita's emotional life, I am indebted to Nigel Nicholson's *Portrait of a Marriage* and to Sally Potter's film *Orlando*, based on Virginia Woolf's novel with the same title. The main character in Woolf's novel is a fictionalized portrait of Vita, and the book has been called the longest love letter in literature. A character based on Violet also appears in *Orlando*. In order to create Vita's voice afresh, I avoided reading her letters and journals, except those Nigel Nicholson (Vita's son) includes in his book, but I did take inspiration from *The Dark Island*, a gothic novel that Vita published in 1934; *Pepita*, a biography written by Vita about her maternal grandmother; and *Challenge*, the long-suppressed novel Vita wrote about her relationship with Violet. *V. Sackville-West*, a biography by Michael Stevens, gave me a detailed timeline and a view of the arc of Vita's life.

I am indebted to my mother, Thelma Strever *(in memoriam)*, and my father-in-law, Paul Troutman *(in memoriam)*, for their memories of growing to adulthood during the Great Depression and their stories about the Home Front during World War II. Other sources of information about the Battle of the Bulge and the Home Front were *Life* magazine and *The Home Front, An Oral History of the War Years in America: 1941-1945* by Archie Satterfield. News reports from *The Hartford Courant* were helpful in providing information about the Hartford circus fire, which occurred on July 6, 1944.

The material quoted from Cedric Foster's radio broadcast came from a reprint my mother preserved in a World War II scrapbook. Entitled "The Story of America's 106th Infantry Division," the program aired over the Yankee Network on January 21, 1945, and the reprint was made available by a Boston insurance company, Employers Group. Thanks also to the veterans of the 106th Infantry Division in Washington State, who twice included me in their annual reunion and gave me their stories: Ken Corrigan,

Myrton Dickerson, Fred Pilkington, George Strong, and especially Ray Johnston.

For background about Charles Lindbergh's transatlantic flight and the Lindbergh baby kidnapping I am indebted to *Lindbergh* by A. Scott Berg; *Anne Morrow Lindbergh: A Gift for Life* by Dorothy Herrmann; *The Airman and the Carpenter* by Ludovic Kennedy; and Lindbergh's own account of his flight in his book entitled, *We*.

The epigraphs that begin each part of this book are from "Going Blind" by Rainer Maria Rilke from *The Selected Poetry of Rainer Maria Rilke*, translated by Stephen Mitchell; from Doris Lessing's *The Summer Before the Dark*; and from *The Illuminated Rumi*, a collaborative work featuring translations by Coleman Barks and illustrations by Michael Green.

Heartfelt thanks to:

My family and friends, whose unerring support and cheerleading keep me going.

Those who have taken me deeper: Pamela Firth, Kim Lincoln, Leticia Nieto, Dian Parker and Kay Ridgway.

My groups: Breakfast Club, Fusion, Olympia Poetry Network, Poetry Book Club, Second Saturday Writers and Team Awesome. It takes many villages.

Vita Laumé *(in memoriam)*, Diana Moore, Tom and Lois Rivard *(in memoriam)*, Shelley Kirk Rudeen and Liz St. Louis, who read the manuscript and gave me their impressions.

Good friends in the forest of publishing: Eido Frances Carney, Susan Christian, M.J. Huetter, Carla and Dean Jones and Marjorie Power.

Debi Bodett, whose vision and design made this book into beauty.

Lee Graves, Jeanne Lohmann, Eileen McGorry, June O'Brien and Kate Severson, who read the manuscript and gave me thoughtful, in-depth feedback. June and Lee read it twice!

June O'Brien, companion on the long, snaking journey of words and dreams.

Barry Troutman—for love, for everything.

About the Author

Linda Strever grew up in Connecticut and earned a Bachelor of Science degree in English Education at Central Connecticut State University. In her mid-thirties she moved to Brooklyn, New York, earning an MFA in Creative Writing at Brooklyn College, City University of New York, where she was awarded the Louis Goodman Creative Writing Scholarship.

Her poetry collection, *Against My Dreams*, was published in 2013. The collection was a finalist for both the Intro Series Poetry Prize and the Levis Poetry Prize from Four-Way Books, the New Issues Press Award in Poetry, and the Ohio State University Press Award in Poetry.

Winner of the Lois Cranston Memorial Poetry Prize from *CALYX Journal*, her work has been a finalist for the Hill-Stead Museum's Sunken Garden Poetry Prize, the *Spoon River Poetry Review* Editors' Prize, the *Crab Creek Review* Poetry Award, the A. E. Coppard Prize for Fiction, as well as in the Provincetown Outer-Most Poetry Contest, the William Van Wert Fiction Competition, and the Summer Literary Seminars Fiction Competition.

Don't Look Away was a finalist for the Eludia Award from Hidden River Arts. Her poetry, fiction and nonfiction have been published widely in journals and magazines, and she is a Pushcart Prize nominee.

She has worked as a proofreader, editor, graphic artist, teacher, trainer, and mediator and lives with her husband in the Pacific Northwest.

photo © Barry Troutman

CPSIA information can be obtained
at www.ICGtesting.com
Printed in the USA
FSHW010742120120
66010FS